The Dead Children's Playground

James Kaine

ISBN 979-8-9867312-7-8 (eBook), 979-8-9905146-0-7 (Paperback), 979-8-9905146-1-4 (Hardcover)

Cover design by: Damonza

Edited by: Louis Greenberg

PROLOGUE

A bel Hargrave felt his massive boots sink into the mud with every footfall. The hulking man was not fleet of foot under normal circumstances but, as the heavy rain pounded down, sluicing off his weathered yellow rain slicker, he reckoned he wasn't moving nearly as fast as he needed to. The conditions were keeping him from safety.

Clamoring voices behind him became audible as Abel's labored breaths burned in his chest. He stole a glance back and panicked as the beam of a flashlight shone right in his eyes, forcing them momentarily shut and causing him to tumble and drop to his knees. He braced himself just in time to prevent a face full of mud. The sludge swallowed his hands to the wrist as he pushed himself off the ground.

Back on his feet, he heard a man's voice behind him. They was close. Too close.

"You're going to burn, you piece of shit!"

Abel pressed his palms against a large red maple to his right, pushing off it to propel himself forward once again. His knees creaked, worn down from supporting his bulk for many years now. Even without the mud impeding him, he would likely feel that he was moving in slow

1

motion as the rabid mob closed in on him.

"Baby killer!" Another voice, a woman this time, pierced through the rain.

The accusation was followed by a thud and a sting on Abel's left shoulder where it met his neck. He didn't see the rock, or who threw it, but he certainly felt it, even through the thick nylon material. Just as the pain eased, another grazed his hood, narrowly missing the ear underneath.

"Monster!" another shout came from behind. The closest one yet.

Abel didn't know what they were talking about. His momma had often referred to him as 'dim,' but he did know things. He knew how to tie his shoes. He knew how to shave. And he knew how to do his job taking care of the cemetery grounds. But what he didn't know is why these folks was so angry with him. He had heard something about their children.

He liked kids. Much more so than the adults, that was for sure. The kids never made fun of him or called him stupid. Sure, they was scared of him from time to time on account of him being so big and all, plus that he could only speak in his head and not out loud, but they was never really mean to him. Just confused.

Now these grown-ups had come to his house and kicked down his door. Lucky for Abel, he had been walking home when they arrived, instead of being at the house. He heard the commotion inside and saw a bunch of folks he didn't know rummaging around his living room with flashlights, the front door hanging off of its hinges.

Abel Hargrave wasn't no genius, but he was smart enough to know that they weren't there for nothing good.

2

He'd moved to the side of the house and ducked down in the grass. It was overgrown, having been neglected as he had been spending more time on his job as caretaker of Maple Hill Cemetery than he had tending to the house his momma left him when she died of some form of tummy cancer going on about three years back, long after his daddy had drank himself to death.

Still, despite the grass being taller than usual, it was nowhere near high enough to hide Abel's six-foot, six-inch frame. He'd been trying to get close enough to take a peek through the side window into the tiny dining area when he heard a shout to his right.

"Here! The son of a bitch is here!"

Abel had turned and saw a skinny, older fella wearing a heavy flannel jacket and a newsboy cap shining a flashlight in his direction. Within seconds, more people, men and women alike, started showing up behind him.

"That's him!" a woman had shouted from his left. Abel turned and saw a lady standing around the back side of the house. She was younger than he was, maybe in her late twenties, but she had a haggard look on her face, pain written all over her features. She seemed awfully mad at Abel but, for the life of him, he didn't know why.

The woman hadn't approached him. She'd just stood there under her umbrella, the rain dripping down around it. Despite her cover from the downpour, her cheeks were wet. Not from the rain though. She was crying.

"You foul creature," she'd said in a shaky voice.

Abel was beyond confused, but he didn't have much time to think about it. He heard footsteps pick up behind him as he turned and saw the group led by the old man in the newsboy hat advancing on him.

If he could speak, Abel would have asked what they

were doing here. He'd tell them he ain't done nothing wrong. Maybe they was looking for someone else. He'd glanced back over his shoulder and saw the woman was joined by another, older lady and two more men about Abel's age, near as he could tell.

No, Abel Hargrave wasn't no genius, but he knew when he was in trouble, so he did the only thing he could. He turned and ran toward the trees.

Now, roughly ten minutes later, he stumbled past Maple Hill Cemetery, the place where he'd been working since he was little more than a kid himself. His grandpappy had worked there, and since he knew Abel wasn't gonna be much for schooling, he had started him working as soon as he could handle a shovel. In all these years, he'd done everything from removing the decaying flowers from forgotten plots to digging some graves on his own. He knew the place like the back of his hand and, even if there weren't much cover to be found, if he could get past the cemetery proper and into the limestone quarry on the other side, he'd hide until hopefully these angry folks gave up looking for him.

Maybe he could find his friend and they could help him hide.

Abel reached the entrance to the graveyard and saw the chain and padlock that he himself had affixed to the gate only a few hours earlier. The cemetery was off limits after sundown, and it was his responsibility to make sure it was secure. He cursed himself for doing that job well because the wrought-iron fence was now standing between him and safety. He knew the chain was wound too tight for anyone to push through, let alone a man of his stature, so he thrust his hand into the pocket of his raincoat and fumbled around for the key.

4

He retrieved it with some effort, the material of the coat sticking in the relentless downpour. Only, as soon as it emerged from his pocket, it slipped from his slick fingers and into the mud below. Abel again dropped to his knees to search for the missing key, but it was too late. He felt an intense pain in the back of his head, saw a flash of light, and then darkness overtook him.

Abel heard voices before his vision returned. They were loud and chaotic, a mix of anguished cries and seething rage. What started as inaudible noise soon took the form of actual dialogue.

"Mayra! My baby! No! No! No!"

"Oh Lord, oh Lord, oh Lord,"

"They... they all dead? How many? How fucking many?"

What was they talking about? Who's dead?

Abel felt wetness splashing on his face. He tried to open his eyes, but they quickly filled with rainwater, forcing them shut again. Keeping them closed, he tried to sit up, but something heavy hit him square in the nose, knocking him back, the rain-softened ground doing little to dull the impact. He swallowed what he thought was more rain, but it tasted of copper. He let out a moan, the only sound he was capable of, having not spoken a word in his whole life.

The voices went silent for a few moments, save for the

5

sobs and cries around him. Abel wanted to get back up but didn't dare try for fear of getting struck again. After what seemed like forever, he heard another man speak.

"Jesus Christ, Wayne. I think this is all of them. I think all them missing kids is down here."

"Son of a bitch," another man replied.

Abel rolled to his side so he could open his eyes without the water pouring down on him. When he did, he was met by a kick to the stomach, which felt like it pushed his gut into his gullet. On impact, he continued to roll until he found himself on his belly. He raised his head, just enough to release the vomit and mucus that had filled his throat.

"Wayne," the first man said, his gruff voice cracking with emotion. "They're all dead."

"Lord have mercy," the second man, presumably Wayne, said.

"What do we do?" the other man asked. "What the hell do we do?"

"You can't arrest him, Wayne," a third man said. "They'll just say he's a cuckoo and put him in a rubber room. That ain't good enough. He's gotta be put down for this, Wayne."

Abel suddenly felt the rain on the back of his head as his hood came down. A sharp tug followed as his head was yanked off the ground. He finally got his eyes open and saw who Wayne was. It was Sheriff Wayne Birken. The police officer looked at him with hatred in his eyes. Abel had never seen anyone that angry with him in his whole life. The sheriff didn't say nothing. Not at first. He just stared daggers into the large, beaten man beneath him. He knew Abel was mute, so it was like he was searching his eyes for some type of answer to a question that the caretaker didn't even know was being asked. Eventually, he must have found his answer.

"String him up."

Abel wasn't sure what that meant but within seconds the other men in the crowd were on him, hooking their arms under his shoulders as they dragged him along the ground. For the first time, Abel saw they were at the old Hermitage Quarry, the three large cave mouths a dead giveaway. In the 1940s, it had been the site of operations for the Madison Limestone Company, something Abel only knew because it was one of the many jobs his daddy had worked before he died, but it went out of business ten years ago in 1952, but the caves remained, about a mile from the playground.

It was where he brought his friends to sleep after they got tired from playing. Was that why they was so mad? Because his friends weren't allowed to play there with him? But was that reason enough to be beating on him like this?

Abel didn't have much longer to think about it because the men pushed him up against another large red maple. If only he could tell them he didn't mean no harm, maybe they'd let him go.

But he couldn't speak and he couldn't read or write, so Abel Hargrave could only grunt and groan as he felt the noose tighten around his neck.

Instinctively, he reached for the rope to force his hands between the thick, corded material and his jugular in an attempt to get some separation, but it was futile. He panicked as the air escaped through his gaping mouth without a new breath to replace it.

The large man thrashed about and a few gasps could be heard among the throng of onlookers as they marveled at his strength. Despite his best efforts to fight, there were just too many able bodies in the crowd and, although it took three of them, they hoisted his heavy frame off the ground, using the thick branches of the maple as a pulley.

"Burn in hell, you bastard!" a woman shouted from the back. Soon, the rest of the crowd joined in, hurling curses and insults at Abel as he hung. Another rock hit him, square on his right cheek this time. It stung worse than any beesting he'd ever experienced as it gashed his skin.

As Abel tried in vain to kick and swing and somehow save himself from his pending execution, he saw another figure off in the distance observing from behind a tree, removed from the bloodthirsty mob. Unlike the others, she wasn't cursing or giving him angry looks. She wasn't even moving. She was just watching.

The woman wasn't like the rest of them. She had dark skin. He couldn't tell how, but something about her was oddly familiar. Even at this distance, even as Abel's eyes watered and his sight blurred, he met her eyes. Something about the way she looked at him calmed him, even in these most dire of circumstances.

Suddenly, he was no longer hanging from a tree. He was by the stream he used to play at back when he was a kid. He looked down at his hands, which were smaller now. The hands of a child. Catching a glimpse at his reflection in the stream, he saw the face he wore in his youth. He didn't know how this was possible, but he was a young boy again.

Abel took a seat on the ground and listened to the running water as he closed his eyes and felt the summer sun beat down on his face, warming him. He was at peace.

In the real world, he stopped thrashing and kicking. He

stopped fighting for his life.

Abel Hargrave accepted his fate and died on the end of that noose.

CHAPTER 1

"**O**nly a few more exits to go."

Kayla Macklin craned her neck around to see the exit sign from her vantage point in the backseat of her father's Tesla. The green and white sign read *Exit 9—Wall Triana Highway/Madison Boulevard.* She smirked.

"Triana? Isn't that the town where that crazy cheerleader butchered all those people?"

"Kayla!" Gretchen Macklin shouted from her position in the passenger seat, turning and shooting her older daughter a glare, her green eyes piercing. "Don't talk like that in front of your sister!"

The nineteen-year-old rolled her eyes at her mother and turned her attention to the co-occupant of the back seat.

"Did I scare you, my fragile little sibling?"

Now it was Kylie's turn to offer Kayla a nasty stare.

The Macklin girls had always been the spitting image of their mother, with fair skin and curly auburn hair, a look that nine-year-old Kylie still maintained. Kayla, on the other hand, had recently opted for a more alternative style. Her hair, now shoulder-length, was straightened and dyed jet black, a color that also dominated her choice of clothing. But they both had those same striking green eyes, of which the younger's were now displaying a distinct irritation with the elder.

Kayla kind of felt bad. Her annoyance was more often than not trained on her mother, but she was aware that Kylie got caught in the crossfire more than she would like. Unfortunately for the youngest Macklin, the best way for her sister to get under Gretchen's skin was through her.

"Okay. I won't mention scary stuff in front of Kylie anymore."

"Thank you," Gretchen said, with no actual appreciation.

Kayla leaned back in the seat and looked out the window as the scenery rapidly passed by. They'd been in the car for the better part of the last day, the trip from their old home in Rockledge, Florida to their new residence in Huntsville, Alabama, clocking just under ten and a half hours. Sure, they'd stopped for meals and bathroom breaks, but to say she was going stir crazy would be an understatement. Not to mention the fact that she was significantly less than thrilled with the entire idea of moving to a new home in a new state, away from what little she had to make life tolerable.

And when Kayla got irritated, her toxic trait was to irritate those around her.

"Geez, it's hot in this car," she said as she unzipped her light hoodie, slipping it off her shoulders. The black T-shirt she wore underneath displayed the grinning bloodstained visage of Art the Clown from the *Terrifier* movies. His mouth wide, displaying yellow teeth jutting from blackened gums.

"Is that supposed to scare me?" Kylie asked defiantly.

Gretchen whirled around.

"Damn it, Kayla! Cover that up!"

"I'm not scared," Kylie interjected.

"That doesn't make it appropriate. Cover it up. Now."

Kayla smirked as she draped the hoodie over her chest, covering the demonic clown.

"If you put half as much effort into your education as you did into tormenting your sister, you may have actually gotten into college."

Kayla's face dropped. She seethed inside at her mom intentionally raising such a sore subject, not even seeing the parallel with her own treatment of Kylie. She swallowed hard and felt a pressure behind her eyes as she did her best to not get emotional. Gretchen's back was to her again, but she could almost feel the smug, self-satisfied smile resulting from that little dig.

"Gretchen." Roger Macklin said from his position in the driver's seat. The way he said her name was enough to convey his opinion that her interaction with their daughter was a low blow.

Roger was the odd man out in the quad. He was tall with dark-brown hair that, at his forty-nine years, was graying around the temples and throughout his neatly trimmed beard. His brown eyes, aided by his wire-frame glasses, displayed a kindness and empathy that Kayla couldn't recall seeing in her mother for a long time. That's not to say you couldn't get him mad. Case in point now.

"Our daughter has been through quite enough without her sister tormenting her, Roger."

"You have two daughters," Kayla muttered, louder than she intended.

"I have had just about—"

"Enough!" Roger bellowed, not actually intending to finish his wife's thought, but absolutely intending to halt the bickering.

Kayla half expected Gretchen to go off on her father, but she kept quiet, staring ahead out the window as the next exit sign passed, signaling that they were getting closer to their destination.

"It's been a long trip and I know everyone is getting cranky," Dad said in the understatement of the year. "But we're almost there. We'll feel better once we're settled."

Doubtful, Kayla thought, but wisely didn't say.

A long trip could not only describe the current car ride, but also the journey to get there. The Macklin family had experienced more than its share of troubles over the past several years, culminating with Roger, an aerospace engineer by trade, accepting a new job in Huntsville, where the industry was prominent. Her parents hadn't shared the reason for the move with Kayla but, from what she knew, it had more to do with medical benefits than her father's career mobility.

Figuring it best to mind her business for the remainder of the drive, Kayla pulled her phone out and started browsing social media. She barely opened the app before the first post hit her like a slap in the face.

It was her best friend Morgan Lanagan's profile. That wasn't a surprise. It was usually the first one that popped up due to whatever algorithm the tech bros had come up with. The surprise was the picture of Morgan and Aiden Dunn, only one of the most popular guys in their graduating class. He was the star forward on the basketball team and one of the most sought-after guys in school. The picture showed the two of them sharing a kiss in the booth of the Waterfront Grill, one of the spots their friend group frequented most.

It's official! Read the caption below the picture.

What the fuck? Kayla thought as she read the comments.

Yay!

So cute!

You look so good together!

Kayla seethed. A lot of girls wanted Aiden and, sure, Morgan had mentioned that he was attractive, but she never thought she had any serious interest in him. Not like that.

But the thing that really pissed her off was that it was *official.* The Macklins only left Rockledge yesterday morning. Kayla and Morgan had talked pretty much every day since middle school. If she had a date with Aiden Dunn, Kayla would have known. But this was more than a date. They were actually together? That couldn't have happened overnight. Which only meant one thing—Morgan had purposely kept this from her. She fought to keep her tears in after her mother's snide comment, but one escaped, falling down her cheek. Kayla, being nothing if not reactionary, added her own comment.

DUDE!! WTF????

She let the device drop in her lap and wiped the tear away. No longer distracted by her phone, she noticed her parents had resumed arguing and were trying, and failing, to be subtle about it.

"I'd appreciate it if you backed me up more," Gretchen whispered through gritted teeth.

"You're too hard on her," Roger replied evenly. "She's been dealing with everything we've been dealing with too."

Gretchen scoffed and it took everything in Kayla's power not to say something. Instead, she looked at her sister. Kylie was staring straight ahead. She had earbuds in and her tablet on, but it rested on her lap. The video she was watching was paused.

She was listening to the argument too.

Kayla was sympathetic. She did love her sister and Lord knows she had been through so much these past few years. She thought about saying something to distract her, maybe try to make her feel better, but emotional connection wasn't the older Macklin girl's strong suit.

It didn't matter because suddenly an image popped up on the Tesla's radar just as Roger pulled off the exit. A person was stepping into the road right by their car, but Roger wasn't reacting as he and Gretchen snipped at each other in hushed tones.

Kayla felt a surge of panic as she suddenly saw the woman in front of their car.

"Dad! Look out!"

Roger turned his attention to the road just in time to swerve around the person crossing the highway in front of the car, narrowly missing her.

"Jesus Christ!" Roger shouted as he righted the vehicle, narrowly missing the barricade. "Freakin' nutcase!"

Kayla turned in her seat and looked out the rear window and saw the woman, who seemed unfazed by nearly getting wiped out by their car. From the brief glimpse she got, Kayla could see she was an older black woman, maybe in her seventies or eighties. She moved slowly but purposefully, as Kayla watched her forage in the overgrown grass.

As they finished rounding the curve off the exit, Kayla could no longer see the woman, so she turned back into her seat.

Welcome to Huntsville.

Fifteen minutes later, the car pulled into the driveway of their new home at 12 Cornerstone Circle. Kayla had seen photos of the house, which was an older colonial that was smaller than the home they left in Rockledge. She wasn't exactly in tune with the family's finances, but given that Mom had left her law practice four years ago to take care of Kylie, it didn't take a CPA to know that their income had taken a major hit.

That, and she'd overheard more than one argument about money over the past couple of years, an occurrence that had become more frequent as they'd prepared for this move.

Dad sighed as he turned off the engine before glancing out the window at the large truck parked on the curb. The liftgate was open and four men stood around chatting while they waited for the family to arrive.

Kayla stepped out and stretched, alleviating some of the stiffness that had really settled in over the last leg of the trip. She zipped up her hoodie, despite the humidity really bearing down in the late morning sun. Not that she gave a shit about annoying her mom, but she really wanted to make an effort to ensure Kylie stopped being collateral damage of her contentious relationship with Gretchen. She'd change into something cooler as soon as she got her bags up to her room.

Kylie exited the vehicle shortly after, mimicking Kayla's stretch without even realizing it. Kayla smiled, an unconscious gesture of her own, but tried to hide it when Kylie glanced her way. Couldn't have her getting *too* comfortable after all. The younger Macklin girl's smirk acknowledged that just maybe the two of them may get along in this new town if they actually made some effort. After all, who else did they have?

"Sorry, guys," Kayla heard Roger tell the movers, "Got a little held up crossing the state line."

"Meter's running, sir," said a bulky man with a long bushy beard. Kayla assumed he was the leader of the crew as he handed a clipboard to her father. "Don't make no difference to us. Sign here."

Roger signed the papers and returned it to the man, who gestured to the other three. They hopped up and climbed the ramp into the back, emerging moments later with the first of the neatly labeled boxes to be brought into the house.

Kayla retrieved her phone and the small bag containing the items she wanted handy on the drive—things like gum, a bottle of water and her phone charger. She sifted through the bag to make sure the pack of Marlboro Lights and the small yellow Bic lighter hadn't fallen out. Mom would freak the fuck out if she knew she was smoking. Even though she didn't particularly care what her mother thought, this wasn't a fight she was in the mood for right now.

As she gathered her stuff, she heard Kylie groan from around the side of the car.

"Kylie?" Gretchen said, her voice stressed. "Are you okay, sweetie?"

Kayla watched as her mother rushed over to her sister and immediately pressed her hand to her forehead.

"Mom," Kylie said, annoyed. "I'm fine. I just had a cramp."

"Where?" Mom asked, stress morphing into panic. "Your stomach?"

"No! My leg! It's fine."

"Are you sure?"

"Yes!"

Gretchen straightened up and rested her hands on her youngest's shoulders.

"Okay, but remember, if you ever feel any type of strange pain, you let me know right away, okay?"

"Okay," Kylie said, pulling away, exasperated, as she reached in and retrieved her own travel bag, along with her tablet and charger.

Gretchen took a deep breath, no doubt calming herself as Kayla rolled her eyes. Her mom was a lot and it wasn't showing any signs of getting better. That made her sad because, at this rate, Kylie would grow up to be one of those people who thought every ache and pain was a predictor of certain death.

As Kayla shut the car door, the sound of another in the distance drew her attention.

Parked at the curb was an older-model silver Kia. A man walked around the back toward them. He was Asian, in his mid-thirties, short of stature, maybe only a few inches taller than Kayla's five foot five inches, but in good shape. He wore a black short-sleeve button-down and matching slacks. Kayla would have wondered what he was doing there, but his white clerical collar gave her a good idea.

Damn it, Mom.

"Hello," the priest said in a pleasant tone while extending his hand toward Gretchen. "You must be the Macklins. I'm Father Thomas Lee."

Gretchen reacted as if the clergyman was a long-lost friend showing up at her doorstep with a present. She beamed a smile at him and shook his hand.

"Father Lee! It's so nice to meet you in person. I'm Gretchen Macklin. We spoke on the phone."

"It's great to put a face to the name." He turned toward the girls, who were now standing next to each other, Kylie confused, Kayla annoyed.

"Hello, ladies, I'm Father—"

"Lee," Kayla cut him off. "I heard you the first time."

"Kayla!" Gretchen snapped. "Be polite."

"Are you our neighbor?" Kylie asked.

"No, young lady," Father Lee responded. "I'm here to—"

Now it was Gretchen's turn to interrupt the priest. "He's here to say a few prayers to welcome us to our new home."

"Oh, cool," Kylie said.

Kayla saw her father emerge from the open doorway, maneuvering around two of the movers as they worked in tandem to carry a dresser inside. She saw him notice the priest. She also saw the frown that formed on his face when he did. Mom's exploration of her Catholic faith was a recent development. And, like many of her mother's endeavors, she dove in headfirst with a fervor that could be excessive, to say the least.

"C'mon Kylie," she said to her sister. "Let's get the rest of our stuff out of the car."

19

"Nice to meet you!" Kylie said cheerily, extending her own hand to the priest, who accepted and shook it before she joined her sister back at the car.

Kayla took her time gathering the rest of her stuff from the back seat as she eavesdropped on her parents and the priest.

"Hi. Roger Macklin," she heard Dad say cordially before prompting for the man's name. "Nice to meet you, Father...?"

"Thomas Lee. Welcome to Huntsville, Mr. Macklin."

"Roger is fine. You guys sure don't waste any time with the welcome committee."

"Well, typically we don't show up along with the movers, but when I spoke to Mrs. Mack—"

For the third time in the past few minutes, a Macklin cut Father Lee off.

"I asked him to come bless the house immediately. I wanted to make sure we started out on strong footing here. You can never be too careful."

"Mm-hmm," Roger muttered. "Well, Father, I thank you for coming. Please feel free to go in and perform your ritual."

"Just a simple blessing, Mr. Mac—excuse me—Roger. Nothing so formal. It'll only take a few minutes. I just need to get my stole from the car."

"Whatever you have to do."

Having retrieved the rest of their belongings from the car, Kayla and Kylie made their way up the walkway to the house. Father Lee had returned to his car and Mom and Dad were whispering to each other. Roger's irritation was palpable, but Gretchen was unfazed, giving him the full brunt of her attitude in return.

This was getting to be too common an occurrence,

even for Kayla, who was at least aware enough of the role she often played in perpetuating it.

"You had no business setting this up without telling me," Kayla heard her father say as they got close enough to decipher the whispers. "Jesus Christ, the girls haven't even been inside the house yet."

"Don't speak like that. He'll hear you," Gretchen shot back. "I want to start off here with a prayer for our family's good health, especially—"

"Girls," Roger said, noting their approach and stopping his wife mid-sentence. "Why don't you drop your stuff inside and then check out the house?"

"Sure," Kayla said, understanding that her usual snark would be more unwelcome than usual in this instance. "C'mon, Kylie."

Kylie followed along, but Kayla saw by the look on her face that she was well aware that Mom and Dad were arguing and it upset her.

As the older girl ushered her sister along while trying to tune out the hushed, angry whispers of their parents, her phone buzzed in her pocket.

She felt a sinking feeling in her stomach when she saw the text message. She didn't know what she should have expected after her comment, but thinking before acting wasn't always Kayla's strong suit.

MORGAN: What was up with that bitchy comment?

Kayla wasn't sure how to respond. She was still pissed, but that didn't mean she hadn't overreacted. She slipped the phone back in her pocket and figured she'd deal with it later.

In her distraction, she hadn't noticed that Kylie was now a few feet ahead of her, but she had stopped just before crossing the threshold into the new house. She looked like she was a million miles away, staring into the interior. Kayla looked over her shoulder, but all she saw were the movers going about their work.

"Hey, space cadet!" Kayla called to her. Kylie turned to her older sibling, a faraway look still in her eyes. "Kylie!" Kayla said, a little louder this time.

Her sister snapped out of it and laughed.

"Sorry, just zoned out."

"Thinking about what?"

"Don't know," Kylie said, before quickly changing the subject. "Where's our rooms?"

Kayla brushed off the oddness of her sister's episode and chalked it up to travel fatigue.

"Let's find out."

CHAPTER 2

K ylie thought the house was pretty nice. Even though it was smaller than their old one, the previous owners had clearly made sure it was well maintained. The hardwood floors were only the slightest bit scuffed in areas, and the walls looked to have been recently painted. It was an open floor plan so you could get a good look as soon as you stepped inside. The rooms were quickly filling up with boxes and furniture as the movers went about their work.

As she watched the workers, she felt that sensation again. The one she felt right before she stepped in. She wasn't sure what it was, but it felt almost as if she were leaving her body, floating out of the physical and into a place where the real world became a movie with busted speakers, the sounds distorted. It wasn't an unpleasant feeling. She'd had way too many of those these past few years as her body fought against her, but it was weird and disconnected.

Her sister's voice brought her back.

"I think we're up here," Kayla said. When Kylie snapped back into herself, she saw her sibling gesturing toward the stairs. "C'mon."

Kylie followed her up to the second floor, turning at the landing halfway up. Their footsteps echoed on the wood as they made their way upstairs. When they got to the top, they saw four open doorways. The one directly at the end of the hall revealed pink tiles and a white pedestal sink, clearly a bathroom.

The first door on the right led to a big bedroom. Mom and dad's dresser was already inside, signaling their parents' claim to the space. Another door inside led to another bathroom. It made sense to Kylie that this was the master bedroom.

Moving down the hall, they looked into the second bedroom. It was a decent size, with light-gray paint and a fuzzy navy-blue carpet. Kylie thought it was kind of boring. As she hoped that the next room would be better, Kayla dispelled any notion of her taking it.

"This one's yours."

"This one sucks," Kylie said, frowning. "Why can't I have the other one?"

"You think Mom is going to let you that far out of her sight?"

Kylie pushed past Kayla and saw that the other room was much more her speed. It was smaller, but the wall and carpet were shades of purple, her favorite color. Plus, the closet was open and she saw it was big enough to walk in. It wasn't a huge space like some of the rich people's closets she saw on TV, and fashion wasn't a big concern of hers, but it would be great to set up a little fort inside. She could stack some boxes with a sheet and read the copy of *Scary Stories to Tell in the Dark* her friend Rachel had given her as a going-away present. She had hidden it in the bottom of her bag because Mom would freak if she found it.

"You hate purple," she observed to Kayla.

"Yep," her sister acknowledged. "But I'd hate to be in

the room next to Mom and Dad even more."

"Why? So, you can have boys over without them hearing?"

Kayla cocked an eyebrow. "What makes you think that?"

"Isn't that what you do? You have boys over and do kissy stuff with them?"

Kayla snorted. It was genuine amusement that Kylie wasn't used to seeing out of her.

"Not exactly."

"C'mon, can't you convince Mom to let me have that room?"

"No," Kayla confessed with a sigh. Kylie saw the gears turning in her head. She knew that Kayla didn't want to be so close to Mom and Dad, but she seemed to be considering it. They both knew the room with the purple carpet was the better option for Kylie. After a moment, Kayla's lips turned up into a smirk. "But I bet we can convince Dad."

Kylie smiled in return and felt silly for not thinking of it. Their father was easily the more reasonable parent.

"Let's go find him!"

As the girls made their way downstairs, Kayla's phone dinged. She stopped on the landing and looked at it, her face twisting at what she saw on the screen. Kylie knew better than to ask, but she saw her sister typing. A lot. She gave her a second to finish, but she kept going. She must have had a lot to say to whoever she was texting.

"Kayla?" she finally asked. The other girl didn't respond. Instead, she just kept at it on her device, looking progressively angrier as she went along. "I'm going to go find Dad."

Kayla still didn't answer her as Kylie continued downstairs. She moved toward the front door, being that was the last place she'd seen her father was out front. But as she approached, her mother rounded a corner with the priest. He was wearing a fancy-looking scarf that was made of a shiny, dark-green material. It had gold frills on either side, right below a stitched cross. He carried a small leather-bound book with gilded pages in one hand and was slipping a small vial half filled with clear liquid into his pocket.

Father Lee seemed nice enough, but Kylie didn't want to get caught up with them, so she quickly turned and ducked into the kitchen. The movers had been there because there were boxes all over the place but, at the present moment, the room was empty. Like the rest of the house, it was smaller than their old kitchen, but everything looked nice enough, she guessed. She heard the faint sound of running water.

Surveying the room, she saw the sink. The faucet had a small but steady stream of water flowing from it, the handle slightly upturned. Kylie went over and pushed it down, cutting off the flow. There was a window directly above giving a view of the backyard and the wooded area behind it. She stood on her tiptoes to get a better look.

The yard, if you could even call it that, wasn't fenced in. That was a disappointment to her. Their old home in Florida had a big backyard with a play set complete with swings and a spiral slide. They also had a big in-ground pool with a diving board. It wasn't unusual for Kylie to cannonball off of it before hopping right out and repeating the process until she was exhausted.

This yard, however, was little more than a patch of grass that backed up to the trees. Without a fence, there wasn't anything to keep people out of their property. The only thing remotely interesting was an old, worn tire swing affixed to a sturdy tree branch.

Boring, Kylie thought to herself.

The thought was almost immediately contradicted when she caught something out of the corner of her eye.

Off in the trees, she saw a little girl skipping around. She looked about Kylie's age with long dark hair that was arranged in loose pigtails on either side. She wore a dress that reminded her of a school uniform with a green-and-black checkered skirt, stockings and buckled Mary Jane shoes. Kylie's school back home had a dress code, but they weren't required to wear any type of school-issued attire other than at phys ed.

Did the school here make you wear a uniform? She hoped not.

The strange girl must have known she was being watched because she abruptly stopped skipping and turned to face the house. She smiled and waved.

Kylie wondered if maybe she was a neighbor. That would be cool if she could make a friend close by. She'd missed so much time with her friends back in Rockledge and, just when she was getting back to some type of social life, they upped and moved here.

I should go introduce myself, she thought.

But where was Kayla? She didn't want to just run off. Mom would be ticked for sure, and Kayla would get in trouble. She didn't want that.

Kylie returned to the front hallway. Fortunately, Mom was outside still talking to the priest so she didn't notice her. The clergyman looked stiff and was checking his watch as she talked rapid fire, no doubt recounting the circumstances leading up to their move.

Kayla was still on the landing, but now she was sitting on the top step, still typing away on her phone.

"Kayla," Kylie said softly, needing her sister's attention, but feeling bad for interrupting.

"What?" Kayla asked without even looking up.

"There's a little girl out back," Kylie said eagerly. "I think she might be our neighbor. I want to say hi."

"Sure. Whatever."

"Let Mom know if she's looking for me."

"Uh-huh."

During the exchange, Kayla remained glued to her phone. Kylie wasn't even sure she was listening, but that wasn't her problem. She'd done what she was supposed to do.

She headed out back.

When Kylie stepped outside, the warm sun felt good on her skin. Even though the doors were open to accommodate the movers, the air conditioning must have been on because the house felt cold. She hadn't realized how cold it actually was until just now. She scanned the vicinity but didn't see the girl right away.

Disappointment sunk in as she made her way to the tire swing, pushing down on it to test its stability before hoisting herself in and swinging. After a few minutes, she felt herself drifting again, lost in the feeling of the fresh air and the songs of the birds as the tire carried her back and forth. But just before she fully sunk into her trance, she saw the girl again.

She was further into the woods this time, but she was looking at Kylie, waving at her. When their eyes met, she gestured for her to come with her. Kylie hopped off the swing and waved back, but didn't step past what she assumed was the boundary of the yard.

"Hi!" she called to the girl. "I'm not supposed to leave the yard!" The girl shrugged and started skipping again, making a circle around a large maple tree, disappearing briefly behind the trunk before emerging again.

Kylie looked back toward the house. She didn't see her parents or Kayla. She thought perhaps she should go back and ask if she could explore behind the house a little, but she knew that wouldn't fly. Maybe if Kayla came with her, but, based on her mood right now, that was a long shot too.

She turned back to the woods and saw the girl was gone.

Darn it.

Kylie thought about it. She *assumed* she wasn't allowed to explore beyond the trees, but no one had explicitly *told* her not to. She could just go find the girl, say hi and come right back. No harm in that, right?

She stepped onto the small path between the trees and headed into the woods.

Kylie felt a little more nervous the further away she got from the house. She'd been walking for a few minutes and told herself she'd come this far and the girl had to be close. Still, she had gone further than her parents would have been okay with.

The path had disappeared a few minutes ago and right when she was at the point where she thought she should turn back, she saw a clearing a few yards ahead. As she got closer, she saw the spires of a big iron fence. Between the bars, she thought she saw a bunch of rocks, arranged in rows. But as she got closer, she saw they weren't rocks. They were tombstones.

It was a cemetery.

Mom and Dad made them move right by a cemetery? Creepy. Kylie figured they must not have read many scary books when they were kids.

She stepped out of the woods and walked up to the gates. There were lots of gravestones inside and it seemed like they were arranged pretty close together. The place was huge. Kylie imagined it would take a very long time to try to walk around the whole thing.

Kylie walked along the perimeter of the cemetery, brushing her hands against the bars. The iron was warm from the sun beating down on it, so she didn't hover on any one for too long. If Mom saw her doing that, she would likely soak her hands in sanitizer just for touching them.

As she moved along, she saw something different

around the side.

A swing set.

Kylie hurried to the swings and saw that they were a part of a small playground. It was open on three sides, but behind the play structures was a large limestone wall that went pretty high up. Concrete blocks were embedded in a dirt mound to the right, forming a crude staircase leading to an unseen path in the woods.

The swings were erected with a green metal A-frame with supports on either end and another in the middle. There were six swings in total—four traditional belt swings and two of the toddler variation.

Behind the swing set was a typical playground slide. From her vantage point in front of the swings, Kylie could see the small plastic climbing wall that led up to the second level of the structure, where there was a rolling tic-tac-toe game board. To the right was a set of stairs and to the left was a climbing bar that reminded her of a twisty straw.

Kylie forewent the stairs in favor of climbing up the bars. They felt kind of slick and had dirt caked on them. She thought again about her mother and her never-ending supply of hand sanitizer.

When she reached the top, she looked around. She wasn't very high, but she had a good view of the cemetery. She wondered if there were any kids buried there. It was a dark thought, but one that wasn't foreign to Kylie. She had often wondered what it was like when you died. Was there a heaven? Did you just go to sleep and never wake up? If so, did you dream? These were all thoughts that no nine-year-old should have but, as Kylie knew all too well, she wasn't an ordinary nine-year-old.

She shook the thoughts off and tuned to see the slide

facing away from the swings. She sat at the top and pushed herself off with the bars, sliding to the ground below, dirt kicking up as she hopped off. It was too short to provide any type of genuine thrill, but it was satisfying in its own way.

Kylie ran around to the front, intending to do it again, when she saw the young girl again. She was on the swings and smiling at Kylie. She approached and introduced herself.

"Hi, I'm Kylie. Kylie Macklin."

"Hi, Kylie Macklin," the girl said in a pleasant tone. "I'm Emily."

"Nice to meet you. I just moved in."

"I saw. Come swing with me."

Kylie smiled and hopped on the swing next to Emily, building momentum quickly to match the other girl's pace.

"You live around here?" Kylie asked.

"Yup."

"That's cool. Where do you go to school? I'm starting at Alexander next week."

"Where are you from?" Emily asked, disregarding Kylie's question.

"Florida."

"What brings you here?"

"My dad got a new job. Something to do with insurance or something. My mom wanted him to have it in case I got sick."

Emily slowed her momentum and eyed her curiously.

"Sick? You don't look sick. In fact, you look very healthy."

"I'm not sick now, but I was."

"Really?" Emily asked, slowing to a stop.

"Yeah, I—"

As she was about to answer, Kylie saw someone else in the distance. It was a man. A very large man wearing a yellow rain slicker. He stood partially behind a tree on the edge of the woods. His hood was up, so she couldn't see his face. She thought it odd that he was wearing a raincoat when there was no rain. Plus, it was really getting hot out as the morning gave way to afternoon. She couldn't imagine the reason behind his unusual choice of attire.

Something about him deeply unsettled her. She couldn't see his eyes, yet she felt like he was staring at her. She suddenly felt cold again, despite the sun.

"Who's that?" Kylie asked, turning to Emily and noticing the other girl's attention was still on her.

"Who's who?" Emily replied.

Kylie pointed toward the woods. But the man was no longer there.

"There was a man. A big man. He was in the woods. Watching us."

Emily shrugged. "Probably The Caretaker."

Kylie stopped swinging. Something about this place had become very unsettling to her. She felt her stomach tighten and cramp as she dismounted.

"Where are you going?" Emily asked, a hint of disappointment in her voice.

"I really have to get back to the house. I need to find my sister."

Emily lit up. "You have a sister? Maybe she can come play with us, too?"

"Um. Maybe."

"The more the merrier! Go get her and bring her back! I'll wait here!"

"I don't know if she—"

Before she could finish, Kylie heard her name called from somewhere in the trees.

"Kylie!"

It was Kayla. She sounded anxious.

"Kylie Macklin, you get over here right now!"

This time it was Mom. That explained Kayla's concern. Whoa boy, was she in trouble.

She saw Gretchen emerge from the trees, her face twisted in an amalgamation of concern and rage. Kayla hurried behind her, trying to keep up with her mother's frantic pace as she stormed toward Kylie.

"See, Mom? She's fine."

"Not a word from you, Kayla!" Gretchen spat without so much as offering a glance in her older daughter's direction. She broke into a light run as she approached Kylie, putting a hand on either shoulder.

"Are you okay? Why are you so dirty? Have you been rolling around in this filth? Here." The words vomited from Mom's mouth as she pulled the sanitizer from her pocket. She forcibly grabbed Kylie's hands and slathered it in the viscous substance . "Rub this in good. Get it all over. You're going straight in the bath when we get back to the house."

"She's fine."

"I said shut your damn mouth!" Gretchen shouted as she whirled to face Kayla. "You are so goddamn irresponsible! I can't trust you!"

"Then fucking don't!" Kayla said, getting in her face. "I didn't ask to be a babysitter. It's not like you have a job anymore. You fucking watch her!"

Kylie cringed. She'd heard her sister curse before and she definitely had seen her fight with Mom before, but she had never seen her talk like this. Mom's face was red and for a second, she thought might actually slap Kayla.

But she didn't. She grabbed Kylie's hand and said, "Let's go."

In the commotion, Kylie had almost completely forgotten about Emily. She turned back to the swing, embarrassed that her potential new friend had to see this ugly fight. She wanted to say goodbye, but there was no one to say goodbye to.

Emily was gone.

CHAPTER 3

The Mackin family sat around the kitchen table for their first dinner in their new home. While they had made some progress on unpacking, there were still boxes surrounding them as they dined on Chinese takeout. The cartons were arranged in the middle of the table as everyone claimed whatever portions they wanted on paper plates.

Silence permeated the room, save for the ticking of the wall clock Roger had put up earlier. He never could stand not knowing what time it was.

Kayla found herself irritated by the rhythmic clacking, but kept her mouth shut. She had already said way too much to her mother at the playground. She partially regretted the outburst, much of it the frustration and fatigue from the move boiling over. Still, her relationship with her mother had deteriorated much over the past few years, making a blow-up inevitable.

When they had returned to the house, Mom didn't say a word to her. She just took Kylie upstairs and ran her a bath after retrieving towels and soap from one of the boxes. Dad had seen them storming in and asked Mom what was wrong, but she just ignored him and ushered her sister upstairs. Dad turned to Kayla and asked her what the deal was, but Kayla had just shrugged and told him to ask Mom.

She saw the exasperation written on his face and felt bad. Dad was always trying to keep a level head while Mom and, yes, even Kayla, as she herself could admit, often ran on pure emotion. For the first time, it struck Kayla just how much Kylie was like their father. She had this matter-of-fact way about her. Even through all the years of doctors' appointments and treatments, Kylie seemed to take everything one day at a time. Sure, there were moments when she was scared, or in pain, or just plain sad, but mostly she handled everything admirably.

Kayla watched her sister as she fumbled with her chopsticks to scoop up some lo mein, most of it spilling back onto her plate. Undeterred, Kylie went back again, this time managing to grab a larger portion. She smiled as she chewed, pleased with herself.

When she looked up, she caught Kayla smiling at her. At first, she looked confused. Kayla had to imagine her sister thought she was mad at her but, after a moment, she returned the smile. The silent understanding delivered, Kayla grabbed her phone next to her and turned her attention to the text chain with Morgan.

Morgan: What was up with that bitchy comment?

Kayla: What's up with u not telling me ur dating Aiden Dunn?

Morgan: Y does it matter????

Kayla: Because I thought we were best friends?

Morgan: U were moving and I didn't want to have a fight before we left.

Kayla: Y would we have a fight?

Morgan: Like u don't know?

Kayla: ????

Morgan: U get weird every time I like a guy.
Kayla: I do not!
Morgan: Every time.
Kayla: Bullshit!
Morgan: It's like u want to date me urself or something.
Kayla: Whatever dude. I'm done. Fuck u.

She got a notification that Morgan had read the last message and she saw the bubble with the dots pop up twice, only to disappear and not return a third time. That was where they left the conversation.

I do not get weird when she dates. That's so fucking stupid. I don't—

"Kayla," Gretchen said, halting her rumination. "Can you please put the phone down and interact with your family?"

Mom's voice was surprisingly level. Her expression neutral. The fact that she hadn't snapped at her threw Kayla. She didn't protest and turned her phone face down next to her plate. Dad seemed surprised too. The tension had been suffocating since they returned, but now Mom was acting like it was normal.

"So, Kayla, I saw that Huntsville Community College is accepting late applications until the thirtieth. Have you thought about maybe taking some classes?"

The college talk again. Mom had switched her attack plan from beratement to guilt trips about her education. Or lack thereof.

"I'm taking a gap year."

"I'm not sure that's wise, Kayla," Gretchen said.

Kayla played it diplomatically. She was exhausted and didn't have the energy for another shouting match.

"I need some time to figure out what I want to do. I... I just don't know yet."

That wasn't a lie. Once Kylie got sick, Kayla had to fend for herself a lot throughout high school. Mom and Dad were so focused on her younger sister's medical care, they didn't push her hard on the educational front. She got middling grades and cared little for the extracurriculars, so she knew she wasn't an ideal college candidate. She spent most of her time partying with her friends, with no eye on the future. Now she was in a new town with no friends and no future.

"You can always take the core courses while you figure out your major."

"It's fine," Roger interjected. "If you don't feel college is right for you, you don't have to go."

Kayla smiled. Gretchen frowned.

"Thanks, Dad," Kayla said genuinely.

"Oh, don't thank me yet," Dad replied. "You don't have to go to college, but you're not going to just sit around all day doing nothing. If you're not going to continue your education, you need to get a job."

Kayla was speechless. Not so much at the edict. She'd actually very much intended to find work. She'd thought about getting her own place for a while now and the blow-up with her mother at the playground cemented the fact that she needed to get out of this house as soon as possible.

No, what surprised her was the coldness with which her father delivered his statement. She had seen him clap back at Mom similarly icy responses, but he'd never shown that lack of emotion with her. It illustrated just how fed up Roger Macklin had become with the never-ending discord in his family.

Kayla felt sad. She had always prided herself on being *Daddy's little girl*. Even as she got older and surlier with her mother, her dad had always been her go-to. While Mom fussed incessantly over Kylie, Kayla felt her father was the one she could talk to when things got rough. Admittedly, she hadn't done her best to foster that relationship recently and now, hearing the matter-of-fact tone in Roger's voice, she regretted it.

"Understand?" Roger asked, prompting her to say something.

"Yes, Daddy," she replied, a little surprised since she hadn't called him *Daddy* in years. She felt like she was Kylie's age again, being scolded for stealing a cookie or something.

"Good," Roger said.

"I'm not sure I agree," Gretchen chimed in.

Oh fuck, Kayla thought.

"How so?" Roger said, scooping a piece of honey chicken into his mouth without looking up.

"What kind of job is she going to get without a degree, Roger?"

"I'm not saying I'm not going to ever go," Kayla interjected. "I just need to figure some stuff out."

"That's how it starts, sweetheart," Gretchen said, the endearment dripping with sarcasm. "You stop your momentum and you can never get it back."

"Interesting you should say that, darling," Roger added, mimicking his wife's smarminess. "Have you considered perhaps going back to work yourself? Maybe start your practice again? At least part time?"

"I don't think that's an appropriate conversation in front of the girls. Especially Kylie."

"But it's appropriate to talk about Kayla's education in front of her?"

"That's different."

"I'm just saying a little extra income would go a long way with the bills."

"I think it's more important for me to be a mother right now."

"Mother to Kylie, you mean."

The room went silent. Kayla hadn't even realized she said the words out loud. She quickly scanned the table. Kylie's eyes were wide. Dad looked shocked. Mom's face was bright red.

"Excuse me, Kayla?" Gretchen asked, venom in her voice.

Kayla felt her eyes water. Fuck it. She'd gone this far.

"Why don't you love me, Mom?"

"Kayla!" Roger scolded.

"No. Why don't you love me, Mom?" Kayla repeated.

"I do love you, Kayla," Gretchen said, her own eyes reddening and watering. "I love you with all my heart. But you know things have been hard. Kylie has needed more from us and I wish that wasn't the case, but it doesn't make it not true. I've done my best to be there for you as much as I can, but *you* have rejected me at almost every turn. I've lain awake many nights, not only worrying about your sister, but feeling like a failure for not being there for you." Kayla sat in stunned silence as tears slipped down her cheeks, defying her will for them not to. "If you want to know if I'm sorry about that, I am. But I can't change it. I can only do my best. So, maybe the question you should ask is: when did you stop loving me?"

Kayla closed her eyes, unable to look at her mother. They burned and itched as more tears fought their way out. She searched her memory, wanting to simultaneously curse her mother yet also to throw her arms around her and hold her tight. It wasn't some grand revelation that the deterioration of their relationship resulted from her feelings of abandonment.

Kylie had gotten sick and Mom had blamed herself. Kayla knew that guilt was why Gretchen had totally dedicated herself to all aspects of Kylie's care, not only in the medical sense, but in the religious as well. Mom had started going to church again, dragging the whole family with her. It wasn't exactly Kayla's first choice to get up early on a Sunday and listen to a priest drone on about the Holy Spirit and dudes with names like Abraham and Jacob. After that, it had just been a steady decline as Kayla did her own thing while her parents, Mom especially, doted on her sick sister.

The worst part of it in Kayla's mind was that she was going through it along with them. She loved Kylie and was just as worried about her. She was dealing with the same stress and anxiety and, while Dad at least would occasionally ask her about how she was doing, Mom just seemed to assume she didn't need a check-in. *Kayla's healthy so clearly she's fine.* It opened the door to resentment that only made her feel guiltier, which, in turn, only exacerbated her anger.

The family sat around the table. Not speaking. Not eating. Just avoiding eye contact in the aftermath of the emotional eruption they'd just experienced until Kayla couldn't take it any longer.

"May I be excused?" she asked, barely above a whisper.

No one responded. She took the silence as permission and left the table.

42

A few hours later, Kayla had unpacked most of her stuff. After she left the table, she had gone straight to her room and shut the door and hadn't opened it since. She was putting away the last of her clothes, some going in the closet on hangers and others folded in her drawer. With the last pile, she dropped a T-shirt that unfolded as it hit the floor. She held it up to refold and felt her stomach knot when she saw the words accompanying the orange ribbon symbol printed on the fabric.

I'm Wearing This Ribbon for Someone I Love.

She turned it over and looked at the back.

Kidney Cancer Awareness.

If she had any tears left to cry, they very well may have started up again. Looking at the shirt she had worn to the St. Jude's cancer walk in Miami last year made her feel guilty again. Her feelings of being neglected were nothing compared to the hell that Kylie had been through. She knew her parents had been hurting too and her petulance had made it harder on them more than once.

I need a cigarette, she thought.

It was late enough. Everyone should have retreated to their bedrooms at this point. She had started smoking a few years back, even though it had become a sort of taboo for her generation. Not that Gen Z had an aversion to tobacco. They just opted to vape it instead.

Like a lot of Kayla's less-advisable actions, her opting for good old-fashioned cancer sticks was out of spite.

She hated to admit it, but she tried them because she wanted to do something unhealthy. At least that's why she smoked the first one. After that, like so many other foolish kids before her, she used stress as an excuse and got addicted.

Back in Florida, she went out a lot and just got her fix then. She was sure her clothes reeked when she came home, but she just blamed it on other people doing it around her. She kind of thought Mom would press her harder on it, maybe throw some of that concern she reserved for Kylie her way, but she always just told her she should try to avoid second-hand smoke and left it at that.

This being day one in a new city and state, however, combined with the late hour, she really didn't have anywhere to go without raising questions she didn't want to answer, so she decided to chance it.

There were two windows in her room, so she opted for the one furthest from the door. She lit a scented candle and placed it on her nightstand. The aroma of lavender filled the air, soon to be locked in combat with the stench of tobacco.

Retrieving the pack and placing the cig between her lips, she turned off her lamp to darken the room before opening the window and sat on the sill, glancing downward to make sure no one was there before flicking the spark wheel, the small flame accompanying the candle as the only source of light in the room.

Just as she was about to ignite her smoke, she jumped as something landed on the sill, the cigarette falling to the floor. She was thankful not only that it landed inside the house rather than on the ground below for her parents to find, but also that it wasn't lit. She had no interest in trying to explain away a burn mark on the carpet.

Leaving it on the floor for now, she grabbed the candle off the nightstand and moved back toward the open window, holding it out to get a better look at what had startled her.

It was a small bird. Kayla had no idea what type. Maybe a sparrow? A finch?

Whatever species it was, it didn't seem spooked. As she got closer, she expected it to fly away, but it just sat there, chirping and staring at her. She stopped a few feet from the window and cocked her head to one side as she observed it. Oddly, the tiny songbird matched the gesture as it watched her back.

Kayla took a step closer. Then another. The bird didn't move. Another step. She was right at the windowsill now, still holding the candle in her left hand. She reached out with her right, not even really knowing what she was going to do if it didn't fly away. Pet it? Shoo it off?

The bird chirped again as Kayla rested her hand on the frame right in front of it. It still didn't budge.

"What's your deal, little dude?" she said as she inched her fingers toward it.

Without warning, the bird thrust its head down like a headbanger at a heavy metal concert, its beak embedding itself momentarily into the back of Kayla's hand.

"Fuck!" she yelled as she quickly placed the candle back on the nightstand, almost dropping it in the process and breathing a sigh of relief when she didn't. A cigarette burn in the carpet would have been bad enough. Burning down their new house on the first night? That would be some bad karma. She clutched her stinging hand and kicked the window frame. This time, the bird flew away and Kayla slammed the window shut.

With the room secure from the aviary assassin, she removed her hand and looked over the fresh wound. It wasn't deep, but it was bleeding pretty good. She transferred her good hand and cupped it underneath, preventing the blood from trickling onto the carpet. The wound needed a Band-Aid.

To Kayla's chagrin, that involved leaving her room and crossing the hall to the bathroom. As she opened her door, she said a silent prayer—the irony of her disdain for her mother's showy piousness not lost on her—that her parents were asleep.

She glanced back and forth and saw all the doors on the second floor were closed, save for the bathroom, so that was a good start. As she stepped over the threshold from her carpeted bedroom to the hardwood floor of the hallway, she took care to step slowly so as not to alert anyone to her presence.

A small nightlight guiding her path, she started toward the bathroom, she heard a commotion from the room behind her. She turned and crept up to the door and heard her parents arguing inside. They were trying, and failing, to keep their voices down.

Kayla couldn't help herself, so she inched toward the closed door and pressed her ear against it.

"It would have been really nice to at least get unpacked before starting up this same old bullshit," Dad said.

"And what bullshit is that, exactly? Your daughter's terrible attitude?"

"Our daughter. And that's the problem. She feels like she's always pushed aside because of Kylie's... situation."

Despite the circumstances, it felt good for Kayla to hear that from her father. Sometimes she felt they didn't even have an awareness of her. His words said otherwise.

Of course, Mom would ruin that a second later.

"Situation? I'd say a cancer diagnosis at five years old is a little more severe than a *situation*!"

"Don't play word games with me, Gretchen. You know what I meant. It's not her fault Kylie got sick."

"I know. It's mine."

"No, it isn't."

"Yes, it is. I should have seen that something was wrong sooner. And I know that we have been through hell over the past four years. And you didn't help things."

"Jesus Christ, Gretchen, I thought we were past this."

"Past you having an affair? You think that's something we just *get past?*"

An affair? That revelation hit Kayla like a slap in the face. She knew her parents had been at each other's throats for a while now, but she had no idea that Dad had cheated on Mom. Her straight-laced father, who would go back into a store and pay for a pack of gum if he accidentally walked out with it, actually stepped out on his marriage?

"It wasn't an affair, Gretchen." It sounded like Dad said that last part through gritted teeth. "I made a onetime mistake. Abigail came onto me. She kissed me and, yeah, I kissed her back, but that was it. I came right home and told you."

"So let me just order your *Husband of the Year* plaque. Sorry if I don't see you as a victim for fucking around while I'm home caring for our cancer-stricken daughter."

There was a long silence after that part. Kayla didn't know what to think. Yeah, her mom could be awful to her, but Dad kissing someone else, especially while Mom was dedicating all her time to Kylie's care, was low. Really low. She didn't know what she thought about her father at that moment.

She didn't have too much time to think about it as she heard footsteps moving toward the door. She quickly ducked into the bathroom and peeking out the door as she watched her father exit the bedroom and make his way to the stairs.

Once he was out of sight, Kayla opened the medicine cabinet and saw that her mom, as expected, had already stocked it. She turned on the faucet and washed away the blood, dabbing it dry with a towel before examining it. The bleeding had mostly stopped, the cut not being deep. She tore open the Band-Aid wrapper and affixed it to the back of her hand.

The first aid finished, she looked at herself in the mirror. As soon as she saw her reflection, she broke down and cried.

CHAPTER 4

T he tapping at the window woke Kylie up.

As she roused from sleep, she heard the rhythmic sound coming from somewhere in the room she couldn't immediately place. Sitting up in bed, she took a second to let her eyes adjust as she was drawn to the sole window in the room, the moonlight from the back of the house providing enough illumination to help her acclimate to the darkened environment. Having gotten her bearings, she looked at the clock on the night table.

11:16 p.m.

The tapping started again and she saw it was coming from a small bird resting on the outside windowsill.

Kylie stepped out of bed and rubbed her eyes as she walked over to examine the little mischief maker. When she was only a few feet away, the bird stopped tapping and seemed to examine her, cocking its head as it did.

She took another step and touched her finger to the window, pressing it against the glass in front of its beak. A tiny circle of fog highlighted her fingertip. The bird tapped again, making a small thunk against the glass as it made contact right where Kylie's finger rested.

Then it abruptly flew off.

Kylie watched as it quickly disappeared through the

trees. The nuisance gone, she intended to get back into bed, but something on the ground below caught her eye. Not just something. Someone.

Emily was standing in the backyard, looking up at her.

The strange girl was still dressed in the same clothes as she had been that afternoon. She was just standing there, smiling up at Kylie. She waved.

Kylie thought it was very odd that a girl her own age would wander around all alone at night on someone else's property, but she was polite and waved back.

Emily's smile widened. She didn't lower her hand, turning it instead and gesturing for Kylie to come down and meet her. She couldn't be serious, could she? Why would her parents let her out this late?

Kylie shrugged and shook her head no. Emily frowned and made a pouting expression. She brought her balled fists up to her eyes and circled them underneath to mock crying. For some reason, this made Kylie laugh.

Emily held one finger up before waving her down again, expressing that she only wanted her to come down for a second.

If I'm quiet, I can go down and say hi and then come right back up, Kylie thought. After all, she was very curious as to what this little girl was doing here at this time of night.

Kylie tiptoed over to her closet and grabbed her sneakers. She didn't want to put them on right away because she knew her footsteps would be too loud if she wore them while she slipped downstairs. She cradled them under her arm and slowly opened her door, looking both ways as if she were crossing the street before stepping quietly out into the hall.

Confident the coast was clear, she stealthily made

her way downstairs, a lump hitting her throat when a step midway down made the slightest creak under even her slight weight. She froze for a long second before resuming her trek downstairs.

As she rounded the corner at the bottom of the stairs, something else stopped her. A glow and faint sounds coming from the living room. She slowed her pace further and crept along the wall to determine the source.

She saw the crown of her father's head jutting up from the back of his easy chair, which was fully reclined. The television she remembered from the family room at their old house was the source of the glow, sitting on the bare console that would eventually have whatever decor Mom decided on. There was an old black-and-white movie playing that Kylie didn't recognize.

With Dad down here, there was no way she could sneak out without attracting attention. She wanted to see what Emily was up to, but she didn't want either of them to get in trouble, so she had no choice but to abort her mission. But, just as she was about to return upstairs, her father let out a truncated snore. He was asleep.

Kylie sighed and headed toward the kitchen. When she got to the threshold of the back door, she slipped on her sneakers and carefully opened it just enough to squeeze outside.

When she was out of the house, she stood on the deck and looked toward the trees. Emily wasn't there. Confused, Kylie scanned the backyard, squinting to see through the darkness.

"Hi!"

Kylie jumped and covered her mouth to stifle a yelp. Emily was standing next to her on the deck, grinning from ear to ear.

"Scared ya!"

"No, you didn't!" Kylie protested before changing the subject. "What are you doing here?"

"I wanted to come get you. So we can play."

"Play? It's the middle of the night!"

"That's what makes it so cool! All my friends are at the playground."

Friends? Kylie thought. *Playground?* "You have friends that are playing there right now?"

"Uh-huh," Emily said as she started skipping around Kylie like she was when she had first seen her earlier that day. "At the playground," she repeated.

"I can't go to the playground. My mom will lose her mind."

"She's sleeping. We'll only go for a little bit and you'll be back before she wakes up. Cross my heart."

Emily punctuated the last sentence by making a cross sign over her chest.

Kylie couldn't believe she was actually considering this. Mom would go absolutely ballistic if she found out she was right outside the house at this hour, let alone walking through the woods to the playground all by herself.

Still, Emily was intriguing. And, if there were more kids at the playground, it had to be some sort of secret club or something. If she was telling the truth, they'd all be risking getting in trouble, too.

As Kylie contemplated if she would go with her, an image flashed in her mind. A memory from two years ago. She was in their old house in Florida and was sitting at the white desk she had decorated with a myriad of stickers ranging from Hello Kitty to Teenage Mutant Ninja Turtles. Her tablet was open and she was watching some show—she couldn't remember which one—on Netflix.

She was so freaking tired of lying in her bed. Her back hurt and her bald head felt weird to her on her pillow. It took a good deal of effort, but she hoisted her frail frame up to a seated position before gingerly getting out of bed and walking over to her desk. She had swiped the multitude of pill bottles off the desk and set up her tablet so she could at least be by the window while she watched her shows.

As she looked outside, she saw Dana and Rachel, two girls she kind of knew from school—at least from what little she had attended since she got sick—riding their bikes along the sidewalk below. She cracked the window a bit, her joints aching as she did. She could hear their laughter through the small opening. They were just having fun, with no idea that anyone was watching them, but it hurt. Their glee felt like a slap in the face to Kylie.

She remembered longing to run outside, to go ask them if she could play. She didn't even have a bike, having outgrown her old one a few years ago. It made her sad to think that she never got to learn to ride one without training wheels. She wondered if she ever would.

As the memory faded back to the recesses of her mind, Kylie smirked at Emily.

"Let's go."

The girls had almost cleared the path into the playground when Kylie's trepidation reared again. She returned to her earlier line of inquiry.

"How are you all out here without your parents knowing?" she asked Emily, who just shrugged.

"Don't have parents."

Kylie felt shocked.

"What do you mean you don't have parents? Where are they?"

"Dead."

Kylie was stunned at the revelation. Not only that the girl's parents were dead, but also by the casualness with which she conveyed the information.

"What... happened to them?"

"They got sick. Died during the pandemic."

"I'm sorry," Kylie offered, as she remembered the craziness of a few years ago when schools shut down and everyone had to wear masks all the time. It was kind of funny. Not *ha ha* funny, but strange to her. She had gotten sick with her own illness a few months after starting kindergarten, not long before the virus had paralyzed the world. Mom was a complete nervous wreck watching the news. Leaving the house for anything but a doctor's appointment was out of the question. And then she was double-masked and slathered with sanitizer if she so much as brushed a surface.

She had to admit it was scary. Not only was there this sickness that everyone was getting, but Kylie had her own to deal with. Her doctor said she was *ee-moon-o compromised*, or something like that. It meant if everyone else had to be cautious, she had to be super ultra mega careful.

And it sucked.

But it must have sucked so much worse for poor Emily. Losing her parents during that time must have been awful.

"I'm really sorry," she said again.

Emily just shrugged once more. "People die. It happens." Again, the girl's casual tone surprised Kylie. She didn't know Emily, but she was sure she had never met anyone like her before. As she tried to figure out what to say next, her new friend broke her train of thought.

"We're here."

As the girls walked out from between the trees and along the cemetery fence, Kylie noted that the moonlight did a good job of lighting up the area. She could see the rows of tombstones that looked almost like they were glowing.

Emily brushed her hands across the iron gates, the same as Kylie had done earlier. She followed suit, sanitizer be damned, as they skipped together toward the playground.

Clearing the fence, Kylie became confused. There was no one else there.

"Where is everyone?" she asked.

Emily flashed her a grin. "Just wait."

"For what?"

Emily didn't answer. Instead, she grabbed her hand and led her to the swings. Kylie thought it was odd that her hand felt so warm because it was pretty chilly out. It hadn't occurred to her until now that it seemed a lot colder than it was when she left the house. It was really strange for a summer night, considering it had been around ninety degrees for much of the day.

They each selected a swing, and Emily let go of Kylie's hand and gripped the chains on either side as she built momentum. Kylie followed suit, and soon they were swinging in tandem. Emily looked blissful. She didn't have a care in the world, while Kylie just felt confused.

As if sensing it, Emily told her, "Don't worry; they'll be here soon."

Kylie had a feeling that something odd was happening, but she wasn't ready for the level of oddness that was about to unfold.

Out of nowhere, something materialized in the sky in front of her. It was some kind of strange orb, glowing even brighter than the moonlight.

It hung in the sky for a moment. It didn't have a face or eyes, but Kylie felt like it was watching her. She felt her breath catch as it moved toward her, but she was more startled by the sudden movement than afraid. It hovered up to her, stopping only inches from her face.

Kylie looked at Emily, who was just smiling at her with an *I told you so* expression.

If someone had described this scenario to Kylie even a couple of weeks ago, she would have expected to be scared, but she wasn't. Something about the way the orb floated in front of her, moonlight reflecting both through and around it. It was oddly beautiful.

She raised her hand tentatively toward it, unsure of what to do. As her fingertips seemed like they were just about to make contact, the orb suddenly spun in the air and the sound of a child's laughter echoed through the night as it flew off.

Kylie was disappointed. "Where did it go?" she asked Emily.

Emily just shrugged and kept swinging. A moment later, the swing next to her started to move on its own. Kylie thought it may have been the wind, but the night was calm and there wasn't much wind to speak of. Especially not the way it started picking up momentum.

More laughter emanated from an undeterminable location. It felt next to her, behind her and around her all at once. The swing on the other side of Kylie swayed as well. Soon all four of the big-kid swings were moving, the two in the middle carrying the girls, the two on either side by themselves.

Kylie heard another laugh. This one was distinctly over her right shoulder. She turned and didn't see anyone, but she heard a slight whooshing sound coming from the slide, followed by a light thunk. Accompanying the last sound was a puff of dirt kicking up from the ground below, as if something had landed in it.

The next thing she noticed was the tic-tac-toe board on top of the slide. The upper left tile swung from X to O. The one next to it moved in the reverse order. Tiles kept spinning at random until the ones marked X formed a diagonal line across the board. A victorious giggle punctuated the unseen player's victory.

The activity continued as Kylie observed it all, mesmerized.

"This is so cool," she said, more to herself than Emily.

"My friends only come out at night. They can be a little shy, though. Usually there aren't this many. They must like you."

"You think?"

"Yeah. There is something... special about you."

Kylie blushed. Usually, when people referred to her as special, it was regarding her illness, not just for who she was. It felt nice.

As she watched Emily, she could suddenly make out the form of another child on the swing next to her. It was a boy about the same age, but he was wearing odd clothes. They looked like something you would see in a movie that took place a hundred years ago. He wore a white button-down shirt cuffed at the collars and long corduroy shorts and knee-high socks along with black leather shoes.

The attire was odd, but his translucent appearance was even stranger. She could see right through him, but he somehow held the chains of the swing. Was he a... ghost? Some poor kid who had not been as lucky as she was and had died, only to be buried in the cemetery next door.

A girl's giggle came from the opposite side. Kylie turned and saw another ghostly figure, a girl in a knee-length cotton dress with an embroidered lace collar. Her Mary Jane shoes looked remarkably similar to Emily's. For a second, Kylie wondered if her new friend was a ghost as well, but she couldn't be. She couldn't see through her. Plus, she had touched her hand and it was warm. She definitely wasn't like the others.

"These are all ghosts?"

"A lot of kids died in this town," Emily said matter-of-factly. "In 1918, there was a terrible virus. They called it the Spanish flu. It hit children hard. A lot of them are buried in the cemetery."

"That's really sad," Kylie said, again reminded of how fortunate she was.

"At least they have this place to play. Every night, they come out and enjoy the playground. A lot of kids died in 1918, but it slowed down after that. At least until the 1960s."

"What happened in the 1960s?"

"A bad man."

Kylie wanted to follow up, but something in Emily's tone gave her pause. It was so blunt and emotionless that she wasn't sure she wanted to know.

It was then that the swings next to them suddenly fluttered in the air, as if the occupants had jumped off. She could no longer see the specters, but she caught glimpses of the grass being trampled and dirt being kicked up as if something were running on it.

"Where are they going?" she asked Emily, who just shrugged nonchalantly again.

Scanning the area, Kylie's blood froze when she saw something on the other side of the cemetery gate.

The large man in the yellow rain slicker. He stood there, staring at them from under his darkened hood.

"There's that man again."

"Yup. The Caretaker."

"Are we in trouble?"

Emily didn't answer. Kylie watched as the man opened the gate and stepped out of the cemetery and into the playground area. The sky darkened above him as gray clouds rolled in, rapidly covering the moon and plunging the area into darkness as if the man had brought the storm with him.

As he approached, Kylie wasn't sure what to do. They could get into a lot of trouble for trespassing. The cemetery man would certainly tell her parents and Mom would freak out, grounding her for the rest of her life.

He was only a few feet away now and Kylie found herself unable to move. Her fear of getting in trouble was fading, being replaced by a concern for her safety. What if this guy wanted to hurt them? Why was Emily so calm? She just kept swinging away as the giant man abruptly stopped in front of them.

"Mister?" The man looked down at her but didn't move. "I'm really sorry, I know I probably shouldn't be here but—"

The man lifted his head and looked off in the distance at something. Kylie turned to ask Emily what was going on, but she was gone. There was no sign of her anywhere. Fear washed over her. She wanted to run, but her body wasn't obeying her. She gripped the swings so tight that the metal dug into her palms, stinging her.

The only thing she could move was her head. She turned to see what had drawn the ominous figure's attention.

Just past the open cemetery gates, an old black woman sat in a rocking chair. She looked like she was over a hundred years old, her body frail and withered, her hair white and wispy. Though she was far away, her face was somehow clear to Kylie, almost as if she had somehow zoomed in preternaturally. Her eyes were a cloudy shade, devoid of irises. Her lips moved rapidly, mumbling something that Kylie couldn't hear.

She turned her attention back to The Caretaker, but he was gone. Like Emily, he was nowhere to be seen. Kylie felt herself regain control and managed to hop off the swing. When she looked back toward the cemetery, the old woman was gone as well.

She was alone.

"Kylie?" a disembodied, yet familiar, voice echoed

from the distance. It was Mom.

She was in a lot of trouble.

"Kylie?" Mom's voice came again, this time carrying a hint of worry.

Kylie was no longer at the playground, but all she saw was darkness. All she felt was cold. At first, anyway. Suddenly, her stomach spun, a tornado working its way up her esophagus as she bolted up in her bed just in time for a stream of vomit to spew from her mouth.

As she came to her senses, she saw she was back in her bedroom and it was morning. She had no recollection of how she'd gotten home.

"Oh my God!" her mom exclaimed. Kylie realized for the first time that she was there in the room with her, a look of utter panic painting her face.

"Roger!" she shouted. "We need you!"

Kayla arrived in the room first, also looking concerned. Dad followed a few seconds behind her, his face twisting in revulsion at the puke-stained comforter.

"Kylie's sick. We need to get her to the ER."

"Gretchen, she threw up. Let's not overreact."

"Don't tell me how to react! It can be a recurrence."

"Gretchen." Roger said again, not raising his voice but driving his point home with his inflection. "You're going to upset her more than she already is."

Kylie's head was spinning. She felt disembodied,

watching the scene from somewhere else, not in her bed covered in the undigested remnants of last night's dinner. Her stomach felt both empty yet somehow full at the same time.

"C'mon baby," Mom said, "Let's get you in the tub."

"I'll get the sheets," Kayla said.

Everyone seemed kind of surprised that she was willing to be so helpful, but Kylie certainly appreciated it. Mom was freaking, Dad was being logical, but Kayla was showing some actual compassion.

Mom and Dad both helped her out of bed, the first time she could remember them working as a team on anything in a while.

"Get her cleaned up and we'll see if we can get her in with the pediatrician," Dad said. "It's probably just a stomach bug."

Mom looked unsure, but nodded as she ushered Kylie out of the room and toward the bath.

CHAPTER 5

L ater that morning, Kayla made her way to downtown Huntsville. The family had only the one car since they'd had to sell Mom's Mercedes shortly before they moved, so Kayla opted to walk instead of ordering an Uber. It was still early, so the sun hadn't yet reached its apex. It was still mild on the approximately twenty-minute walk into town.

Her thoughts wandered to Kylie. Dad's practicality was often a counter to Mom's overzealousness, but sometimes she thought maybe he went too far in the other direction just to balance the pendulum that constantly swung over their heads. Sure, it was probably just a stomach bug, but given her sister's history, you couldn't really blame anyone for freaking out when she just threw up out of nowhere like that.

Kayla grimaced as she recalled the smell. She had gathered the comforter up, careful not to let the foul substance spill over as she carried it to the washing machine. She deposited the comforter inside and started the machine before going back to check on Kylie. Mom had already gotten her out of the tub and was running the blow dryer over her hair, all while peppering her with questions about how she was feeling. Did her stomach hurt? Was she having trouble going to the bathroom? Did she have any other weird pains? She had to admit; she felt bad for Mom in that moment. Despite their issues, she had no doubt that she legitimately loved Kylie, and the pain and worry written all over her face had made Kayla sad.

She crossed the street into the town proper and observed the rows of shops lined on either side of the street. It was a mix of cafes and boutique stores peddling various items. Kayla had to admit there was a certain charm to it.

It was a little after 11 a.m. on a Monday. Some of the locals, at least Kayla assumed they were locals, were moving about from shop to shop. She'd gone from seeing very few people to an increasing number as she got further toward the center of the town. It felt like the quiet before the storm of lunch hour.

She had seen a few stores were looking to hire people and bookmarked them on her phone and was going to hit them in order, starting with the closest one, a small clothing shop which, according to her map, was two blocks up and one block over on the right.

Kayla passed the first block and stopped at the end of the street, the light red and the *Don't Walk* symbol illuminated with its familiar orange glow. As she waited for it to turn, she suddenly felt the stress of the morning bubble back up. Not to mention the revelation that her parents' marital issues were even deeper than she thought. She hadn't really stopped moving until just this moment, and that brief respite was enough for the morning's events to press down on her. She needed a cigarette.

While it was probably not advisable to walk into a job interview reeking of tobacco, especially at a clothing store, she didn't really care, opting for the quick fix to ease her anxiety over professionalism. She retrieved the pack from her purse and placed the Marlboro between her lips before going back for her light. As she sparked the flame and moved it toward the tip, a voice startled her.

"People still smoke cigarettes?"

Surprised that she was being watched, she instinctively extinguished the flame and snatched the smoke from her mouth as if a teacher had caught her behind the middle-school bleachers before turning toward the unknown observer.

Her breath caught in her lungs when she saw the girl. It almost made her cough, which would have been quite ironic if she thought about it.

The girl was beautiful. She was leaning against the side of the corner building, which Kayla could see through the window was a small delicatessen. She smirked at Kayla, her blue eyes sparkling with a mix of curiosity and amusement. The girl was comparable in height to Kayla, slender and athletic, with long blond hair tied back in a tight ponytail. She wore jeans and a plain white T-shirt covered by a red apron that read *Big Al's Deli*, the same name stenciled on the window. Her posture was relaxed as she took a pull on a vape pen, holding for a moment before exhaling a blueberry-scented plume. But the most striking thing to Kayla was her deep blue eyes.

On one hand, Kayla felt annoyed. Who did this girl think she was talking to a stranger like that? On the other hand, something about her reminded her of Morgan, and it was instantly disarming to her. Her instinct was to give her an attitude, but her snark was diluted when it actually came out.

"Don't think you're one to talk," Kayla said, nodding toward the vape pen. The girl laughed. It was hearty and, when she heard it, it felt like Kayla's heart skipped a beat. But she tried to keep from getting flustered. "Oh, is that funny?"

"Hilarious," the girl said, grinning ear to ear as she held out her vape. "Come on. Are you really going to compare those stinky death sticks to this thing, which leaves no odor clinging to your clothes whatsoever?"

"Smoking's smoking."

"Bullshit. Try it," the girl said as she took a step toward Kayla, the vape still out in front of her.

The proposal surprised Kayla. "You're mighty brave, offering a total stranger a hit off your vape. How do you know I don't have cooties?"

The girl cocked an eyebrow. "Do you?"

Now it was Kayla's turn to laugh. "Haven't gotten tested recently." The girl chuckled as Kayla took the device and examined it. She saw a smudge from the girl's red lipstick encircling the tip.

"Shit!" the girl said, taking it back and wiping it on her apron to remove the stain. "Sorry about that."

She offered it back to Kayla, who accepted it and took a pull of her own, inhaling the vapor and holding it in before exhaling. She had to admit; it was more pleasant than the cigarette. And the deep inhalation eased her anxiety a bit. Although she had an inkling that maybe this girl's energy had something to do with it. You can't really know someone from a thirty-second conversation, but she gave off such a free-spirited vibe that Kayla found herself drawn to it.

Kayla handed the pen back to the girl, who took it and again wiped it on her apron. Kayla looked at her, feeling slightly offended. The girl noticed and smiled again.

"You never confirmed you didn't have cooties."

Kayla laughed despite herself as the girl took another pull on the vape. As she did, something caught her eye and she quickly removed it from her mouth and put her hand behind her back, awkwardly slipping it into her back pocket as she held in her exhalation.

"Desiree!" a man's voice shouted from the entrance to the shop. "Break's over! We gotta prep for the lunch rush!"

"Sorry, Daddy," the girl said, the vapor escaping from between her lips despite her best efforts.

The man who had shouted at the girl Kayla now knew as Desiree was short and stout, his bald head red and glistening as a droplet of sweat dripped into his dark, horseshoe hairline. He snorted, which made the hairs on his bushy mustache that was badly in need of a trim bristle. He wore a similar outfit to Desiree's, complete with the same logoed apron. It looked better on her, though.

"Are you vaping?" the man asked through gritted teeth. "How many times have I told you that shit is worse than cigarettes! You wanna get popcorn lung?"

Desiree opened her mouth to defend herself, but Kayla cut her off.

"Sorry sir," she said. "It's mine. I shouldn't have offered it to her."

"Uh-huh," the man said, unconvinced. "Even if I didn't just witness my daughter trying to exhale, I know her a little too well to believe that you'd be the bad influence. And I've never even met you."

"Sorry, Daddy," Desiree repeated.

"Yeah. Yeah," he said, nonchalantly. "Get your ass back

in here and get to work. If your friend Jasmine didn't flake out on me all the time, I wouldn't a had to fire her and we'd have some extra help around here!"

"My friend here needs a job," Desiree said, cocking her head toward Kayla.

"How'd you know that?" Kayla whispered.

Desiree grinned a knowing grin. "Well, let's see. You're about eighteen, nineteen, but not in school, and you're walking around downtown Huntsville on a Monday morning. You're wearing jeans, but they look like they're one of your nicer pairs, along with wedges when you strike me as more of a Chuck's type of girl."

Kayla was stunned. "You can tell all that from looking at me?"

"Not really," Desiree said, pointing toward Kayla's waist. "Your resume is sticking out of your purse."

Kayla looked down and confirmed that it was. She rolled her head back, unsure whether to laugh or groan.

"This is all very fascinating," Desiree's dad said, "but I got a bunch of hungry folks about to storm this place in the next twenty minutes, and I can really use some help here, so you're hired. Desi, grab her an apron and tell her to wash her hands."

"I'm starting now?" Kayla said in shock.

"You want an orientation to serve sandwiches?" the man said before heading back inside.

Desiree followed in her dad's direction, patting Kayla on the shoulder as she passed.

"That's Big Al for ya," she said. "All business."

"So, what do I actually do?"

"Nothing to it. Just follow my lead. Welcome aboard...?" Desiree stopped, fishing for an actual introduction.

"Kayla."

"Welcome aboard, Kayla!" Desiree said with a salute as she went back into the deli, the bewildered new employee following a few steps behind.

CHAPTER 6

K ylie felt the paper lining the examination table crinkle underneath her as she shifted her weight, trying to get comfortable. Her nausea had passed and, all things considered, she actually felt pretty good. Even so, there was no way Mom wasn't going to make her go to the doctor, so she didn't bother trying to argue.

The pediatrician's office looked a lot like her old doctor's back home. Her old one, that is, before she had to go to the other specialists. Those were a lot less cheerful. The doctor who did her regular checkups before she got sick had a lot of toys and charts and funny posters showing where things were on the body. The children's hospital was much the same in decor, but Kylie remembered the waiting room. While the regular doctor treated sick kids, they were mostly runny noses and sore throats. The hospital had kids who had lost their hair or wore oxygen masks. Some couldn't even walk, so they sat in wheelchairs while their parents looked really sad and nervous in the seats next to them.

Even though this office was more like her old pediatrician's, Kylie had more than her fill of doctors over the past few years. The look on Mom's face. That old trepidation she used to have when they went for her checkups brought her back to those scary days and made her very antsy to get this over with.

After what felt like hours, a small woman in scrubs and a familiar white coat with a stethoscope dangling from her neck entered the room. She had a friendly demeanor, along with a confident smile that put Kylie at ease.

"Hello," she said in a sing-song tone. "My name is Dr. Zelman, but you can just call me Dr. Z."

"Hi!" Kylie said.

"Hi, Doctor," Mom said before the doctor had a chance to even ask what was wrong. "Kylie got very sick this morning and threw up as soon as I woke her up."

"Oh no," Dr. Z said sympathetically. "Let's take a look at you."

Mom continued. "She didn't say much about pain, but she had this dazed look about her."

"Well," the doc replied nonchalantly as she ushered Kylie to sit up straight. She took her stethoscope and gently put the chest piece on her sternum, moving it about. "There's always stuff going around. Now that the school year is starting, it's only going to get worse, I'm afraid."

"Kylie is immunocompromised," Mom explained.

Dr. Z finished with the stethoscope and paused the examination. "How so?" she asked.

"She's in remission from kidney cancer. Wilms tumor."

The doctor nodded, but didn't change her facial expression. Mom looked annoyed that she wasn't more concerned.

"Well, thank goodness you're in remission. How long ago was she diagnosed?"

"When she was five, I was giving her a bath and her stomach seemed really bloated to me. I felt around and found a mass that I could feel if I pressed down. They did an ultrasound and found the tumor."

Dr. Z nodded. "Wilms is the most common form of kidney cancer in kids. You're very lucky you caught it in time."

Mom's face dropped. It didn't go unnoticed.

"Mrs. Macklin?"

Mom composed herself. "No. I mean yes. I just didn't catch it in time."

"What do you mean?"

"When Kylie was a baby, I used to massage her with calming lotion before bed. I thought it looked like her right side may have been a little bigger than her left. There were more folds in the skin of her legs on that side. Once we started the cancer treatment, I was told she had a rare genetic condition called hemihypertrophy."

"I'm familiar with it," the doctor acknowledged. "It's very rare."

"One in a million," Mom said. "Something about the way the chromosomes formed. Thankfully, with Kylie, it wasn't progressive, so you can't really even tell."

"No, you can't," Dr. Z agreed, flashing a smile at her patient. "She's a beautiful young lady."

Mom got emotional again. "But when the doctors told us that this condition put her at risk for liver and kidney tumors, I was shocked. I'd never heard of this. I had no idea."

"Most people haven't," the doctor assured her, but Mom just kept going, spewing the tale like she was in a confessional.

"If I had followed through when I saw this, they would have put her in a monitoring protocol: bloodwork every three months until she was four to check the liver enzymes and ultrasounds every three months until she was eight to make sure there were no masses on the kidneys. By the time she was diagnosed, she was already in stage two."

Dr. Z was sympathetic, nodding as if she didn't know all about the protocol Mom was explaining. She just let her unload. "Mrs. Macklin, most kids with hemihypertrophy go undiagnosed. And most don't develop these cancers. The risk is elevated, yes, but it's only about five to ten percent greater than a child without the condition. Many parents would not have handled it any differently. The important thing is that Kylie is in remission and healthy."

"I know," Gretchen said, putting her head down, feeling guilty even though the guilt was coming from herself and not the doctor.

The doc turned her attention back to Kylie and moved the stethoscope around to her back, asking her to take a series of deep breaths as she examined different spots.

"Lungs sound good," she said, more to herself than her patient. A few more checks followed, including looking in her ears and throat with the light and having her lay down so the doc could press on her belly. It was a little uncomfortable, but nothing like the pain she felt when she was dealing with the cancer treatments. Finally, Dr. Z said, "Okay, sweetie, you can sit up."

"Should we get bloodwork?" Mom asked.

"I don't think that's necessary, Mrs. Macklin," the doctor responded. "She seems perfectly healthy. My guess is she ate something that didn't agree with her. You folks came in from Florida?"

"Yes, Rockledge."

"That's a pretty long drive. Ten, eleven hours. That can take its toll too. I'd say make sure she drinks plenty of fluids. Water. Maybe even some Gatorade for the electrolytes. If she gets sick again, we can run some tests, but for right now I'd say rest up for the day and she should be good to go to school tomorrow."

Kylie was thrilled. She really didn't want to miss her first day at her new school. Mom, on the other hand, didn't look nearly as relieved.

"Are you sure, Doctor?"

"Absolutely. I think Ms. Kylie has probably been poked and prodded enough during her treatment. No need to do anymore unless absolutely necessary."

Mom still didn't look convinced, but nodded. "Thank you, Doctor."

CHAPTER 7

Kayla wiped the sweat from her brow as the last of the lunch rush customers shuffled out the door. Kayla was amazed at just how many hungry patrons had stuffed themselves into the tiny space that was Big Al's, clamoring for Reubens and turkey clubs. As she took a bite into the Italian hoagie Desiree had made for her, she could understand why. It may very well have been the best sandwich she ever ate.

"Damn, this is legit," she said, eschewing manners and delivering the compliment with the food still in her mouth.

Desiree laughed. "Yeah, Daddy grew up in New York. I guess poor boys are a big deal up there. But he calls them heroes."

Kayla chuckled to herself. Hearing Desiree's southern accent, it was hard to believe she was only a generation removed from the northeast. Her family must have moved here before she was born. Or at least when she was very young. "We just call them subs in Florida." She took another bite. "But I don't care what you call it, this is a damn good sandwich."

"Best you'll ever eat," Al said as he exited the kitchen and stepped behind the counter, surveying Kayla, who, for a moment, thought she'd be in trouble for eating on the job. "You did good today, Kelly."

"Kayla!" Desiree corrected in a snippy tone. Al put his hands up in a mea culpa.

"Sorry, pumpkin," he said, Kayla noting just how different his accent was. "Didn't mean no offense, just met the girl five minutes before a hundred people stormed the place for lunch." He turned his attention to Kayla. "You did good today, Kayla. If you want to stay on, I'm about to revise the schedule for next week, since my daughter's friend Jasmine proved unreliable."

"I prefer to think of myself as a free spirit," a female voice came from the entrance.

Kayla turned to see a young black girl about her age standing in the doorway, sporting a shit-eating grin. She had short, spiky hair that was dyed neon green and her nose and eyebrow were pierced. She looked like she was about to step on stage and grab the mike at a punk rock show.

She wasn't alone either. A tall boy, again of similar age, stood behind her. His long shaggy blond hair hung down over his shoulders and his tanned arms were bare in a sleeveless Operation Ivy T-shirt, displaying a myriad of tattoos up and down their length.

Al rolled his eyes at the girl, but it was more playful than any type of ill will. He smirked.

"That's why you're *free* to work somewhere else, Jasmine."

The girl exaggerated a pouty face. "You still love me, though. Right, Mr. Costello?"

"Like the daughter I never wanted." Desiree smacked his arm and he winced. "Alright, alright. I gotta go take care of a couple of things. Desi, can I trust you to watch the shop for an hour now that the craziness is over?"

"I'll try not to burn the place down," she agreed.

Al removed his apron and hung it on a hook against the back wall, grabbing the car keys on the hook next to it before walking to the door. As he left, he placed his hand on Jasmine's shoulder and told her, "You realize your employee discount is no longer valid, right?"

Jasmine laughed. "I'll just go eat down the street at Grace's Diner."

Al scoffed. "Have fun with that, kid." Jasmine stepped aside to let him exit. As he did, he patted the boy on his inked-up arm and winked at him. "You got your hands full with this one, Ben. Good luck."

As he left, an older black woman entered the store, pushing her way past Jasmine and Ben without saying a word as she approached the counter as if on a mission. She looked to be in her seventies, with a distinct, no-nonsense demeanor about her. She also looked familiar to Kayla, but she couldn't quite place her.

"You could say excuse me, Auntie Ethel," Jasmine said.

"And you could stop jibber jabbering and let me pass. I guess we both could learn some manners now, can't we?" Kayla put her hand to her mouth to stifle a laugh at the cantankerous customer. When the woman glared at her, she bit her lip to repress her amusement further. "And you, young lady. How about you pack me a container of that bland-ass potato salad you sell here?"

"Auntie!" Jasmine chided.

"Pshaw," Ethel huffed, waving her niece away.

Desiree laughed. "Coming right up, Aunt Ethel."

"See?" Ethel said to Jasmine. "This one has a bit of respect."

"Oh, you're just salty because you never found your mama's recipe book. I guess her potato salad wasn't so bland?"

The smugness on Ethel's face melted into something that Kayla couldn't quite grasp. It was serious. Almost angry.

"That book has a lot more in it than potato salad," she said. "Recipes you couldn't even dream of."

Kayla watched the exchange with fascination. To say she'd met an interesting cast of characters today would be an understatement. As she watched Jasmine and her aunt bicker, she suddenly realized where she had seen Aunt Ethel before. She was the woman they had seen foraging in the field off of the exit when they had driven into town. The one her dad almost hit.

She figured it was best to keep that tidbit to herself.

"Here you go, Aunt Ethel," Desiree said as she handed the woman a plastic bag with the plastic container of the bland-ass potato salad. "Enjoy!"

"Harrumph," the old woman grunted, as she accepted it. "Pay the woman, Jasmine."

Jasmine gave her a half-lip smirk as she dug into her pocket and produced a crumpled twenty-dollar bill, handing it to Desiree before extending her hand to Kayla, likely realizing that they had been ignoring her while dealing with her cranky old aunt.

"You must be the new me," she said. "Jasmine."

"Kayla."

"Nice to meet you. That's my boyfriend Ben."

Ben, who was milling over by the drink cooler, keeping his distance from Ethel's warpath, smiled and up nodded. "Sup," he said. His voice was deep, but warm.

"Hi," Kayla said to him.

"Hi, Ben!" Desiree waved and blew him a kiss before Jasmine reached over the counter in a playful attempt to slap her that she dodged easily.

"Uh-uh!" Jasmine said. "You had your shot! He's mine now!"

"You can keep him," Desiree laughed.

Kayla felt a twinge of disappointment at the thought of Desiree and Ben together. She didn't quite understand why. She'd only just met these people. But she'd felt an instant connection. The mind can go to some strange places pretty quickly, she supposed.

"My brother's still single," Ben said with a smirk.

"Ew," Desiree said. "Your brother's ten years old."

Kayla saw the opportunity to join the conversation.

"Cool! I have a nine-year-old sister. She's starting fourth grade over at Alexander this week."

"Sweet," Ben replied. "I guess her and Drew will be in the same class."

"Cool," Kayla repeated, cringing a little that she couldn't think of a better response than *cool*. She guessed that's why writing was never her strong suit.

"Small world," Ben said, opening the cooler and grabbing a bottle of iced tea. Kayla looked over to Ethel, who was frowning as she perused the plastic display case full of lottery scratch tickets, thinking that indeed it was.

"Well, listen," Jasmine said as Ben stepped up behind her, towering over the much shorter girl, reaching over to hand Kayla the iced tea along with a five-dollar bill. "Big Al ain't so bad to work for. Just show up on time and try not to flake out too much."

"Uh-huh," Desiree said as she waved Ben's hand away, indicating the drink was on the house. "But that was just too much for you?"

"Like I said," Jasmine answered with a wink toward Kayla. "Free spirit."

The group laughed before Ethel played the role of buzzkill.

"We gonna leave soon, or should I just arrange for my wake to be in this damn store?"

Jasmine rolled her eyes. "Okay, Auntie. We're going. See you, Desi. Hope to see you around, Kayla."

"Cool," Kayla answered again, mentally slapping her head. She really needed a thesaurus or something. The others weren't as concerned as she was with her lack of vocabularic variety.

"See ya," Ben said as the trio exited the store, Ethel in the lead.

"She's a trip," Desiree said when they were out of earshot.

"Clearly," Kayla agreed, pausing for a second before deciding to let her new friend in on the knowledge she already had of the woman. "You know, I saw her walking around in the grass off of Exit 8. She was picking flowers or something."

Desiree wasn't the least bit surprised. "Yup, that's Auntie Ethel."

"She does that often?"

"Yep. She's lucky she hasn't been hit by a car yet." Kayla nodded, remembering how she narrowly got hit by her dad. "She forages. Looking for plants and stuff."

"For what?"

Desiree's grin widened, knowing that Kayla wouldn't be expecting what she said next. "She practices Hoodoo."

"You mean Voodoo?"

"No, Hoodoo's different. Don't ask me how. But I made the mistake of calling it Voodoo once and I thought Ethel was going to rip my head off. I actually had a bit of, let's say, intestinal distress the next day. I always wondered if it was related."

"For real?"

Desiree shrugged. "I also drank a bunch of beer and obliterated a plate of hot wings that night, so who knows?"

The girls laughed.

"She really believes all that, huh?"

"Yeah. Her mother was big into it. Apparently, she got real deep when all those kids disappeared in the sixties."

"What do you mean?"

"So, I'm guessing you haven't been made aware of Huntsville's sordid history yet?" Desiree asked.

"I guess not," Kayla replied. Despite what she said next, her curiosity was piqued. "Do I want to know?"

"Depends on how easily you get freaked out. We got everything here. From plagues to serial killers to haunted playgrounds!" That last one perked Kayla up. "Wait. What playground?"

"Maple Hill Park. It's next to the cemetery off of McClung Avenue."

"You know it?"

"It's practically in my backyard."

Desiree lit up. "No fucking way!"

"Yes, fucking way," Kayla said, feeling unsettled but trying not to show it. After all, ghosts weren't real. Despite that, something about that place had creeped her out.

"So, what's the deal with it?"

"Oh no," Desiree said, now wearing a full veneer of mischief. "I'm not going to tell you."

"What?" Kayla said. "You can't just drop something like that on someone and not fill them in on the details!"

"Sure I can! It's better if I show you!"

JAMES KAINE

"Show me?"

"You doing anything Friday night?" Desiree asked.

"Don't think so," Kayla answered, knowing damn well she didn't have plans.

"So, that's a no," Desiree said perceptively. "I'll pick you up at seven. We can go grab some grub, then I'll show you!"

"Uh, sure!" Kayla said, excited at the prospect of building some type of social life- even if it involved potential ghost encounters.

"Awesome!" Desiree said. "It's a date!"

CHAPTER 8

E xcitement and trepidation filled Kylie as she stepped into the classroom. At first glance, it wasn't all that different from her old school.

The walls displayed papers and posters depicting various subjects ranging from upper and lower-case letters to multiplication tables to illustrations of historic events.

All around her, boys and girls were filing in and taking their assigned seats at one of five colorful tables, each one surrounded by four matching chairs. Kylie frowned. The others already knew their seating assignments. She didn't.

Now it was Thursday, the third day of school. Even though she had felt better by the time they had left the doctor on Tuesday, her mother had still insisted on keeping her home. Originally, Mom's plan was to keep her home the whole week, but Kylie and her father finally wore her down until she begrudgingly agreed.

But to say she wasn't happy would be an understatement.

Instead of letting her take the bus with the other kids—"Those things are germ farms," she had said—she insisted on driving her there herself. Dad had offered to take her on his way to work, but Mom shot him down.

She was pretty mean about it, too. On the car ride over, she had said little other than the laundry list of things Kylie shouldn't do, peppered with the occasional "This is not a good idea."

Mom's attitude followed her out of the car and right up to the school's entrance. When a pleasant young teacher, not much older than Kayla, stopped them at the door asking if she could help, Mom told her she was escorting her daughter to her classroom. When the teacher explained that they didn't permit that because of security protocols, Kylie saw her mother's face redden. Although she hadn't raised her voice, acidity laced her words.

"This is a special circumstance," Gretchen said.

The young woman may or may not have felt intimidated, but if she did, she deserved credit for not showing it.

"Then you'll have to discuss that with the administration. The main office is on the east side of the building. But I'm more than happy to escort Miss..."

"Kylie!" the young girl had answered before her mother had the chance, her enthusiasm a stark contrast to her parent's abrasiveness.

"I'll be more than happy to escort Miss Kylie to her class," the teacher said with a wink.

Gretchen paused for several moments. Kylie could tell she wanted to press the issue. In fact, it surprised her when she said in a softened tone, "She's registered with Miss Evans. Fourth Grade."

"Awesome," the young teacher said. "Please don't worry, ma'am, we'll take good care of her."

Mom nodded, unconvinced. She bent over and firmly placed her hands on her daughter's upper arms. "Your sanitizer is in the front pouch of your backpack. Use it often, okay?"

Kylie nodded, knowing full well that she and her mother had different ideas of how often that should be.

"One more thing," Mom said, reaching into her pocket and retrieving an all too familiar blue-and-white medical face mask. Kylie grimaced at the sight of it, the thought of having to wear one of those again knotting her stomach.

"Make sure you wear this while you're in the building."

"Mom!" Kylie protested.

"Oh, we don't require those," the teacher said.

"I'm requiring it," Gretchen said, the acid burned back into her tone.

The teacher didn't say anything else. Instead, she simply nodded and offered the new student and her mother a tight-lipped smile. Kylie didn't protest, but her dissatisfaction was evident on her face, even after she reluctantly covered it with the mask.

Mom smiled in relief and pulled her in for a too-tight hug. "Have a great first day, sweetheart!"

Kylie hugged her back, knowing both the gesture and the words were genuine. That was the great paradox of life with Gretchen Macklin. She could be caustic and hard to deal with but she also genuinely cared, with most of her less-than-pleasant character traits born out of a place of fear. "Thanks, Mom," she said.

Gretchen hesitantly broke the hug and let her daughter enter the building. Kylie planned on walking away but couldn't help but steal a glance back before turning the corner, seeing her mother watching her intently as she wiped a tear from her eye.

Despite her sympathy for her mother's feelings, Kylie still yanked the mask off her face the moment she rounded the corner, stuffing it in her pocket so she could put it back on after school and walk out wearing it to appease her overprotective parent. She thought the teacher may press her to put it back on out of concern for facing Mom's wrath, but she just smiled and gave her another, more conspiratorial, wink.

Kylie had a good feeling that she would like it here.

Now, despite her enthusiasm, she anxiously surveyed her surroundings, searching for an indicator of where she should sit.

"You must be Kylie Macklin," a cheerful voice said from her left.

Kylie turned to see a woman about her mother's age, but with a distinctly more congenial demeanor, smiling down at her.

"Yes, ma'am," Kylie answered.

"And well-mannered too," the woman said. "I'm Miss Evans. We've missed you these first couple of days. Are you feeling better?"

"Yes, I am. Thank you, Miss Evans."

The teacher ushered her to the front of the room as she continued speaking.

"Good to hear. Don't worry. You didn't miss too much."

She turned her attention to the rest of the students, most of whom were already seated, but not yet settled. "Everyone," she said, "let me have your attention." The students quieted quickly, a sign of the command the teacher already had over her young charges. "This is Kylie Macklin. She's been a little under the weather the past couple of days, but she's feeling much better, so please let's welcome Kylie to our class."

"Hi Kylie!" the class chimed, almost in unison. Some of the voices were genuinely enthusiastic and welcoming of the new student. Others were wholly disinterested and robotically following their teacher's prompt.

"Hi," Kylie said, raising her hand in a tentative wave.

"Kylie just joined us from Florida," Miss Evans continued. "I know you'll make her feel welcome." She gestured toward an empty chair at the table closest to the window. "Kylie, please take a seat over there and we'll get started."

Kylie eagerly made her way to the table and sat down next to a short, stout boy with shaggy blond hair. He smiled at her with a hint of shyness.

"Hi," the boy said. "I'm Andrew Gatto, but everyone calls me Drew."

Kylie returned the smile and offered her hand. "Kylie. Kylie Macklin," she parroted.

The boy shook her hand and giggled at the touch. Two other students, both girls, introduced themselves as Jessie and Trina. They were all very friendly and Kylie felt a warmth spread throughout her. It felt so good to be social with kids her age.

With formalities out of the way, Miss Evans began taking a roll call. As she did, Kylie glanced out the window. The classroom was at the back of the school and she could see the blacktop with swings and slides, not unlike the playground through the woods behind her family's new house. The school's recreation area, however, also had basketball courts on either side of the paved area and soccer nets off in the grass. Kylie always wanted to play soccer.

As she daydreamed about kicking a ball up and down the field, motion by the slide caught her eye. She turned her full attention toward the area and saw a young girl skipping around the structure into her view.

Emily.

Is she a student here? Kylie thought. *Why isn't she in class?*

As if Emily knew she was being watched, she abruptly stopped skipping and stared through the window at Kylie. She smiled widely and waved. Kylie wasn't sure how to react, so she hesitantly raised her hand and returned the gesture, not unlike when she had waved to the class just a few minutes earlier.

"Kylie," Ms. Evans' voice again broke her concentration. She turned to face the teacher.

"Yes, ma'am?"

"Something interesting out there?" she asked, her voice a touch sterner then during the introduction.

Kylie looked back out the window and, once again, Emily was gone.

"No, ma'am."

She took one last look before turning her attention back to the class. Something about that girl was very strange.

CHAPTER 9

I t was Friday night and Kayla found herself in the unusual position of being excited about something. She hadn't expected to make friends in this new town, especially not so soon. But now not only had she made new friends, but she felt an actual connection with Desiree. Hell, Morgan had blocked her after their argument, yet Kayla had barely spared a thought for her former lifelong best friend since she'd walked into Big Al's Deli. She'd only worked the one shift on Tuesday so far and she really wanted to pop in on either of the subsequent two days, but she didn't want to come off as desperate, so she played it cool even though she almost cracked a few times.

Now on her third outfit choice, Kayla felt satisfied with her cute but casual choice. After all, she was going to check out a haunted playground next to a cemetery with a new friend. It wasn't a date.

Although Desiree *did* say *It's a date*. Could that be what this was?

The chime of the doorbell interrupted her ruminations on the matter. She felt a rush of excitement as she bounded down the stairs to answer the door before her parents could beat her to it. Alas, she was too late. She made it around the landing, only to see her father opening the door.

"Hi!" Desiree said, "Is Kayla here?"

"Um, yes she is," Dad replied. "Is she expecting you?"

Her smile was warm and disarming. She extended her hand to Roger, who accepted it.

"Yup! I'm Desiree Costello. I work with Kayla. We're hanging out tonight."

"Hi!" Kayla said as she made her way down the rest of the stairs, trying to cut her father off before he said anything that would embarrass her. "We're just heading out to a... movie." Desiree gave her a side-eyed glance, but didn't blow up her spot. "See ya!"

She tried to step past her dad, but he held up a hand. "Whoa, wait a sec. Did you forget you were babysitting?"

"What?" Kayla said in shock, noticing the suit her father was wearing for the first time. "That's next week!"

"No, sweetheart. It's tonight."

Her parents had mentioned a dinner party at her father's new boss's house they had coming up. They told her they'd need her to watch Kylie that night. Since this had come up weeks before they'd actually had moved, she'd agreed, assuming she wouldn't have plans. Now she cursed herself because she knew she had only been half listening and now had clearly confused the dates. She felt her heart sink under the crushing disappointment, knowing that she couldn't argue her way out of this.

"Date night?" Desiree asked innocently, unaware of the strain the Macklin's marriage was under these days. Kayla cringed as the thought of her father kissing another woman again invaded her mind. She tried to shake it off as quickly as possible.

"Work function," Roger answered politely.

"Oh. Well, would it be cool if I hung out here and

helped babysit?"

"I think that'd be okay," he agreed.

Kayla felt the weight dissipate. Sure, they wouldn't be able to go out, but that wasn't the appeal of tonight. She'd get to hang out with Desiree and, if they had to do it here, that was just fine with her. She was just grateful that it had been her father who answered the door and not her mother. Gretchen would have probably insisted on a full medical history before dismissing the girl because she had chicken pox when she was five or something.

"Awesome!" Desiree said as Roger stepped aside to let her in. She surveyed the area and commented, "You have a really nice house here, Mr. Macklin."

"Thank you, Desiree," he said, offering a conciliatory smile to Kayla that she returned with gratitude to her father for not completely ruining her night.

"So, when do I meet Kylie?" she asked.

"Now!" Kylie said, leaping out from around the wall connecting the foyer to the dining room, her hands up in an unsuccessful attempt to scare her sister and her friend. She looked disappointed as Desiree laughed instead of jumping.

"Hi Kylie, I'm Desiree. I'm friends with your sister." She reached out and brushed the girl's auburn curls. "Your hair is so pretty!"

"Thanks!" Kylie said. "Kayla's hair is the same color, but she dyed it black because she likes to be goth."

Kayla stuck her tongue out at her little sister. "You don't even know what goth means."

"Who's this?" Gretchen asked from the stairs Kayla had descended only a couple minutes prior. She wore a green cocktail dress and pushed her hair over her shoulder to one side while affixing an earring to her left lobe as she made her way to join the group. While her husband's demeanor toward the visitor was one of confusion, hers presented as irritation. Desiree maintained her cheerfulness and again extended her hand.

"I'm Desiree, I'm friends with—"

"Kayla didn't tell you she was babysitting tonight?"

"I got the dates mixed up," Kayla confessed, figuring acknowledging her error was the best course of action.

"Mm-hmm," Gretchen said. "Well, I'm sure you two can find something to do another night."

Desiree chimed in before Kayla could stop her. "It's cool. Mr. Macklin said I could stay and help babysit!"

If Gretchen had laser vision, her husband's head would have turned into a hollow cavity with the stare she gave him. "Did he?"

Desiree read the room. "I... hope that's okay."

To Kayla's surprise, Gretchen composed herself and even smiled at the girl. "I suppose it is."

"We should head out," Roger said, touching his wife's upper arm. She tensed, but didn't recoil. Despite her attempt at subtlety, the tension didn't go unnoticed. Desiree seemed like she felt bad, and Kayla felt embarrassed. Kylie, as always, was an innocent bystander to the train wreck that was her family.

"Yes, dear," Gretchen said in an icy tone.

"Have a good time," Roger said with a smattering of defiance. "There's money for food on the table. Kylie needs to be in bed at 8:30."

"Got it, Dad," Kayla said, before mouthing *thank you.*

Roger nodded and blew a kiss to Kylie. "Nice to meet you, Desiree."

"You too, Mr. Macklin! Have a great night!"

CHAPTER 10

Kylie glanced over at the clock and noted the time. 8:12 p.m. She frowned, fully aware that her bedtime was upon her. It was disappointing because this had turned into a fun night. Kayla's friend Desiree was super cool and nice to her. In fact, just having her around seemed to make Kayla nicer, too.

The three of them had ordered pizza and ate it while watching a movie. Desiree asked if she wanted a scary movie, to which Kylie had enthusiastically agreed, despite her actual exposure to the genre being limited to Disney zombie flicks. She put on a movie called *The Monster Squad*. It was about a bunch of kids who fought Dracula, The Wolfman, The Mummy and the Creature from the Black Lagoon. It was PG-13, but pretty violent and had a lot of bad words. Some kids even smoked cigarettes! When she pointed it out, Kayla said movies in the 1980s were just different. And she better not dare tell their parents they'd watched this. She swore silence.

Kylie thought the pizza was pretty good, but Desiree was unimpressed. She told them they'd have to come over and have her father's homemade tomato pie sometime. Big Al was adamant that you'd never find a better pizza than in New York or New Jersey. Desiree backed that sentiment, confirming to the Macklin girls that her father made the best pizza she's ever had.

"I can come too?" Kylie had asked.

"Of course!" Desiree said before lowering her voice a bit, but not enough that Kayla couldn't hear her. "I actually like you better than your sister."

Kylie and Desiree laughed while Kayla rolled her eyes. "Ha ha ha," she said, enunciating each word to emphasize how not funny she found the joke. Now it was her turn to glance at the clock. "Okay, kid. Go brush your teeth."

"Aw, come on," Kylie protested. "Just one more minute?"

"No way. You've been pulling that *one more minute* shit since you were five. It always means at least fifteen."

"Ugh," Kylie said, as she got up and headed to the stairs. "You're no fun."

"Tell you what," Desiree interjected. "If you can get ready and get in bed quick, I'll come tell you a ghost story before you go to sleep."

Kylie lit up. "Deal!" she agreed before taking the steps two at a time.

Five minutes later, her teeth were brushed and she had changed into her pajamas before hopping into bed and pulling the sheets up.

"Ready!" she shouted downstairs.

Desiree pulled the small stool from Kylie's vanity up next to the bed while Kayla took a seat at the foot. She smiled as she turned off the lamp on the night table and flicked on the flashlight on her phone, holding it under her chin, the low light source projecting ominous shadows on her face.

"Did you know this town is haunted?"

Kylie nodded.

"Oh, you do?" Desiree asked, breaking character a bit, having not expected an affirmative.

"There are ghosts at the playground."

"Where did you hear that?" Kayla asked.

"I had a dream about them."

"You did?" Desiree asked. "What did you see?"

"I woke up on a swing in the playground. There was another girl there, too. Her name is Emily. I met her the other day, but I don't think she's a ghost because I can see her and touch her."

"What?" Kayla asked.

"The other day. When you and Mom found me at the playground. She was there in my dream too. That's when all the other kids showed up, but I couldn't see them. They were just these... floating balls of light. The swings started moving on their own and I could hear them sliding down the slides. But there was a man there too. He was big. Really big. He was wearing a yellow raincoat."

Desiree flicked the lamp back on and turned off her flashlight.

"What did he do?"

"He scared all the kids away. Then he came up to me, but there was another old lady sitting in a rocking chair. She was like mumbling something behind me. When I turned around, he was gone. Then I woke up and got sick."

"Wow," was all Desiree could say. She eyed Kayla,

something in her expression saying that there may be more to this than a nine-year-old's overactive imagination. "Where did you hear about all this?"

Kylie shrugged. "I told you. Emily brought me there to play."

"Has anyone told you the story of the Maple Hill Park?" Desiree asked Kayla.

"Like Kylie said, she ran off to play there the day we moved in, but I had no idea about any kind of hauntings until you mentioned it the other day." She turned her attention to Kylie. "Why didn't you tell me about your dream?"

She shrugged again. "It was just a bad dream. I get them sometimes. They're not real."

Desiree put her hand on the young girl's head. "That's right. Bad dreams can't hurt you."

"So, what's the deal with the playground?" Kayla asked.

Desiree took a deep breath like she wasn't sure how much she should say about it. "People say that the ghosts of the children buried in the cemetery come out to play at night."

"Do a lot of kids... die... here?" Kylie asked, showing actual fear for the first time since they started on the subject.

"Not for a very long time," Desiree said. "There was a terrible virus over a hundred years ago called the Spanish flu. A lot of kids got it, but it's not something we have to worry about now." She looked like she regretted offering a bedtime ghost story at all. "But if you believe the ghosts are real—and I'm not saying they are—they're not evil. They're just kids looking for a place to play."

"I like that," Kylie said with a small smile.

"You do?" Desiree asked, surprised.

"Yeah. I was really sick before we moved here. I could have died." Desiree exchanged a look with Kayla, who confirmed with a nod. "Oh, my God," Desiree said, pressing her hand to her heart. "I'm so sorry."

"But I'm better now. I'm back at school and even made some new friends—Jessie, Trina and Drew!"

"Drew Gatto? He's our friend Ben's brother!" she said, pointing back and forth between her and Kayla. Kylie noticed that something about the way Desiree said *our friend* made her sister smile.

"I guess it's nice to know that the kids still have somewhere to play, even after they die," Kylie said.

Desiree nodded. "Yeah. As long as that playground is there, they'll always have a place to play." A silence hung in the air. None of the trio was really sure what to say next. Finally, Desiree took a deep breath and planted her hands on her thighs, pushing up off of the chair. "Okay, I think that's enough of the spooky stuff for one night, wouldn't you say, Kayla?"

"I'd say so," Kayla agreed, getting up as well. She walked over and reached for the lamp to turn it off, but before she did, she asked, "You okay without the light?"

"Yup!" Kylie said, "Good night!"

"Good night," Kayla and Desiree said in unison. They exited the room, leaving the door cracked enough that a sliver of light peeked in from the hallway.

Kylie turned on her side and, within a few minutes, fell asleep.

CHAPTER 11

"**I**s Kylie a heavy sleeper?" Desiree asked when she and Kayla were back downstairs.

"Yeah," Kayla replied. "She can pretty much fall asleep anywhere and it takes a lot of effort to wake her."

"Good," she said with a half smile. "Because I have to show you something."

"What?"

"It's easier to show you. Jasmine and Ben are going to meet us at the cemetery."

"I can't leave her."

"What time are your parents going to be home?"

"Around 11:30, they said."

"Then we have three hours. We won't need more than one."

Kayla thought it over. Deep down, she knew it wasn't a good idea, but they weren't going to be away very long, and she couldn't remember the last time Kylie woke up in the middle of the night, especially since she'd recovered.

"Okay, I'll leave a note just in case."

After checking on her sister, who was, in fact, sleeping soundly, and scribbling a note that they'd be back soon on the off chance she woke up, Kayla and Desiree were walking through the woods toward the playground. The night was humid, and Kayla could feel the droplets of sweat beading on her forehead as they traipsed down the path to the playground.

"You can't just tell me what we're doing?"

"Uh-uh," Desiree said. "You wouldn't believe me."

"I swear to God, if this is some kind of prank—"

Desiree stopped abruptly. Kayla tried to as well, but planted her left foot too quickly and stumbled forward. Her friend managed to catch her, hooking her arm around her waist and pulling her back upright, turning her to face her as she did. When Kayla regained her balance, she found herself almost nose to nose with Desiree. She expected the other girl to back away at the invasion of her personal space, but she didn't. Instead, she laughed while keeping her hands on Kayla's waist.

"First day with your new legs?"

"Funny," Kayla said, her sarcasm dimmed as she looked into Desiree's unforgettable steel-blue eyes, that locked with her own. She felt light in the aura of her friend's effervescence. She felt an overwhelming urge to kiss her, but she didn't know if that was appropriate. Maybe Desiree wasn't into girls. After all, she and Ben had maybe been a thing. And if she was into Kayla, she certainly didn't want to scare her off.

"Still with me?" Desiree said, breaking into Kayla's rumination, but still refraining from creating distance. It was Kayla that took a step back instead, Desiree's hands sliding away from her as she did.

"Yeah. Sorry."

"No. This is not a prank. I promise."

"That sounds just like something a prankster would say," Kayla quipped, trying to lighten the one-sided awkwardness she was feeling.

"We can go back then," Desiree said, calling her bluff.

Kayla curled a lip in an exaggerated sneer, knowing Desiree had gotten her. "No. Let's go. Just let's put a move on."

Desiree hooked her left arm in the crook of Kayla's and ushered her down the path. "Better make sure your clumsy ass doesn't stumble again."

"Oh, bite it," Kayla said as she playfully pushed her away, regretting it as soon as she felt the absence of her touch.

Desiree giggled as she regained her balance from the light shove. She went to say something else, but looked ahead as something in the distance diverted her attention.

"What is it?" Kayla asked, feeling a shot of ice in her bloodstream.

"I saw something."

She reached over and grabbed Kayla's hand, pulling her close. Kayla was happy about the return of the physical contact, but didn't like the idea of someone else lurking in the woods with them. Both girls jumped when they heard a tree branch snap behind them.

"Boo!" a female voice came from behind them.

Both girls jumped, but Desiree whirled and swung her

fist in a wild haymaker that Jasmine just managed to duck.

"Whoa!" she said. "Take it easy, slugger!"

"Damn it, Jazz!" Desiree said as she put her hand over her chest, feeling her heart thump under her palm. "You scared the shit out of us!"

"Sorry," she said between laughs, as the figure from the distance came into view, revealing himself as Ben. He came up behind Jasmine and put his arms around her waist. "I couldn't help it. You okay, Kayla?"

Kayla was a little pissed, but she also wanted to show restraint. It was just a joke, after all.

"Yeah," she said with a slightly forced smile. "Good one."

"I'm going to get you for this," Desiree said. "Mark my words."

"Sure, sure."

Kayla was feeling apprehension at how much time had passed. There was still time before her parents would be home, but it was getting too close for comfort. "Guys, we can talk about prank wars later. Can we just see what we're here to see?"

The playground had a much different feel at night. As soon as they crossed the clearing and the swings and slide came into view, the humidity in the air seemed to dissipate, replaced by a breezeless chill. But, more than that, the place was quiet. The swings were still, and there wasn't any evidence of anything supernatural as far as she could tell.

"So, where're the ghosts?" she asked with a smattering of annoyance.

Desiree looked at her phone. "It's 9:15. Legend says the hauntings start after ten."

"You've never seen anything here?"

"Not personally. I've even come out here late a few times, but nothing."

"So, what are we doing here?" Kayla said, now the annoyance really coming out. Her sister was home alone, and she still had no idea why they were here.

"The thing I want to show you isn't here."

"Enough with the mystery. Can you just tell me what's going on?"

Desiree gave her an apologetic look. "The woman in the rocking chair."

"What about her?"

"Desiree texted me about what Kylie said. It sounds like she was describing my great-grandmother," Jasmine said. "Auntie Ethel's mother. She's buried here in the cemetery."

Kayla still didn't quite understand, but she followed as her friend led her to the cemetery gates. She was expecting them to be locked and was quite surprised when Jasmine effortlessly pushed them open. Once inside the cemetery grounds, the air actually regained its humidity, as if somehow the chill only swirled around the playground. They didn't talk as Jasmine led them to an above-ground crypt. It was one of a row of many similar structures standing like sentinels in the moonlit graveyard. Above the weathered stone doorway, the slate had the name *Weeks* carved into it in large font. While everything about the crypt was old, the keypad to the right of the entryway was a more modern addition, one that Kayla surveyed curiously, finding it odd for an old structure to have such a hi-tech touch.

"My dad had this lock installed a few years ago. Easier than having to remember a key every time we come out here," Jasmine explained as she punched in a six-digit code, after which a beep and a click signaled the door was now unlocked. She turned on her phone's flashlight. The others followed suit as they stepped inside the darkened tomb. Between the flashlights and the faint shafts of moonlight filtering through the narrow windows, Kayla could see the interior well.

The floor echoed with the group's footsteps as they stepped inside. A veil of cobwebs hung from the corners of the ceiling. Kayla felt an energy permeate the air. It was strong, but not suffocating. It wasn't dark, but it enveloped her like a protective shell, offering a feeling of security. As she surveyed the recessed alcoves of the dusty walls, she saw the nameplates above the slots where the caskets rested.

Ethel Weeks 1946–

Martin Weeks 1944–2015

Eunice Weeks 1921–2019

Jasmine shone her flashlight on Eunice's name. "That's my great-grandmother." She then moved the beam to the opposite corner of the crypt where, for the first time, Kayla saw the old rocking chair in the corner. She felt a distinct chill at the sight of it. Its wooden frame bore the marks of age, with a myriad of cracks and grooves permanently etched into it. The seat had become worn and curved from the many years of use prior to its owner's demise. Its arms showed the same, with a slight sag from countless hours of rocking.

"I... don't get it," Kayla said. "You're saying this is the chair that Kylie saw in her dream? The woman was your great-grandmother?"

"I don't know," Jasmine said. "My dad has always been tight-lipped about it, but people talk like Great-Grandma Eunice was some dark arts practitioner or some shit."

"Hoodoo?" Kayla asked.

Jasmine offered a half smirk. "I see Desiree filled you in on some things."

Desiree shrugged. "It's not exactly a secret around here, Jazz."

"Guess not," Jasmine agreed. "Here's the real rundown on this place. They built the park sometime around the 1860s. But the ghost stuff didn't happen until after the Spanish flu outbreak in 1918. A lot of kids have always been buried here. In the early 1900s, a bunch of mills opened in the area and there weren't exactly child labor laws back then, so they figured kids were a prime source of labor. A lot of accidents. A bunch of death. Then the flu came along in 1918. They don't know exactly how many kids died, but they figure it's in the hundreds. And they're all buried right here."

"How do you know all this?" Kayla asked.

"My family's been obsessed with this place for as long as I can remember. Auntie Ethel and my grandpa Martin talked about it all the damn time. From what I understand, it all comes from their mama. She felt some type of obligation to this place."

"Why's that?"

"Back in the 1960s, more kids died. But it wasn't the flu this time. It was a serial killer. They called him The Caretaker."

"The Caretaker?" Kayla asked.

"A guy named Abel Hargrave," Jasmine explained. "He was the caretaker here at the cemetery—hence the name. He was a really big dude from what they say, but he couldn't talk, mute since birth or something. A bunch of kids disappeared from town over a few months. Eventually, they found the bodies in the old quarry just off the edge of the graveyard. Strung old Abel up right then and there. No trial or nothing."

"How'd they get away with that?"

"The sheriff was the one who gave the order. What's he going to do, arrest himself?"

Kayla nodded, fascinated by the tale. "I guess not."

"Anyways, from what my grandad and Aunt Ethel told me, Great-Grandma Eunice said she had to watch over the kids here. That's why every night she would sit in her rocking chair in this cemetery and watch over the ghosts of the kids while they played. She used her Hoodoo spells for their protection. My grandad and Auntie Ethel thought it only right they kept the chair here."

Kayla felt a little overwhelmed by all the detail. Could Kylie have really seen the ghost of Jasmine's great-grandmother in her dream? Shit, was it even a dream at all?

"When I first wanted to show you this place, I thought I'd just bring you in on some of our town's more infamous history, but what Kylie said weirded me out a little," Desiree said. "Look, I've seen nothing here to make me believe this is anything other than just some spooky

105

story, but the way your sister described her dream hit a little too close to home. Especially about the guy in the raincoat."

"What about it?"

"She said he was big, right?"

"Well, yeah."

Jasmine stepped back into the conversation. "Eunice always warned the kids in the family that if they ever saw a big man in a yellow raincoat, to stay far away. And to tell her if it ever happened."

"Why?"

"She wouldn't say, but she was adamant about it."

"Did you ever see him?"

"No, never. But isn't it kinda weird that your sister had a dream that involved ghost children, an old black lady in a rocking chair and a big dude in a yellow raincoat?"

Kayla thought about it. It was definitely weird. Almost too weird to be true.

They're totally fucking with me right now.

"Okay, good one, Desiree."

Desiree looked genuinely shocked and held her hands up in a gesture of innocence. "I didn't make any of this up, I swear!"

"Uh-huh," Kayla said before turning to Jasmine. "I gotta admit, you had me going for a minute there."

"You can believe me or not," Jasmine said, annoyed. "But it's the truth."

"Right," Kayla said as she walked over to the rocking chair, running her finger over the sheen of dust on the right arm. "This rocking chair protects the ghosts of kids from the ghost of a giant serial killer, and my little sister somehow saw all of this in a dream?"

"Whatever," Jasmine said as she grabbed Ben by the

arm. "Just trying to help."

Jasmine and Ben left the crypt and Kayla followed behind, giving Desiree a disapproving glance as she made her way to the exit. Desiree grabbed her arm to stop her. Kayla didn't wrench away from her grip but turned to face her. "We're not lying to you."

Kayla wanted to believe her. She practically needed to, but friends had burned her before. Morgan's recent betrayal came to mind. Morgan had known damn well that Kayla had feelings for her, but she'd never outright shot her down. Now Kayla felt like she had always led her on, making her think she'd had a chance while she'd been pining for Aiden in secret. Desiree was probably no different. Just a tease who liked the attention of someone as vulnerable as Kayla. She felt her eyes water as the rising tide of emotion threatened to burst her dam.

Before it could, the crypt door suddenly slammed shut, plunging the room into total darkness. Even the windows somehow were blacked out. The girls both screamed as their vision failed, along with their phones' flashlights. She couldn't even see the light from the windows anymore. In a wave of panic, Desiree released her grip on Kayla.

"Jasmine!" Desiree yelled. "What the fuck?"

"This isn't fucking funny!" Kayla added.

Jasmine's muffled voice came from the other side of the door, interspersed with the chime of keys being pressed and the buzz of their failure to open it. "It wasn't us! It just slammed! I can't open it!"

Kayla tapped her phone screen, trying to light it up enough to restart the flashlight app, but the screen wouldn't illuminate. She stretched her arms out in front of her, trying to feel around for something but, no matter which direction she tentatively stepped, her hands didn't make contact with anything. It seemed impossible, as if the room had expanded into an endless void.

"Desiree?" she called, trying not to sound panicked.

"I'm here," Desiree answered, but she sounded far away—much further than the small space should have allowed.

"Where?"

"Here."

She sounded even further away now, but Kayla had a general idea of the direction of her voice. She took a step in that direction, but her body and blood froze simultaneously as an ominous hiss broke the silence. Unlike Desiree's voice, this sounded like it was right in front of her.

"Desiree," she whispered, her voice cracking. "Do you hear that?"

She didn't answer. The room was once again quiet and dark. The silence felt oppressive, like it was hiding something deadly. Kayla felt paralyzed, every one of her senses eluding her. It felt like time slowed down to a crawl and she didn't know what to do when the hissing sound rose again, closer this time.

She was about to call for Desiree again when she suddenly saw two reddish, slit-shaped eyes open right in front of her. Illuminated by an unknown light source, two ivory-white curved fangs appeared, accompanied by another hiss. A hideous amalgamation of a human and reptile emerged from the shadows in front of her. Fleshy scales covered its face and thick mucus spilled from its ever-widening mouth as the monstrosity moved toward Kayla.

She shrieked in terror as she moved backward, trying

to escape the creature. As she did, her foot caught on something and she fell, landing on something that immediately gave out under her weight, the sound of splintering wood echoing through the tomb. As she hit the floor with a thud, suddenly all the light returned to the room as the door swung open and Jasmine and Ben reentered with their flashlights trained on her. Desiree was on the opposite side of the door. Her chest heaved as she tried to catch her breath, a look of panic slowly fading from her face.

With an additional light source now available, Kayla looked around and saw that she was lying in the wreckage of Eunice's rocking chair. She pushed herself up onto her elbows and Desiree rushed over to help her up. As soon as she was off the ground, she wrenched herself free from the other girl's grip and dusted herself off. When the others reemerged, she had momentarily forgotten the reason she'd fallen, and a rush of fear washed over her as she surveyed the tomb.

"Where is it?" she asked frantically as she turned her own flashlight back on, waving it haphazardly around the room.

"Where's what?" Ben asked.

"Some fucking giant snake thing!" she said.

The others joined in, pushing the flashlight beams to the ground, searching for the reptilian intruder.

"There!" Jasmine shouted as the others shone their lights on the same spot just in time to see a large snake with a red, black and yellow banded pattern slither over the shattered remnants of the rocking chair and into a hole in the right corner of the room, escaping with an ominous hiss.

"Oh, shit!" Ben said. "That's a coral snake. They're

109

venomous, dude!"

"Fuck!" Kayla yelled as the group rushed out of the crypt as fast as they could, slamming the door behind them.

Once outside, Kayla bent over and put her hands on her knees as she tried to let her heart rate slow.

"Jesus Christ," Jasmine said. "I'm so sorry. I have no idea how that happened."

"We couldn't get the damn thing open," Ben added. "Must have typed in the code like thirty times before it just worked again."

Kayla, less afraid, but angrier, stood upright. She looked each one of them in their eyes, searching for the truth. She only glanced at Jasmine and Ben, but locked onto Desiree, who looked apologetic. But remorse didn't belie wrongdoing. She wanted to go off on all three of them, but just checked the time instead. It was a little before ten. Her parents still wouldn't be home for a while, but she suddenly felt an urge to get back to her sister as quickly as possible.

She turned her back on the group and headed toward the path home.

CHAPTER 12

Kylie found herself again watching the swings at the playground. But this time, she wasn't there. At least she didn't feel like she was. She felt like she was floating right outside of the fabric of reality. The park was still, to the point where Kylie wasn't even sure she wasn't looking at a painting.

But then it started.

The chains of the swings creaked as they started to move. Slowly at first, they picked up speed until they were making full rotations over the top of the A-frame. The slide made noises like a hammer striking a garbage can as the metal warped under the weight of the unseen. Each noise was followed by the squeak of the phantom slider before large plumes of dirt erupted at the base. The tic-tac-toe wheels spun so fast that they could flay the skin off the hands of anyone who tried to touch them.

Amid the cacophony, a chorus of children's voices sang out, reciting an odd rhyme.

I had a little bird.
Its name was Enza.
I opened the window.
And in flew Enza.

The sounds of little footfalls accompanied the sing-song lyrics, stamping the ground around the swings as smaller tufts of dirt popped from the terrain.

The rhyme gained speed, similar to a video that had its playback speed increased two or three times.

Ihadalittlebird itsnamewasEnza Iopenedthewindow andinflewEnza.

The rhyme got faster and faster until the words became indistinguishable and the sound dizzying. Just when it hit a point where Kylie felt nauseated by the auditory assault, it slowed as quickly as it had crescendoed. Only now, tapping replaced the words. The pattern of the rhyme soon gave way to a metronomic beat of something small tapping on a pane of glass.

Suddenly, Kylie was awake. For a few moments after her eyes opened, she remained on her back, looking up at the ceiling where the fan spun soundlessly on its medium-level setting. The cool air it whipped up dried the sweat that had beaded on her forehead.

Night sweats had always fouled Kylie out. Mostly because they were a staple of her time with cancer. She long ago lost count of how many times she'd woken up with the cotton fabric of her sheets drenched and clinging to her. The first time it had happened, she'd sobbed, thinking she had wet the bed. Now she knew better, but that knowledge didn't make things any more pleasant.

She continued to lie back, getting her bearings and enjoying the airflow from the fan. As she did, she noticed the tapping sound again.

As clarity won out over drowsiness, she recognized it.

Sitting up in bed, she realized two things: this episode of night sweats had been mild, a fact for which she was grateful, and the tapping was, once again, from the small bird seated on her windowsill. It would tap twice, pause, then tap twice more.

Tap. Tap.

She surveyed the small creature curiously. Last time she had seen it, it had signaled Emily's presence in her backyard.

Tap. Tap.

She pulled the covers off of her and swung her legs over the edge of the bed and onto the floor. The carpet felt good under her feet. It made her feel grounded in the real world, away from her dream.

Tap. Tap.

She took a tentative step toward the window, concerned—not so much about the bird—but rather about what awaited her down below.

Tap. Tap.

Steeling herself, Kylie walked slowly but steadily toward the window.

Tap. Tap.

When she was close enough, she again reached out her finger toward the bird. Her finger contacted the glass, and, as before, a small ring of fog materialized around the tip. She anticipated two more taps, but the bird broke its rhythm and stared up at her, its black eyes locked on Kylie's green ones.

Without warning, the bird jerked its head forward toward the glass. The impact, previously a tap, now registered as a disproportionate thud. Two more sounds followed in rapid succession.

The first was the crack of glass as its tiny beak embedded itself in the windowpane, fresh fissures spider-webbing around the point of collision.

The second was another crack, but this time it was the small bones in the bird's neck shattering upon impact.

Kylie watched in horror as it hung on the sill until its beak dislodged and it plummeted in a spiral to the ground below.

The curiously macabre incident turned out to be only a precursor to something more sinister. Pulling her focus away from the dead bird, Kylie turned her attention toward the trees, expecting to see Emily once again. But she didn't. What she saw chilled her to the bone.

The man in the yellow raincoat stood in the backyard, only a scant few feet from the dead bird. There was no rain, but his hood was up, a black void where his face should have been. He was breathing heavily, his massive shoulders heaving with each exhalation.

Kylie felt frozen with fear. This was now the third occasion on which she had seen this sinister figure, but something about this time was different. He appeared ready to strike, coiled like a snake. She scanned the area behind him, hoping against hope that maybe the old woman would be back. She couldn't be sure that she was the reason he hadn't got to her at the playground, but she also had nothing else to go on.

The standoff continued for what felt like an eternity. Kylie was afraid to move for fear that would spur the monster to advance.

Where was Kayla? Did he already get her?

"Kayla..."

She tried to call out to her sister, but her voice only came out in a cracked whisper. It was barely audible, even to her, but the hulking specter below cocked his head to one side as if she had called to him directly.

Then he started toward the house.

Terror washed over Kylie, and she found her voice.

"Kayla!" she screamed as loud as she could, the sound

stinging her throat as her cry echoed through the silent house.

Kylie spun on her heels and bolted toward her bedroom door.

She flung it open and made the sharp turn toward her sister's bedroom, slipping on the hardwood floor and landing hard on her left side, a lightning bolt of pain shooting through the elbow that took the brunt of the impact, down her forearm and to her hand, the palm and digits instantly tingling with a rapid onset of numbness.

Doing her best to ignore it, she used her other hand to push herself up and off the floor. She ran to Kayla's room and turned the knob, relieved to find it unlocked but dismayed to see that it was unoccupied.

"Kayla!" she screamed again, her most desperate plea for help yet.

Kylie rushed over to the window and dared to peek outside. The man was standing on the deck directly below. Somehow, he knew she was there because he looked up again, but she still couldn't see what was underneath the hood.

In a panic, she turned and ran out of the room, moving so fast she smacked into the railing, nearly tumbling over. She saw the hint of a light peeking around a corner downstairs and prayed that she would find her sister there... and that the scary man wouldn't be able to get in the house.

No longer concerned with how much noise she was making—the man knew she was in there—she bounded downstairs toward the light source, toward safety, only to find that she was still alone, the light from the range hood above the stove her only companion. She frantically surveyed the room, looking for anything to help her.

There was no phone in the house, so she had no way of contacting Kayla or her parents.

Running around the island, she eyed a Post-it note on the marble surface. It read *Had to run out. Be back in a few minutes*. Where could Kayla have gone? Why would she have left her alone like this? Mom was going to kill her. Kylie just hoped she was still alive to see it. As she contemplated her next move, she glanced toward the kitchen window and again saw that hooded face, its features lost in a dark void, directly outside the window over the sink. She screamed again, the scream now mixing with tears as she ducked behind the island as if that would somehow provide her sanctuary.

She got down on her stomach and army-crawled out of the kitchen and into the living room. With nowhere else to go, she found the only place she could think of to hide—in the tiny space between Dad's recliner and the wall. She pushed herself forward, her left arm still feeling like pins and needles, but not caring that it did. Her tears dripped onto the carpet with each push toward the chair.

Squeezing as far as she could into the condensed space, she curled into a ball, drawing her knees up to her chest, pulling them in as hard as she could. She sobbed, praying like she had with her mother during her treatment. Imploring whoever or whatever God was not to let her die. He hadn't let the cancer win; he couldn't let this monster have her.

As she cried and prayed, she was afraid that this time her appeal to a higher power wouldn't work.

The knob rattled as the front door opened.

CHAPTER 13

"**K**ayla! Wait up!"

Kayla was having none of it as Desiree chased her down the path back toward her house, walking as fast as she could without breaking into a full run. She was furious. She was scared. But most of all, she was hurt. She had let her guard down with these people, something she rarely did this quickly. Maybe it was the hurt of what happened with Morgan coupled with the loneliness and isolation she felt, not only from moving to a new state, but also from her family itself. She needed a smoke and a cry.

"Come on, Kayla!" Desiree shouted as she closed the distance.

"Fuck off!" she said without looking back, hoping her pursuer didn't notice the crack in her voice.

That prompted Desiree to move even faster, closing the last of the ground between them and grabbing Kayla's arm, hooking it to first stop her pace. Kayla didn't resist, but she also didn't face her until Desiree gently yanked her by the elbow to force the turn. She looked like she was about to cry herself, and that softened Kayla's rage. But it didn't go away.

"Listen to me," Desiree said. "I didn't do that. Neither

did Jasmine or Ben. That would have been a fucked-up thing to do and that's not us."

"Why should I believe you?"

She put her hand on Kayla's cheek. It was tender and reassuring, and the angry girl felt the irritation melting away as she continued to fight the tears lurking just around her eyes.

"Don't mess with me, Desiree. I've been burned by people I care about too many times. I can't fucking deal with it again."

Surprisingly, the first tear came from Desiree, a single drop that danced down her cheek. "I swear, Kayla. I'm not the type of person to scare someone like that. I wouldn't even do it to someone I don't like."

She likes me?

That was the takeaway from what Desiree said. She liked her too, but did she like her or did she *like* her? The last of the anger was gone, and she nodded as her own tears started. Desiree pulled her into a hug. Kayla let her arms hang low before she wrapped them around her as she cried. It was a release of everything that had built up since the day they found out that her sister had cancer. She had tried so hard to push it all down somewhere deep where the emotions couldn't escape, where they couldn't get out to hurt her, but that tank had been filled to the brim long ago. It finally burst.

Desiree didn't say anything else. She just held Kayla until the flood subsided. When she was ready, it was her that broke the hug. "I'm sorry, that was scary as shit."

"What was that monster I saw? Do you think it was just that snake?"

Kayla thought about it and wondered if she had actually seen what she thought she did. They were in a cemetery. At night. After hearing a scary-ass story about dead kids and serial killers. And, to top it all off, they'd ended up trapped in a damn crypt. The others had seen that normal snake after the door opened. That must have been what she saw. Her eyes had to be just playing tricks on her.

Kayla finally stepped back from the embrace.

"It had to be."

She didn't know if she was trying to convince Desiree or herself. She looked to her for reassurance.

"You don't believe all this stuff about ghosts, do you?"

Kayla hoped Desiree would give her a definitive no, but she didn't. She just said, "I don't know. I'd like to believe there's something out there. Wouldn't you?"

She thought about it. The idea of her body being relegated to a husk that would disintegrate into the dirt without anything after was decidedly unappealing. It made her sad to think about all those children buried in the cemetery. Their lives were over before they could even start. If things had gone differently, that could have even been Kylie.

Oh fuck.

The thought of her sister was a reminder that she was still at the house, all by herself.

"Shit!" she exclaimed in a panic. "I gotta get back to Kylie."

"Go." Desiree said. "I'll smooth things over with Jasmine and Ben."

Kayla nodded and turned to leave, but Desiree grasped her hand.

"I'll see you at work tomorrow?"

She nodded again.

"You want to maybe hang out after? No scary shit. I

119

promise."

"I'd like that."

Desiree smiled and pecked her on the cheek, her lips warm where the streaks from Kayla's tears had cooled. Any irritation that she may have held onto was gone.

"See ya tomorrow."

Without another word, Kayla ran the rest of the way home.

It only took a few minutes to reach the house. Without hesitation, she opened the back door and froze at what she saw inside.

"Where the hell were you?"

Roger Macklin's face was red as he posed the question to his older daughter. His eyes displayed a fury that she could never remember seeing before.

"I asked you a question," he said, his voice calm and measured yet permeated with anger.

Kylie was huddled on the couch in Gretchen's embrace. They were also staring at Kayla. Her younger sister was not crying, but her eyes betrayed that she had been. They were red and swollen. Even though they didn't register anger toward Kayla, there was an abundance of hurt, and that was even worse.

But what Kylie lacked in wrath, her mother more than made up for it in spades. Beyond the unbridled fury within them, there was something else. They were glassy and bloodshot, but not as if she'd been crying. She looked drunk.

Her father looked as if he was going to explode if he didn't get an answer soon. Even then, depending on her explanation, he may do so anyway.

"I thought I heard something out back and went to check."

"Bullshit!" Gretchen snapped, the word slurred, confirming her intoxication.

Kayla wasn't a detective, but it didn't take one to understand what had happened here. Mom had gotten drunk, precipitating their early exit from the work function. That also probably didn't help her father's current temperament, although Kayla couldn't deny her own culpability.

"We've been calling you for the past twenty minutes," he said, struggling to maintain that even tone.

"What?" Kayla exclaimed, genuinely surprised as she checked her phone. "My phone didn't—"

She cut herself off as the screen lit up. There were many notifications. She quickly scrolled through, counting eleven missed calls and about fifteen text messages, all with variations of asking just where the hell she was. The messages lined up with the time she was in the crypt, but even when she had her phone out to use her flashlight, no messages or calls had come through.

"You're grounded," Gretchen spat.

"What? You can't ground me! I'm a fucking adult!"

"We're still waiting for the day you start acting like one!" her mother countered.

"Enough!" Roger bellowed, even more forcefully than he had during that initial journey to this new home that was already fraught with tension and acrimony. He lowered his voice and asked, "When do you get paid?"

The question threw Kayla, but she felt it best to answer.

"Sometime next week. Friday, I think."

"As soon as that paycheck hits, you're going to give me sixty-five dollars for your cell phone bill, or you can go sign up for your own plan. I'll leave it up to you."

"Are you fucking serious?" she blurted, regretting it before even finishing the sentence.

"And you're going to watch your mouth while living under my roof."

Kayla was flabbergasted. Her father had *never* been this harsh with her. She looked to her mother, half expecting her to take umbrage with the *my house* comment. But she remained silent, continuing to hold Kylie close.

"Dad..." she started without really considering what she was going to say.

"Take a couple of days and think about whether you want to be a part of this family or just a tenant. If it's the latter, we can discuss rent."

CHAPTER 14

For much of the next day, the Macklin home was quiet as a tomb. It was Saturday, so Dad didn't have work. Even though he and Mom were both home, Kylie noticed they didn't speak to each other at all. Mom would normally have this angry look on her face in situations like this, but today, she just looked sad. At least in her interactions with Dad.

Kayla was another story.

Dad had been angrier the night before than any time Kylie could remember. She knew a lot of it was rightfully focused on Kayla, but even at nine and not particularly well-versed in adult relationships, she also felt her father's anger was directed at her mother for whatever had happened while they were out.

Her parents had come in while she was hiding behind Dad's recliner.

She had watched through the small sliver of space through the chair and the wall as her father led her mother in by the arm. As soon as they crossed the threshold, she wrenched her arm away and ordered him to "Get your fucking hands off me!" Mom's voice sounded funny. Her words came out slowly and she didn't pronounce certain letters correctly. It reminded her of the time Kayla got her *smart* teeth taken out and came home loopy with a mouthful of cotton gauze. They had all had a good laugh at her sister's expense but this time, even if Kylie hadn't been cowering in fear for her life, it wasn't funny.

"Just trying to make sure you don't fall and embarrass yourself any more than you already have tonight."

Who knows how much longer or more intense the argument would have gotten had Kylie not released a sharp exhalation of breath she hadn't even realized she was holding in, alerting her parents to her presence.

What followed was a blur as Kylie sprang from behind the chair and flung herself into her father's arms. After the initial shock of finding their youngest child hiding alone downstairs, they started asking her a rapid-fire succession of questions.

"What were you doing back there?"

"Why are you by yourself?"

"Where's your sister?"

And the one they asked multiple times, "Are you okay?"

She broke down and cried as she told them about the man she had seen outside and that she didn't know where Kayla was. Dad had immediately rushed upstairs, searching for her sister. She heard him banging around the rooms for a couple of minutes before he returned, holding a gun. She hadn't even known that her father owned one. It looked like a smaller version of the one Rudy used to kill the werewolf in the movie. He went outside, weapon in hand, while Mom led her over to the couch and held her tight while continuing to ask if she was alright.

A few minutes later, Dad had come back inside and announced that there was no one outside, not even Kayla. Over the next fifteen minutes, her father called and texted his missing daughter many times, not receiving a reply. Until the moment Kayla walked back in, his face was tattooed with worry. The anger only came after he saw she was okay.

So, yeah, Kylie had never seen her father that angry before. But she had also only seen him look that scared one other time she could remember—when they found out she was sick. It was the worry that gave way to the rage.

The argument that followed was intense. Dad had commanded everyone's attention, having reached his limit with his family's problems. After he'd asked Kayla if she was a part of the family or a tenant—a word that Kylie wasn't familiar with—he had pivoted from her and spread his ire across the group as a whole.

"I am beyond tired of living like this," he said, his voice lowered back to a conversational level, but no less lacking in authority. "We are the luckiest family in the world. Our daughter beat the odds and survived something that a lot of kids don't."

The words chilled her and, had Roger not been so angry, he may have chosen them more carefully. "But instead of being grateful and embracing this second chance, we're all diving deeper into our own bullshit. Do we even love each other at all anymore?"

His voice cracked on the word *love*. He removed his glasses and wiped his eye with his sleeve, snuffing out a tear before it could escape. He took a deep breath and returned the glasses. The broken father and husband surveyed his stunned family one more time before walking upstairs without another word.

Mom and Kayla engaged in a brief stare-down before Kayla followed her father's lead.

Kylie quietly cried, no longer out of fear of the ominous man, but out of sadness for the state of her family. She felt like this was all her fault. If she had never gotten sick, they would all still be happy. She didn't mean to make everyone so angry all the time.

"Come on," Mom said gently as she rose off the couch and reaching her hand to Kylie, which she took without hesitation.

Her voice sounded more like herself, as if something about the argument had flipped a switch and fixed whatever was causing her to sound funny.

The remaining Macklins headed upstairs. Both Dad's and Kayla's doors were shut all the way. Mom brought Kylie into her bedroom and tucked her into bed. She kissed her gently on the forehead and said, "I love you."

Kylie had expected her mother to leave, but she kicked off her high-heeled shoes, not bothering to straighten them after they landed haphazardly on the floor. She climbed onto the bed over the covers next to Kylie. Gretchen's back was to her daughter and Kylie wondered if she was going to say anything else, but within a minute she was lightly snoring.

Not long after, the emotional exhaustion siphoned the last of Kylie's adrenaline, allowing sleep to take her. She didn't dream that night.

For that, she was grateful.

Now, as the family listlessly went about their day, unsure of where they would go from here, the tension between Mom and Kayla was threatening to bubble up to the surface yet again. Her parents had largely written off the threat of the large man to a bad dream. There was no evidence to the contrary.

But the idea that Kayla had left her little sister all alone in the house at night, knowing there was no phone, was clearly eating away at Gretchen, preventing any type of real repair to the family dynamic.

The matriarch's eyes never left her eldest daughter as she popped a slice of bread into the toaster and poured herself a lukewarm cup of coffee. Kayla didn't brave a glance in her mother's direction, but did offer Kylie a tight-lipped attempt at an apologetic smile. The younger girl returned one of her own.

Kayla left for work and returned home around dinnertime. There was no attempt at a family dinner tonight. Mom whipped up chicken nuggets with a side of mac and cheese for Kylie. To her surprise, she offered some to Kayla when she walked in, but her sister politely declined, holding up a plastic bag with a torpedo-shaped object wrapped in waxed deli paper to evidence that she had taken care of dinner on her own. Her parents, to her knowledge, didn't eat.

After she ate, Kylie retired to her room and watched TV while she doodled in her notebook. Mom stopped in around eight to make sure she was ready for bed and instructed her to turn everything off and go to sleep at eight thirty.

Ten minutes before her designated bedtime, Kayla knocked lightly on her door, but entered without an invitation. Kylie sat upright on the bed and muted, but didn't turn off, the TV. Kayla took a seat on the opposite side and reached out for her sister's hand.

Kylie accepted it. Her sister squeezed it gently.

"I'm sorry," Kayla said.

Kylie nodded. "I know." She paused before posing the question: "Why did you leave me here alone?"

She watched as Kayla searched for the words, even though she knew the answer. The hesitation was to determine how much she should actually disclose. When she answered, she chose honesty.

"Desiree wanted to show me something. At the cemetery." Kylie didn't ask what it was, but rather sat in silence, beckoning Kayla to continue without using her words. She continued. "The way you described your... dream was very... specific. You saw things that there was no way you should have known about." Kylie still kept quiet. Somehow, she knew what Kayla was referencing, but she wanted to hear her say it. "She showed me the rocking chair. It belonged to Jasmine's great-grandmother. How did you know about it?"

"I saw it in my dream," Kylie confirmed. "What else did you see?"

"Nothing else," the speed of her reply coupled with the slight stammer told Kylie that she wasn't being truthful. She didn't call her out, though.

"There's something wrong with that playground," Kylie said. She expected Kayla to contradict her. To tell her she was being silly and letting her imagination get the better of her. But she didn't.

"I think you should stay away from it."

Kylie nodded. Sure, it was nice to have somewhere to play so close to her house, but there was weird energy in the air. She hadn't seen anything ghostly while she was there during the day, only in her dream.

It was a dream, wasn't it?

And the girl, Emily. Everything about her was strange. On their first meeting, she was willing to overlook her peculiarity, her desperation to make friends leading to view their encounter through rose-colored glasses. But now, having met other kids at school, combined with the weird, haunting dreams, convinced her she should stay far away from the odd child.

Both girls fell silent, sitting in consideration of both each other and the growing list of concerns between them—a new home, new relationships, fractured old ones, their parents' ever-deteriorating marriage. Oh yeah, and the minor matter of ghosts possibly hanging out less than a mile from where they currently were.

Kylie's face twisted from contemplation to apprehension as the events of the past few days pushed their way to the forefront of her mind.

"Are we in danger?" she asked her big sister.

Kayla's heart melted at the question. Kylie had shown maturity and bravery well beyond her years, ever since the day she'd received her devastating diagnosis. But now, she was just a nine-year-old girl who was terrified about what lurked in the dark. Her sister pulled her in and hugged her tight.

"No," she said unconvincingly. Even so, Kylie appreciated her saying what she needed to hear. She felt Kayla start to pull back, but didn't let her.

"Will you stay with me for a while?"

"Of course."

When Kylie next opened her eyes, she was no longer in her bed. She was once again on the swing in the park. Unlike last time, there was no chill in the air, but one ran through her body as a wave of fear and confusion washed over her.

"Hi, Kylie!"

The voice next to her was familiar and different at the same time.

It carried the tone and tenor of a child her age but this time a sinister undercurrent hid underneath those two simple words.

She turned to her left and saw Emily swinging next to her, a sardonic smile stretched across her face.

"What are you?" Kylie mustered the courage to ask.

"What do you mean? I'm your friend, silly!"

"Why don't you go to school?"

"I told you. My parents are dead. No one makes me go, so I don't."

The explanation wasn't satisfactory to Kylie. She figured she didn't have anything to lose by just coming right out and asking the question.

"Are you a ghost?"

Emily looked her over curiously, as if the question didn't register with her at first. But, after a moment, she burst out in a belly laugh, as if she'd just been told the funniest joke of all time. When she finally settled, she answered, "No. There aren't any ghosts here. Not anymore."

"What about your friends?" Kylie asked, her fear somewhat diluted by frustration at Emily's evasiveness.

"Look around," the other girl said, her amused expression morphing into a sneer. "Do you see them?"

Kylie dared to look away from Emily long enough to observe the area. The strange girl wasn't lying. There were no orbs and none of the swings moved on their own. The slide was quiet and still.

If the ghosts were here, they weren't making their presence known. Despite the lack of spectral activity, the girls weren't alone.

"Hi, Kylie."

Drew Gatto said from the swing to her right. The greeting was no different from the one Emily had used only a couple minutes ago, but Drew's carried nothing but warmth.

"What are you doing here?" she asked him.

Drew frowned at the question. Kylie wasn't trying to be mean, but she was genuinely surprised to see the boy there at the playground, explaining the abrupt question.

"Emily invited me."

The mention of her name made Kylie realize that, in the shock of seeing Drew, she had momentarily forgotten about Emily, who she still thought might be up to no good. She turned back to the other girl, who wasn't paying attention to either of them. She was just swinging away while reciting a familiar rhyme, each propulsion of the swing punctuated with the next verse.

"I had a little bird. Its name was Enza. I opened the window. And in flew Enza."

She turned back to Drew. He dragged his feet along the ground to stop the momentum of the swing. Just before it came to a complete stop, he hopped off and gestured

131

for Kylie and Emily to follow him.

"Come on!" he said cheerily, "Let's go on the slide!"

"Drew! Wait!" Kylie called. He stopped, but everything in his posture screamed impatiently to get to the next activity.

"What?"

"Do your parents know you're here this late? Aren't they worried about you?"

"I dunno," he said nonchalantly. "Come *on*!" With that, he ran toward the slide and climbed up before quickly descending with a gleeful declaration of "Yeah!" As soon as he hit the ground, he repeated the process.

She looked back at Emily, who had stopped swinging, her dark eyes staring almost straight through the confused child. Kylie repeated her earlier inquiry.

"Where are the others?"

Emily shrugged again. "Don't know. But it doesn't matter. I have you and Drew to play with now."

Something about the way she said that made Kylie very uneasy. She wanted to get out of this place as soon as she could. Longing for the safety of her bedroom, she shut her eyes tight and tried to will her way back there. When she opened them again, she was still at the playground with Emily and Drew, the former's sinister smile still painted on her face.

"Kylie!" a muffled voice called from the distance. It was faint, but it was there.

She surveyed the area, petrified that she would see the large man who had stalked her the night before, but all she saw was the eerie stillness of the trees.

"Kylie, sweetheart," the voice came again. It was a little clearer this time. It sounded like her mother, but, unlike that first day here, it was calm. There was no panic or urgency in the tone.

Emily winked at her and spoke. Her voice seemed different, as if run through a voice-changing device that created an ominous, reverberating pitch.

"See you soon, Kylie."

"Kylie," Mom's voice said again, as she found herself roused from sleep. She felt her mother's hand stroking her shoulder. When her vision cleared from her slumber, she saw she was indeed back in her bedroom. Kayla was no longer there, but Gretchen was sitting on the edge of her bed.

"Mom?" she asked, her voice dry and cracked.

"I'm here, baby. What do you need?"

"Huh?"

"You were calling me."

Kylie wasn't sure she heard her right, but the words were enough to stimulate her mind the rest of the way awake. She sat up in bed and told her mother, "No, I wasn't."

Gretchen's face registered initial confusion, followed by a realization. "You must have been talking in your sleep. It's been a while since you've done that."

Kylie was also confused. Mom was right. When she was sick, it was common for her to talk in her sleep, the result of delirium born out of her pain. But she always woke feeling restless and disoriented. This time, it felt more like when she had woken up from her surgery. Before they started, they had put a mask over her face and asked her to count down from one hundred. She remembered making it to ninety-eight. The next thing she knew, she was awake. Even though it only felt like a few seconds had passed, it also somehow felt like days, as if she had experienced the deepest sleep of her life. That's how she felt now.

"I didn't... realize."

Gretchen smiled warmly and it was comforting to her daughter. Her mom could be over the top for sure, but she never doubted her love. "It's okay, sweetie. Go back to sleep."

Kylie felt the grogginess returning, but she was afraid to close her eyes for fear of ending up back at the playground with Emily. Whatever she was. Any notion that she was just a normal kid that lived nearby was gone. She never wanted to see her again.

But she didn't want to tell her mom any of that. She would only worry more and probably keep her from going to school. Where she had real friends. Like Drew and the others. She hoped Drew was okay, but there was nothing she could do about that right now.

"I love you, Mommy."

Gretchen's face took on a level of softness at the declaration, as if the words had touched her heart. "I love you too, sweetheart." She got up off the bed and kissed her daughter on her forehead. "I'll leave the door open a crack so I can hear you if you call again."

Kylie wasn't convinced she had called her the first time, but she didn't argue. She just smiled and shut her eyes while she listened to her mother exit the room.

She continued to fight off sleep but, even awake, all she

could see in her head was Emily's wicked grin and that rhyme.

I had a little bird...

"Shhhhh." An ethereal voice came from the direction of her bedroom door.

Kylie froze. She squeezed her eyes shut, afraid to see who or what made the sound. She counted in her head. First to ten. Then twenty. Then thirty. At forty, she opened her eyes. They strained through the darkness as she focused on the bedroom door, which, as her mother promised, was left ajar.

A pair of white eyes without irises stared back at her from the darkness outside the door that led to the upstairs hallway. As her vision adjusted further, she saw they belonged to a little girl. She was wearing a similar outfit to Emily, but it wasn't the menacing girl from the playground. It was a child she had never seen before. Below her eyes, her skin cracked and a faint white glow emitted from just below the surface, as if light had taken the place of her blood.

Kylie was scared, but not sure if she was in danger. The girl drew her finger to her fissured lips and again said, "Shhhhh."

Kylie could no longer hold her eyes open and blinked.

When she opened them, the little girl was gone.

CHAPTER 15

K ayla hung out at the deli on Sunday, even though she wasn't scheduled to work. It was better than just sitting around her house and there was really no one she'd rather spend time with than Desiree.

Big Al was actually happy to see her. He told her if she wanted to earn a couple of bucks, she could work a half shift during lunch hour. It wasn't as busy as during the week, but a decent number of hungry patrons made their way in and out of the sandwich shop, including a few that she already recognized as regulars.

Beyond that, much of the day was uneventful. The girls had only talked briefly about the incident at the crypt the day before, and they hadn't mentioned it at all today. Instead, they talked about their lives. Kayla talked about her life in Florida, how she was mainly on her own while her parents tended to Kylie during her illness. She mentioned her friend Morgan and how they didn't talk anymore because she'd hooked up with Aiden.

"What's the big deal?" Desiree asked, non-judgmentally. "You have a crush or something?"

"Ew. Definitely not. Aiden is not my type."

Desiree gave her a wry, knowing smile. "No shit. I meant Morgan."

Kayla felt her face flush. Sure, there had been

136

an ongoing flirtation—at least that's how she saw it—between the two of them, but she hadn't confirmed her sexual orientation to her new friend, who hadn't confirmed hers either. Kayla didn't necessarily consider herself *in the closet*, but she hadn't come out to anyone either. She knew her parents wouldn't have an issue with her being gay, but she had no desire to discuss her relationships with them, romantic or otherwise, so it just hadn't come up. She was never sure how her friends would react, so she never really went there with them either. As much as she crushed on Morgan, she was afraid that if she ever professed her feelings for her, she'd scare her away. She knew her friend only had an interest in boys. If she knew Kayla was interested in her, she feared, it would make things awkward and ruin their friendship.

I guess I took care of that, she thought, recalling the snarky social media comment followed by the heated text exchange.

"It was... complicated," Kayla confessed.

"It shouldn't be," Desiree said, putting her hand on top of Kayla's on the counter. She let it linger there.

"What about you?" Kayla asked.

"What about me?"

"Do you have a boyfriend?"

Desiree cocked an eyebrow at the question, as if it wasn't the one she was expecting.

"Don't you think I would have mentioned one by now?"

"Good point. So what was the deal with you and Ben?"

Now she smirked. "We hooked up a couple of times. It was alright, but he's not really my type."

"What is your type?"

The smirk morphed into a full-blown, flirtatious smile. Kayla realized that Desiree still hadn't moved her hand from on top of her own. "I like to keep my options open."

"I'm sure you have your share."

"Maybe. But I'm pretty picky. I have to see something special in someone if I'm going to give them my time."

Kayla became aware that during the conversation, the two had drifted closer. She was definitely picking up the signals that her new friend was giving her, but still she hesitated, afraid of what misreading the situation might mean for their budding relationship. Still, she needed to know what this was.

"Do you have anyone special in mind right now?"

"Maybe," she said again, a spark in her eye. "But I wonder if this person knows just how special they are. Something tells me they don't."

Kayla felt her stomach somersault. Desiree was being coy, but she was clearly referring to her. They both fell silent, but it was comfortable. Desiree coiled her fingers around her hand and squeezed it. Kayla turned her palm upward and cupped it back as they looked into each other's eyes.

"You damn fools!"

The old woman's voice killed the moment, causing the girls to release each other's hands as if they had been burned. Kayla turned to see that Ethel Weeks had stormed into the deli and was barreling toward the counter on a mission that, from the rage written on her face, wasn't to procure potato salad.

"Auntie Ethel," Desiree started before the septuagenarian cut her off.

"Don't you Auntie Ethel nothin', young lady! Do you have any idea of what you've done?"

"What are you talking about?" Kayla asked, even though she could venture an educated guess.

"You know goddamn well what I'm talking about. Which one of y'all broke Mama's rocking chair?"

The girls tried not to look at each other, knowing a glance in either's direction would serve as an admission of guilt.

"We don't know what you're talking about," Desiree lied. "I swear."

"Yeah," Kayla abetted. "What rocking chair?"

The old woman narrowed her eyes and clenched her teeth, not buying the denials for a second.

"You listen to me and you listen to me good. You have no idea what kind of evil you've unleashed."

Kayla froze, not knowing quite what this woman was talking about, but she thought back to what she had seen in the crypt. She knew in her heart that it was more than just a run-of-the-mill snake. She just didn't want to believe it.

"What evil?" she asked.

"You let it out. That chair was the only thing that tethered Mama's spirit to the living world. Without it, she's lost. And without her, them kids is in danger."

"Kids? Auntie Ethel, what kids?" Desiree said, trying to calm the agitated woman.

"The kids in the cemetery. Without Mama to protect them, that thing is going to feed on their souls. And when it runs out of them, it's going to come for the living. Because it's forever hungry."

The girls dropped the subterfuge and ventured to look in each other's direction. They didn't know how to react to any of this.

"I gotta find it."

"Find what?" Desiree asked.

"I gotta find Mama's recipe book. It's the only thing that

can save them kids now."

Kayla thought about her sister. Was Kylie in danger? Actual danger?

"Ethel—" Desiree started.

"I done told you not to Ethel me!" the woman was apoplectic. "Don't you see? I got no notion of where that damned book is and without it, that thing is only going to get stronger! It's only going to need to feed more!"

"What thing?" Kayla shouted, her patience for Ethel's ranting gone.

Before the woman could answer, Jasmine burst in through the door, her breath labored as if she'd been running.

"Auntie Ethel!" she exclaimed at the sight of the woman. "There you are!"

She rushed up to the counter and hooked her arm in her aunt's. Ethel didn't resist, but continued to stare daggers at Kayla and Desiree.

"You damn fools," she spat once again before allowing Jasmine to guide her to the exit. Jasmine turned to her friends and mouthed the words *I'm sorry* as she led her agitated aunt out of the deli.

Desiree laughed. "Man, Ethel can be tough, but I've never seen her that riled up."

Kayla didn't see the humor. "What if she's telling the truth? What if that rocking chair was some kind of... tether... or whatever the hell she called it."

"Kayla..." Desiree started, without really knowing what she was going to say.

"You know this is fucking weird, Desiree. Kylie's dreams. Getting locked in the crypt. That fucking thing inside."

"I thought you said it was just a snake?"

"*You* said it was just a snake and I didn't want to believe anything otherwise."

Desiree put her hands on Kayla's shoulders as if she were going to shake some sense into her. She didn't, though. She just squeezed reassuringly.

"Yes. Weird shit happens here, but there's no evil entity preying on the souls of dead children."

When she put it like that, it certainly sounded ridiculous. Kayla's mind was waging a war between things she'd both seen and heard that defied rational explanation and her long-held belief that everything in the world had some type of rational explanation. She had the same conflicting feelings about the move to Huntsville. Sure, she missed her old home and friends—whatever friends she still had, which she wasn't convinced were any at the moment—but she also developed new friendships like the one with Desiree. Friends with the potential to be perhaps something more.

Assuming they hadn't just unleashed some type of evil that would destroy everyone in the town, but that was a bit too far-fetched.

Right?

CHAPTER 16

Kylie was anxious as she walked into the classroom on Monday morning for her third day at Alexander Elementary. Of all the eerie things she had experienced since moving here, her dream with Emily and Drew at the playground was the most disturbing. It was the first time she'd seen a glimpse of Emily's true nature beneath her innocent facade, and she knew there was much more to discover. None of which she was eager to. But mostly, Drew's appearance at the playground had her worried. She didn't know her classmate well, but he was sweet and friendly. She didn't want anything bad to happen to him. First thing, she needed to know how he'd ended up there. If he even remembered at all.

So when she looked around the room and didn't see him there, her anxiety immediately spiked. She took her seat at the table while Jessie and Trina were already settled and going about their business, waiting for class to start, Jessie doodling in her notepad and Trina flipping through a *Diary of a Wimpy Kid* book.

"Hi," Kylie said to the girls, trying not to sound nervous.

The girls both greeted her, but didn't make much more effort to engage. Not out of rudeness; they were just wrapped up in their own activities as fourth graders are wont to be.

"Is Drew here today?"

"I dunno," Jessie answered with a shrug without looking up from her scribbles.

Trina, however, put her book down and smirked at Kylie. "Ooooh," she said, drawing out the *oo* sound. "Do you have a crush on Drew?"

It was dumb and Kylie didn't have the time or patience for it. "No," she answered pointedly.

"I think you do!" Trina replied, undeterred. "I think you have a crush on Drew and want to kiss him and marry him and have babies!"

Kylie was dealing with a sleep deficit and maybe ghosts or even worse monsters behind her house, so her patience for her classmate's teasing wasn't in abundance this morning.

"Shut up," she said with an authority that rendered Trina speechless.

"*Excuse me!*" Miss Evans said from the front of the room. "What makes you think you can speak like that in this classroom?"

Kylie wanted to channel her mother and go into full lawyer mode, defending her actions by saying the other girl, who had pretended to refocus on her book when she was actually listening to the interaction, was the one who provoked *her*. But she had bigger problems than schoolyard squabbles.

"Sorry, Miss Evans."

"I'll bet you are. You're getting clipped down for that one, Kylie."

Miss Evans had a chart in the classroom with everyone's names on colorful paper clips. On the paper were levels from one to five, charting the students' behavior, with level five being they were perfect angels with impeccable academics to level one being reserved for the future hooligans of Huntsville. Kylie fumed internally as she watched her teacher move her paperclip from level three—where everyone started and most still were, it being so early in the year—to level two.

This is bullshit, she thought, using language in her head she wouldn't dare say out loud. That was the crux of the problem here. Kylie loved school. She felt thrilled to have the ability to come here every day, an appreciation gained when this simple task that so many took for granted had almost been stolen from her forever. To be seen as anything other than a model student who was forever grateful for the opportunity to get an education was unpalatable to her.

She shot a dirty look at Trina, who she caught peering over the top of the book at her before quickly glancing back down at the pages. Miss Evans had already moved on from the discipline and was now addressing the class, starting with the morning roll call.

When she skipped Drew's name, Kylie raised her hand, knowing that she was inviting further derision with what she was about to ask. She also didn't care.

"Yes, Kylie?" the teacher asked, with a modicum of exasperation.

"Where's Drew today?"

As she expected, the snickers surrounded her as the developing minds in the room assuming the inquiry was borne out of a romantic interest rather than genuine concern for the boy.

"Settle down," Miss Evans instructed, and the class obeyed. "Drew is not feeling well today, so he's staying home."

She went back and called the next name. Kylie raised

her hand again.

"Kylie," she said, her patience now razor thin. "This is not the time for questions."

Ignoring her, Kylie asked, "Is he okay?"

More snickers. Miss Evans glared at the students. Taking the hint, they abruptly silenced themselves.

"Kylie, I'm sure he's fine, but it is not appropriate for me to discuss other students with you."

The answers were wholly unsatisfactory. He could have a simple cold or he could be deathly ill and in the hospital. Whichever way it went, she knew she would not get the answer from her teacher and was only going to risk her ire by pressing further. She folded her hands on the table while her teacher finished taking attendance.

When Miss Evans called for recess, Kylie stepped out into the sun and the warmth felt good on her face. It was a beautiful day, for which she was grateful. There had been too much darkness and cold surrounding her in recent days. She observed the other students. Some were dribbling basketballs on the blacktop courts, others ran around playing haphazard games of tag, while still others made use of the school's playground equipment.

No thanks, Kylie thought as she looked at her classmates laughing on the swing set.

She walked over to a large red maple tree, which was a little way from the designated play area, but not so far as to get her in trouble. She took a seat underneath, pulled out her notebook, opened it to a blank page and started drawing. What started as doodles eventually took the form of a girl with dark hair on a swing. It wouldn't go on display at an art gallery, but it was also not unclear what it was. Or, more specifically, *who* it was.

Emily.

Kylie narrowed her eyes and tried to understand what compelled her to draw the one thing she wanted to avoid. She hadn't even realized she'd done it until the drawing was finished.

"Kylie," a small voice broke her concentration.

Startled, she felt her body tense as she slapped the notebook shut. She looked up and saw Trina and Jessie standing over her. She now recognized it was Trina's voice that had broken her concentration.

"Whatcha doing?" Jessie asked. It sounded more like innocuous small talk rather than some type of set up question.

"Just... drawing." She said.

"Cool!" Jessie said without a follow-up. She looked at Trina as if she were waiting for her to say something. When she didn't, Jessie nudged her without subtlety.

"I'm sorry," Trina said, sounding genuine despite the apology's need to be prompted.

"It's okay," Kylie said.

"I know you were just worried he might be really sick," she continued. "Like you were when you had cancer."

Kylie was thrown. As much as the conciliation was unexpected, this was even more startling. She hadn't told anyone in school that she had been sick. She had no idea if her teacher knew or not, but given that she wouldn't disclose the reason for Drew's absence, it was hard to believe she would have shared Kylie's cancer fight with the class. Maybe her mom had said something? But, even then, who would have told these girls?

"How did you know I had cancer?" she asked, before adding, "I'm okay now. It's not like something you can catch or anything."

She both hated the need to qualify it and felt it was necessary. The way the world had been during the pandemic, everyone was afraid of getting sick, not just from the virus, but from other things that could make the virus worse. Even deadly. *Underlining conditions* was what she thought they had talked about. Her sickness was her fight alone, but she still felt compelled to tell people she couldn't make them ill. Adults seemed to know that already, but other kids didn't always understand that.

"We know," Jessie said. "And we know that you're all better now."

Kylie shook her head, as if trying to clear it of some trance she found herself in. *How did they know this? Who told them?*

While she contemplated how to respond, Trina asked, "You live by the playground at Maple Hill Park, right?"

Another unexpected turn in the conversation.

"Uh, yeah."

"That's awesome!" Jessie said. "Maybe we can all go hang out and play there sometime?"

You need to stay far away from that place, Kylie thought, but didn't verbalize. Instead, she said, "I don't really like it there. It's kind of boring."

The response was clearly unsatisfactory to her classmates, who wore disappointed expressions.

"That's not what we heard," Trina said. "She told us it

was the coolest playground in town!"

"Who?" Kylie asked, both knowing and fearing the answer.

"Our new friend Emily."

The name sent a shiver through Kylie. How many of these kids had Emily set her sights on?

"Who's Emily?" She tried to play off. Trina's face screwed up with irritation.

"She said you'd lie to us. Said you wanted to keep the playground all to yourself."

Kylie stood up to face the girls. She knew that willful ignorance wasn't going to work, so she pivoted to be more direct.

"How do you know her?"

"She came to my house last night," Jessie said. "I found her skipping around my backyard. I thought it was a little weird, but she told me all about the playground. She said all the kids want to play there."

Kylie turned her attention to Trina. "Is that what happened to you, too?"

Trina nodded and crossed her arms, clearly the less congenial of the two.

"You shouldn't go there," Kylie said. "And you shouldn't talk to Emily, either. She's—" She wanted to say *dangerous*, but that was only going to make her sound crazy which, from the looks at the expressions on the other students' faces, they already thought she was. "She's a bad kid," was the explanation she opted for.

"That's mean!" Trina said, the irony of how she had treated Kylie in class earlier lost on her. "You just want to keep the playground all to yourself! Emily said you'd say that!"

"Emily's a liar!" Kylie yelled, loud enough to attract the

attention of the other kids and, worse, Miss Evans.

"Kylie Macklin!" the teacher called as she stormed over. "What is going on here?"

"Nothing," Jessie said, trying to maintain the peace. "We were just... playing a game."

"Is this true, Trina?" Miss Evans asked.

Kylie stared the girl down. She must have done an adequate job of conveying that Trina would be best advised to keep her mouth shut because she said, "Yes, Miss Evans. We were just playing."

The teacher now looked at Kylie, who nodded in concurrence. She didn't look wholly convinced, but she also clearly wasn't in the mood to deal with any more minor disciplinary issues today. She looked at her watch before addressing the trio again.

"Time to line up. Recess is over."

As Kylie and her classmates returned to their room and took their seats for the next lesson, Kylie couldn't concentrate. All she could think was that whatever was going on with Emily and the playground wasn't going to go away on its own. In fact, it was getting worse.

She kept her eyes glued to her book and the front of the classroom, not sparing even the quickest glance out the window for fear that she'd see the malevolent little girl staring at her from the distance.

CHAPTER 17

Kayla sat on her windowsill and exhaled the cotton-candy-flavored vapor out her window, watching it dissipate into the night sky. She smiled as she turned the vape pen over in her hand, examining it. She had to admit, it was definitely less harsh than smoking cigarettes. When she'd finished her last pack, she had gone to the store to get another, but decided to try the vape instead. She knew smoking was a turnoff for lots of people and, until now, she didn't give a shit. But when you have people around you that you're interested in, maybe it was time to start.

She never saw herself as the type of person who would change up their behavior for a potential romantic interest, but, in her mind, giving up something as almost universally loathed as smoking cigarettes wasn't the worst compromise. It also wasn't like Desiree had told her she wouldn't be interested if she kept smoking. That actually made it easier. It was a choice she made to better herself with no actual pressure from anyone else. Yeah, she was still smoking, and vaping carried its own unique set of risks, but it was something her friend did too, so it wasn't like she could cast aspersions on Kayla for doing the same thing.

Friend, she thought. That part was obvious at this

point. She and Desiree were friends. But could they actually be more? The potential was there. She had all but confirmed that she was open to a relationship with a girl. Now it was just a matter of if, and when, they took that next step.

She thought back to the moment they shared at the deli. But the problem in doing so was that she also remembered what had happened next.

The odd encounter with Jasmine's aunt brought the less positive aspects of her new life here to the forefront of her mind. Sure, Auntie Ethel seemed like a kooky old woman, maybe she even had dementia or something, but the anger was real whether it came from a place of truth or delusion. But the anger also seemed like it was tinged with fear. The one thing she could tell with absolute certainty was, whether it was true or a delusion, Ethel *believed* everything she said.

After the incident, neither Kayla nor Desiree continued their flirtation. They had debriefed about what had just happened, closed up the deli, then met up with Jasmine and Ben for dinner at the diner Jasmine had joked about the first time they had met at Big Al's.

Jasmine apologized profusely for her aunt and said something about how her mental acuity had deteriorated over the past few years, resulting in her becoming not only confused but also downright mean at times. She told Kayla not to put too much stock in what she said and that her family had always been something of a pariah in the community because of her great-grandmother's dalliance with Hoodoo. Her father had tried to distance them by living as normally as possible, working in finance and taking part in the community, often through events at the local Baptist church of which they were members.

But, when his father died in 2015, he felt an obligation to his aunt, so they had all done their best to disregard her quirks while integrating them into their family as best they could. She still lived a few miles away in the small house where she had lived with her mother her whole life, never marrying or having children of her own. Jasmine's parents had tried unsuccessfully for years to convince her to move in with them, but she'd resisted at every turn. Jasmine admitted her dad had growing concerns over Ethel living on her own, especially as she grew more agitated and erratic in her advanced age. She had apparently even tried experimenting with different spells on her own, but she often grew frustrated at her lack of success with them.

All this was to say that Ethel's doomsaying was not to be taken seriously. This made Kayla feel a little better, but she had still seen too much that she couldn't explain to dispel the notions entirely.

Still, Kayla had a good time with her three new friends. They all laughed and talked about music—Ben, unsurprisingly, was a punk rock purist. Jasmine also liked punk, but professed a love for metalcore, at which Ben rolled his eyes. Everyone went silent when Desiree said her favorite artist was Taylor Swift, with Jasmine particularly giving her friend her own version of Dwayne "The Rock" Johnson's *people's eyebrow*.

"Bullshit!" she called her out. "You said your favorite band is *A Day to Remember*!"

Desiree broke down and laughed before the rest of the group joined in. It made Kayla happy to hear because ADTR was one of her favorites as well, having formed in Ocala only two hours from where she'd grown up. Having something else in common with Desiree gave her a warm feeling and, a couple of hours later, they had walked out of the diner, belting out the chorus to "All Signs Point to Lauderdale."

But, now back home after what had turned out to be a pretty good night, Kayla again found her mind returning to the darker things that had been occurring in her life. She had gotten home a little after eight o'clock and had popped in to say hi to Kylie before heading to her bedroom. She had been making more of an effort to bond with her little sister to make up for abandoning her the other night.

As soon as she entered the room, she could tell something was wrong. Kylie looked drawn and was quiet, only mumbling a "hey" when she had walked in.

"What's wrong?" Kayla had asked.

"Nothing."

Kayla walked over and gently took her sister's tablet away, placing it on the other side of the bed.

"Why don't I believe you? Did you have another bad dream or something?"

"How long did you stay after I fell asleep the other night?"

"I don't know. A few minutes. I made sure you were asleep before you left."

"Did anything strange happen?"

Kayla wasn't sure where she was going with this. "No, you fell asleep and I left. What do you mean, strange?"

"Did you see Drew's brother tonight?"

Now Kayla was really confused. Her sister was all over the place.

"Yeah, actually. We all had dinner together."

"Did he say anything about Drew?"

"Um, something about him having a cold, I think.

153

Why?"

"But he's okay?"

"Other than having a cold, I guess so." That seemed to make Kylie feel better. Her demeanor changed and she looked as if a weight had been lifted. Kayla posed the question again. "Why do you ask?"

"He wasn't in school today. I just hoped he was okay."

"Oh," Kayla said, wondering if there was more behind this. "Do you like him?"

This made Kylie mad for some reason. Kayla obviously wasn't aware of the teasing her concern had resulted in at school, so she wasn't sure why she had reacted that way.

"No! I just wanted to make sure he was okay!"

Kayla put her hands up as if she were being mugged. "Okay, geez. It was just a question. What aren't you telling me here?"

Kylie sighed. "I had another dream the night before he wasn't in school. I was back at the playground, but this time the ghosts were all gone. But Drew was there. With *her*."

"That girl you told me about? Emily?"

She saw her sister tense at the mere mention of the other girl's name, and she regretted mentioning it.

"I was going to ask him about it, but he wasn't at school today. I was afraid something happened to him."

Kayla felt bad for Kylie. Her sister had been through so much on her own it would be easy to forgive if she lacked the same compassion for others, but she still had that good heart of hers. It was one quality Kayla admired most about her. She thought of something and held up a finger on one hand to tell her sister to give her a second while grabbing her phone with the other and deftly typing and sending a text message.

She smiled at Kylie, who surveyed her curiously while she put her phone on the bed between them.

"What are you doing?" Kylie asked.

"Give it a minute."

It was less than a minute before the ringtone from Kayla's phone broke the silence. The incoming call was labeled *Ben*. Kayla tapped the *Answer* button and Ben's face popped on the screen.

"Hey, Kayla" he said. Kylie peered over into view of the screen and he added, "You must be Drew's friend, Kylie."

"Hi," Kylie said shyly.

Ben disappeared from the screen and the girls could see he was walking as the video feed moved with him. When the camera stopped shaking, they could see Ben again, but he was kneeling next to a bed with a boy about Kylie's age tucked in up to his chest, only his arms free, wearing long-sleeved pajamas. There was a nightstand visible over Ben's shoulder where Kayla could see a box surrounded by crumpled tissues, a glass filled a third of the way with what looked like orange juice, and an empty bowl with a spoon resting inside.

"Hey, Drew," Ben told the boy. "Your friend Kylie wanted to check and see if you were okay."

Kayla watched as her sister inspected the screen. Drew definitely looked like he didn't feel well. His skin tone was pallid, save for the angry shade of red that circled his nose that he had undoubtedly blown many times. His lips were chapped and he had heavy bags under his glassy eyes. No, he didn't look like he felt well, but he also looked like any other kid with a cold. Especially since she had a frame of reference, having seen Kylie during her much more severe battle with a decidedly deadlier illness.

"Hi," Drew said weakly, but with a glint of cheeriness at seeing his friend on the screen.

"Hi, Drew," Kylie said with relief creeping into her voice. "How are you feeling?"

"Like poop," he said, laughing at the word as any ten-year-old boy would.

"I'm sorry," Kylie said. "But I hope you feel better soon. We miss you at school."

"I'm staying home again tomorrow, but I hope I can come back on Wednesday."

"I hope so!" Kylie said, her worry further melting away as the conversation continued and she could see that he was, in fact, just dealing with a little cold. "Feel better!"

"Thanks!" Drew replied, his enthusiasm cutting through the sickness.

"Okay," Ben had said, filling up the screen once again. "Little man needs his rest, but we appreciate you checking up on him. You ladies have a good night."

They had hung up and Kylie went to bed, relieved.

That was a few hours ago and Kayla had meandered about a bit, too charged up to sleep. She exchanged some texts with Desiree, browsed social media and now was vaping and thinking about the recent events of her life. Her parents still weren't talking much, so that wasn't ideal, but at least she was finding her own way a bit in this new locale. And her relationship with Kylie seemed to be improving, which made her happy too.

Just as she was thinking about Kylie, something caught her attention below. Like her sister's, her room faced the back of the house, giving her a clear view of the backyard up to the threshold of the woods. Those same woods where she now saw a figure darting into the trees. A figure in the shape of a young girl.

Kylie.

What the hell is she doing?

Kayla looked at the clock and saw it was almost midnight. The house was quiet and she hadn't heard any of the doors open. It couldn't be her sister, could it?

She left her room and hurried to Kylie's, turning the knob only to find it locked. That was strange because her sister never kept her room locked, mainly because she wasn't allowed to. Kayla tried again just to be sure before tapping gently on the wood, not wanting to wake her parents.

"Kylie," she whispered as loud as she could without raising her voice to a level that would attract their attention. "Kylie? Why is the door locked?"

When she didn't get a response, she considered her options. She could start pounding on the door, not caring if she disturbed her parents or not. Or she could just wake them up and let them know Kylie may or may not have run out the back door and into the woods. Neither of those options seemed appealing, so she settled on a third choice, which—while probably not the most responsible alternative—was really the only one in her mind.

"Kylie!" Kayla called for the first time above a whisper level once she was confident she was far enough away from her house. "Where are you?"

157

She scanned the trees in all directions, looking for a glimpse of the girl she'd seen, no longer convinced that it was her sister, but still needing to verify. Without really thinking about it, she realized she was on the path to the playground. It made sense, though. Somehow that's where Kylie kept ending up in her dreams, so why wouldn't that be the place to look?

Kayla made it to the clearing and the cemetery came into view. The night was clear and still, with an almost-full moon providing a good deal of light. But she didn't see Kylie or any other children anywhere. The night was eerily quiet as she jogged along the cemetery's iron fence to the playground.

When she made it to a spot where the swings and the slide were in view, she again confirmed that no one was there, Kylie or otherwise. There weren't any ghostly happenings either. The swings were motionless, and the slide was quiet. But, more than that, there was something in the air, a heaviness that didn't feel right to her. She started to think coming out here had been a bad idea.

Having confirmed that her sister wasn't at the playground, she started back toward the path in the woods. As she reached the cemetery, she heard a faint sound coming from somewhere inside the gates. It sounded like a child's voice. A young girl.

Kayla ran around to the cemetery gate she had entered the night of the incident at the crypt. She was both surprised and relieved to find that it was still unlocked. There really wasn't much security here at all.

She pushed through the gate and looked around, listening for the voice, but for the moment everything was silent again. Kayla didn't want to, but she started moving in the direction of Jasmine's family tomb, that being the only landmark she knew and, like it or not, what seemed to be the source of all this madness.

As she got closer to her destination, she heard the voice again, clearer this time. It was reciting an odd kind of nursery rhyme.

I had a little bird.

At the sound of the word *bird* her hand stung. She rubbed the spot where the mostly healed wound from the beak of the small bird outside her window remained.

Its name was Enza.

She picked up her pace as she identified the direction. The next line was the clearest yet.

I opened the window.

Kayla glimpsed a shadow behind one of the tombstones as the voice recited the last line.

And in flew Enza.

As the voice stopped, she saw something peeking out over the top of the tombstone. It was the top of a child's head. However, its hair was not the same auburn color as her sister's. It was more of a dirty blond. The child moved up to glimpse over the stone memorial, giving Kayla a better idea of what it looked like. What Kayla saw terrified and saddened her in equal measure.

The child was a girl and, as she suspected, she appeared the same age as Kylie. Well, she would have been the same age as Kylie if she were still alive. The little girl's skin was gray, and deep cracks ran in all directions throughout her cheeks and forehead, with a dim glow emitting light from underneath. Its eyes were completely white with gray orbs where the irises should be. Her ghastly features were exacerbated by the mask of fear she wore. Kayla wasn't the only one scared here.

She froze, not sure if she should approach or run. As

she contemplated the latter, the child spoke, its voice sounding like a poorly recorded audio file rife with static.

"Is he gone?"

"Is... who gone?" Kayla replied.

"The bad man. He's been chasing me. I was hiding in the woods, but he saw me."

"There's no one here," Kayla said, daring to take a step in the ghost's direction.

The child looked around and ducked back behind the tombstone. After a moment, the rhyme started up again.

"I had a little bird. Its name was Enza. I opened the window. And in flew Enza."

Kayla tentatively stepped toward the gravestone. She read the name etched into the marble:

Janet Perkins
1908–1918

She wondered if this was the little girl's grave. Based on the dates she would be about ten years old, which matched up with her appearance. She felt cold as she looked around the stone and saw the little girl huddled behind it, knees drawn into her chest. Seeing her up close, Kayla got a good look at her old-fashioned clothing. She wore a long-sleeved, high-necked nightgown in a muted shade of pink, embellished with a lace ribbon just below the neck. The specter looked up from Kayla and a glowing droplet, a tear, escaped from her eye.

"I'm scared," the child said.

Kayla crouched to her level and smiled, fighting through her own fear in an attempt to comfort the lost soul.

"It's okay," Kayla said in a shaky voice. "There's no one else here."

"Are you sure?"

She wasn't, but this girl didn't need to know that right now, so Kayla nodded and said, "I'm sure." The girl looked out over the tombstone again to verify what Kayla told her before ducking back down again. "Is your name Janet?" Kayla asked.

"Yes, ma'am," the girl replied. "Janet Perkins."

"Who are you afraid of?"

"The bad man. He takes kids like me. He takes them and they never come back. He's not like the other lady. She was nice."

"What lady?"

"The old colored lady."

Kayla winced at the problematic description, but couldn't fault a girl who'd died in 1918 for not being privy to modern sensitivities. "Was her name Eunice?"

"I think so," Janet said. "She used to sit in her rocking chair and, if the bad man ever came around, she would say some stuff and he would go away and let us play in peace. But now she's gone and he can get to us. That's why we're hiding."

Kayla felt sick to her stomach because this little girl had all but confirmed that what Ethel had said wasn't the delusional ranting of an elderly woman with dementia. They may have actually released an evil into this place and onto these poor souls.

"What was that rhyme you were saying? About the bird?" Kayla asked.

"Our parents taught it to us. When everyone was getting sick and dying, we had to stay inside and keep the windows closed. They said the rhyme was a reminder

161

to not let the sickness in. Without the woman to protect us, I hoped maybe the rhyme could. Like a spell or something."

Kayla was confused, fascinated and terrified all at once. She wanted desperately to help this girl, but didn't know how or even if she could. Her inability to aid the child became abundantly clear in the next few moments.

First, the girl's dead eyes widened and terror twisted her already broken face at something she saw behind Kayla. Kayla stood and whirled on her heels in time to see a massive man thundering toward them, wearing black pants and boots and a large yellow rain slicker with the hood up, making his face impossible to see as it was swallowed by a blackened void.

"Run!" Kayla shouted at the girl, who was already moving to do so. Kayla turned as well and followed behind. The young woman and the ghost child ran for their lives, unsure of where they could even go to escape their pursuer.

Kayla looked over her shoulder and tensed as she saw the man rapidly gaining ground, his long strides helping him bridge the distance. That decision cost Kayla, as she didn't see the rock on the ground in front of her and she tripped, crashing to the grass below. She couldn't spare the time to assess how much the fall had hurt because the man was almost upon her. She pushed up to her hands and knees; her left knee screamed in pain having landed square on the rock that had felled her. Defenseless, she felt the shadow of the giant fall over her and she braced herself for his attack.

But it never came.

She felt an extreme burst of cold as the lumbering ghost passed through her, ignoring the human, in pursuit of the little ghost. Kayla pushed herself to her feet and moved forward, limping from the knee injury as she tried to catch up with the spirits, even though she had no idea what she could do to help.

She watched as the little girl disappeared through the wall of a tomb similar to the one owned by the Weeks family. The large man followed close behind and, within a few seconds, an ear-splitting scream came from within.

Kayla stopped in her tracks as she observed the stone structure, unsure if there was a way to access it and, if there was, definitely hesitant to go inside given what she had seen the last time she was in one of those.

While she considered her next move, she heard another scream and saw the man exit through the wall perpendicular to the one he had phased through to get in. Only this time he was carrying the ghost of the little girl who was screaming and reaching out toward Kayla.

"Please!" the desperate specter shouted. "Please help me! I don't want to die! I don't want to die again! It hurts!"

Kayla rushed forward again, doing her best to catch up, but the large man was moving faster now, even though his gait presented itself as a walk. Even without the throbbing in her knee hindering her, she doubted she could have caught up to him.

"I had a little bird!" the girl shouted through her panic. "I opened the window. And in flew—"

She never got to the finish the sentence as the man along with his captive disappeared when they reached the edge of the cemetery.

"No!" Kayla screamed as she continued toward the fence. She looked on the other side, but only saw the quarry with its limestone walls shining in the moonlight. The monster and the little girl were gone.

Kayla reentered her house almost an hour later. She had circled the cemetery and playground twice, trying to make sure that Kylie actually wasn't there. She didn't see any other supernatural phenomena. Her knee had screamed at her the entire journey back through the woods. She felt numb. Her failure to help the girl was made even worse by the knowledge that by breaking that rocking chair, she'd been responsible for her ghastly fate.

She tiptoed up the stairs, taking care not to wake her parents. When she reached the second-floor hallway, she tensed when she saw that Kylie's door was now cracked open. She moved gingerly toward it and peeked in through the slight opening. She could see only the foot of her sister's bed, so she gently pushed the door open to see, to her relief, that Kylie was in bed.

For a moment, she couldn't tell if Kylie was breathing and she felt panic set back in, but, before she could enter the room to check, Kylie let out a little snore and shifted positions to turn on her side.

Kayla took a deep breath as she felt a rush of emotion coursing through her. She just made it to her room and managed to quietly shut and lock the door before she slid down to the floor and drew her knees up to her chest, covering her face with her dirt-smeared hands as she sobbed.

CHAPTER 18

"I think you're overreacting."

Kylie sighed as she heard her father say that while she was walking down the stairs. It was another school day and, although she knew Drew wouldn't be back today, she felt good being able to video chat with him last night and see that he just had a typical cold.

But that didn't mean she was thrilled to be walking into the middle of yet another argument between her parents.

"And I respectfully disagree," Gretchen said. "But there is clearly some type of outbreak at that school and I think our immunocompromised child should stay home until it's safe."

Outbreak? What was Mom talking about?

Kylie crouched down on the landing and eavesdropped.

"They only said they had a few more callouts than usual," Roger countered. "That doesn't constitute an outbreak."

"Dear parents," Mom said, sounding like she was reading. "While this is not a cause for alarm, I am writing to let you know that we have had an unusually high number of students out sick today. While classes will proceed as scheduled, we wanted to write and ask you to remind your children of proper hygienic precautions to prevent illness, including washing hands, utilizing hand-sanitizing stations and staying home when sick. While the school is not requiring masking at this time, you may have your child do so at your option. Miss Evans, Fourth Grade." She returned to her usual speaking cadence. "You don't think keeping her home until we at least find out what is going on is *overreacting*? Jesus, Roger, they just sent this thirty minutes before we have to take her to school and we shouldn't at least ask a couple of questions before we just ship her off?"

Dad didn't answer for a few seconds, Mom having clearly lawyered him off guard. When he responded, it was through a slight, but noticeable, stutter.

"I... I just don't want her to fall behind. She's missed so much and we're less than a month into what was supposed to be her first normal school year since the start of kindergarten."

"Is that worth her health, Roger?" Mom said, her voice even. "I know you think I'm over the top. And you know what? You're right. I am because I'm so damn scared of her going through anything like that again. Aren't you scared of that, too?"

"Of course I am," Dad said, sounding emotional now. "But I'm also scared of her not getting to live a life. I don't want her to be in constant fear for her health."

"It's not fair that she has to be," Mom said, her own voice breaking a bit. "But life isn't fair. You know that."

Another long pause before Dad said, "I know." Another pause. "But let's talk to her. Let her make the choice."

"Roger..." Now it was Mom's turn for a drawn-out pause. "I don't think that's wise."

They both fell silent for the moment, and Kylie

decided that she wasn't going to be left out of the decision-making process, so she moved the rest of the way downstairs. She didn't even pretend she didn't know what was going on.

"I'm going to school," she said bluntly as she entered the kitchen.

"Sweetie, that's not your decision," Mom said.

"Why not?" Kylie asked defiantly.

"Because you're still a child and your health is our responsibility," Dad said, to both Kylie and Gretchen's surprise.

"You said I should go!" Kylie protested.

"I was having a discussion with your mother, and we hadn't come to a decision yet."

Gretchen's expression turned from surprise to satisfaction. In Kylie's mind, however, this was an unwelcome development. For months, she had longed for her parents to get on the same page. Now she had gotten her wish, but it was at her expense. Just when she thought it couldn't get worse, Kayla entered the chat.

"Maybe it's not the worst idea to keep Kylie home today," her big sister said as she entered the kitchen.

Now all three of them stood in shock. Mom and Dad agreeing was one thing. It had been a while, but at least there was precedent.

Kayla taking their side was a rarity akin to hitting the lottery.

Kylie gave her sister a death stare, but dialed it back when she saw the fear in her expression. It wasn't that she was worried about what would happen if she got sick. Something had seriously rattled her.

"Listen," Kayla continued. "They just found out about this, so maybe they'll take the day and sanitize the place

167

after dismissal. That way she can go back tomorrow."

The family all considered the scenario, each deciding if it was not only plausible, but the best course of action. Beyond that, the level of compromise and communication threw them all off balance.

"Okay," Kylie said. "I'll stay home today." Mom looked relieved and Dad actually did too. She wondered if it was more because they were avoiding another major argument than concern for her attending school. She looked Kayla dead in the eye when she said, "But I'm going tomorrow."

Gretchen took out her phone and said, "I'll make sure they get your classroom cleaned tonight."

For the first time in a long time, the air between her parents felt lighter. It was as if talking things out civilly and showing compassion for one another were crucial elements of a healthy relationship. But where the acrimony between Gretchen and Roger had somewhat faded into the background, whatever was bothering Kayla was weighing heavily on her.

"I gotta get to work," Dad announced as Kayla took a seat next to Kylie at the kitchen island. "Love you, girls." He kissed them each on the top of their heads in succession as he hurried toward the living room and out the door. Gretchen had stepped out into the living room to make the call to the school, so it was just the sisters in the kitchen now.

"What the heck, Kayla?" Kylie asked. "Since when do you agree with Mom?"

"Do you trust me?" Kayla asked.

"I don't know," Kylie replied. It was a little meaner than she wanted it to be, but Kayla hadn't always been the nicest to her. Sure, she had been kinder the past couple of days, but that didn't mean Kylie had just magically forgotten just how bad her sister's attitude had been toward her at times.

"Well, you need to," Kayla snapped back before taking a second to assess her own tone. "I saw him."

"Who?"

"The man in the raincoat. Last night. At the cemetery."

"What? Why were you there?"

"I can't get into it now, but I'm going to find out. Please. Please trust me."

Before she could answer, they heard their mother's voice grow louder as she reentered the room. "Thank you. I'll call tomorrow morning to confirm the room has been cleaned before sending her back." She hung up the phone and addressed her daughters. "They've assured me they'll have a cleaning crew in tonight." Neither responded, piquing her curiosity. "What are you two talking about?"

The girls exchanged a look before answering in unison. "Nothing."

Gretchen didn't buy it, but she also didn't want to put her family back to its default setting of domestic strife, so she let it go.

"Your teacher is going to put today's classwork in the portal so you can complete your assignments from home."

This prompted another dirty look in Kayla's direction, conveying that, whatever she was going to find out, she had better find it quick.

"I'm going to go get some answers," Kayla reassured. "Until then, please stay in the house. And whatever you do, stay away from the playground."

CHAPTER 19

"Y'all need to have your heads examined for this one," Jasmine said as they walked up the overgrown pathway to Ethel's front porch. The small, one-story ranch had probably seen better days, but that wasn't any time in recent memory, judging by the state of it. The mint-green paint was peeling off the weathered, rust-stained siding and the window frames were covered with so many layers of white paint they didn't look like they'd even open. They also looked as if they weren't even functional with the fog between the panes evidencing broken thermal seals. Nothing about the house was inviting, but it was the only place that might offer the answers Kayla needed right now.

She had called Desiree right after talking to Kylie in the kitchen. With the growing weirdness in town, she took little convincing to help her.

Jasmine was another story. When she hadn't answered their texts, they went to her house. Both her and Ben's cars were outside, and they knocked until Jasmine, groggy and irritable, her green hair tousled and her nightshirt wrinkled, answered the door.

She still lived with her parents, but they were away for a few days, hence her sleepover with her boyfriend, who had sleepily shuffled in behind her, looking every bit as disheveled. Must have been a wild night.

Once the initial annoyance waned, Jasmine's demeanor turned to skepticism. But Kayla remained fervent in her belief that something sinister was going on and that Aunt Ethel was the key to learning more.

So, even though she wasn't sold, she agreed.

Now, Jasmine led the way as she, Kayla, Desiree and Ben climbed the steps of Ethel's peeling front porch. She raised her arm to knock on the door—there was an empty socket where a doorbell would have been—but the rickety old door swung open before she could bring it down.

Ethel's slight frame filled about half the doorway, her face scrunched as if she had just sucked on a lemon.

"You really done gone and made a mess now."

"So whatcha all expect me to do?" Ethel asked as she took a seat in her recliner, an old leather chair worn and cracked, having needed replacement years ago.

"Tell us what we're dealing with," Kayla said, losing patience with the curmudgeonly woman, but trying not to show it for fear of getting stonewalled.

"What do you think, young lady? There's a demon preying on this town, and that playground is its favorite place to feed."

The girls and Ben exchanged glances, none of them really sure what they should have expected.

"What kind of demon?" Kayla asked.

"The kind that feeds on children. Living or dead."

"How do we stop it?" Kayla asked as the others regarded her with surprise that she'd jumped past the part about a demon without even questioning it. But they hadn't seen what she had.

"I don't know," Ethel said bluntly.

"You don't know?" Desiree chimed in, asking before Kayla could. Kayla wasn't sure if Desiree bought in to all of this, but she was being supportive and that was enough to endear her to Kayla all the more. "I thought you knew about this stuff? Hoodoo and all that?"

Ethel's face looked odd to Kayla as she considered Desiree's question. It took her a minute, but she realized that, for the first time in multiple encounters, the elderly woman was smiling. As if that wasn't strange enough, the smile was followed by a hearty laugh, a wet choking accompanying the sardonic chuckle.

"This is funny?" Kayla asked.

The laugh cut off abruptly and Ethel went stone-faced so fast Kayla briefly wondered if she'd seen her laugh at all.

"No, girl. It's goddamn tragic."

"Then help us!"

"I ain't equipped to go toe to toe with no damn demon."

"You can't use the magic your mother did?"

For a moment, Ethel's face softened, looking more morose than angry at the question.

"I can't do the things Mama did. Never could."

Kayla wasn't expecting that answer. Desiree had said she practiced Hoodoo. They had seen her foraging in the field when they first arrived in Huntsville. If she couldn't help them, who could?

172

"I thought she taught you all that, Auntie," Jasmine said.

"She showed me some. Basic spells like health or love—although fat lotta good that one did me—or how to handle someone who wronged you. I reckon with the right spell, I can make someone shit their pants from clear across town." With the last example, she gave Desiree a curious look, causing her to frown and rub her stomach as if experiencing a gas pain. "But Mama knew more than most. She practiced magic so powerful that it could cause some real problems in the wrong hands. She never trusted me or my brother with it. That's why she always hid that damn recipe book."

The recipe book. Suddenly, it all clicked for Kayla. That book that Ethel had gone on and on about really wasn't for making potato salad. It contained all of Eunice's spells. That was their key to fighting this thing.

"And you have no idea where to find it?"

"If I did, don't you think I would have used it by now?"

Kayla abruptly stood up, taking a step toward Ethel, causing her to push back into the worn leather of the chair.

"I've had just about enough of this shit!" she said.

"*Excuse me?*" Ethel said, taken aback.

"I'm sorry that you're angry. I don't really know why you are and I don't rightly care, but my little sister is in danger and if you can't help us, then you're wasting our damn time!"

The two women of different generations stared each other down in silence for several long moments. Ethel narrowed her eyes, sizing up Kayla as if trying to determine just how much resolve the young lady carried inside her.

"Fuck this," Kayla said.

She took a step back to leave, but stopped when she felt Ethel's surprisingly firm grip on her wrist. The vitriol that had painted the old woman's demeanor was gone, replaced with a reflection born of the loneliness that lurked under her gruff exterior.

"Sit, Kayla," she said calmly, using her name for the first time instead of some variation of *girl* or *missy*. "Please." Her sincerity was convincing enough that Kayla reclaimed her seat on the couch next to Desiree. Ethel looked like she may even cry, but if the tears were gathering, she staved them off. "Kids always had a way of dying round here. When they opened the quarry around the turn of the century—the last one, not this one—they used kids as cheap labor. Lots of accidents. Lots of death." Kayla nodded, trying not to be impatient even though Jasmine had already told her about this part that night in the crypt. "Then the Spanish flu came round in 1918 and lots more died. My mama was born in 1921, two years after it ended. Once it did, it seemed like the kids was gon' be okay. At least for a while."

"Why do you think that was? Did your mother have anything to do with that?"

"Naw," Ethel said after contemplating it for a moment. "Don't reckon it was anything like that. Can't give you a good reason. But that all changed back in 1961. That's when the kids started disappearing. Now, Mama was forty years old by that point. My brother, Martin, he was eighteen and I was sixteen, so we wasn't in any danger because the kids that vanished was around nine and ten."

Kayla and Ben exchanged a nervous glance with their siblings being in that target range. Ethel continued, "It all stopped the next year, though. The townsfolk got wind that it was the cemetery caretaker, a man named

Abel Hargrave, that was stealing them kids. Brought them down to the old quarry where he killed them."

"So, Abel is the demon?" Kayla asked as a flash of the large man carrying away the ghost of the little girl ran through her mind.

"Mama never said. She got real tight-lipped when it came to Abel. If we even asked about it, she shut us down quick. All she said was to stay away from the playground by the cemetery. And if we ever seen a big man in a yellow raincoat, to run back home and tell her straight away."

"I saw him," Kayla said, her voice barely above a whisper.

"Where?"

"At the cemetery. Last night. I saw a little girl hiding behind a tombstone. The man came out of nowhere and dragged her away screaming."

Ethel dropped her head and rubbed her eyes with one hand, exhaling deeply as Kayla confirmed her fear.

"Then Mama really is gone. And The Caretaker is back."

"What does that mean?"

"It means every child in this town is now in danger."

CHAPTER 20

"Ugh!" Kylie said as she slammed her laptop shut, afraid for a moment she may have broken it. She really didn't care about the school-issued device, but also didn't care for a lecture from her parents if it was broken. Raising the screen up, she confirmed it wasn't cracked and could still light up before closing it again, gently this time.

She'd been staring at the stupid math assignment for the past forty minutes, not thrilled about not only having to stay home, but having to do schoolwork on top of it. It felt like she was in prison, just like when she was sick. Only it was worse this time because she wasn't. She felt great, in fact, other than the irritation. It wasn't fair that Mom and Dad and now even Kayla got to decide what she could and couldn't do.

If it wasn't for her sister, she may have protested more fervently, but thinking back to the look on her face when they were talking, she knew that something had seriously rattled her sibling. A week ago, Kayla didn't even believe her about her dreams and the weirdness surrounding the playground, but now she was even more frightened than Kylie was. What could she have seen that had her so badly shaken?

Kylie made her way over to the bed and plopped

down. She picked up her latest book, *Smile*, off of the nightstand and opened it to where she had left off, removing the bookmark and placing it on the bed next to her. She started reading but, after scanning the same paragraph five times, she slammed the book shut, even more frustrated than she was with the laptop. Maybe the TV would provide an escape.

Clicking it on, a commercial was the first thing she saw. It was a recruitment ad for a mining company. In it, a young boy not much older than Kylie, wearing a dirty jumpsuit and a helmet with a light affixed to the front, was walking through what looked like some type of cave. His face was caked with soot and his voice sounded raw and cracked when he spoke.

"Come work down at the Hermitage Mine! All the kids are dying for a job here!"

This was the strangest commercial Kylie had ever seen. Why would they have kids working at a mine? She changed the app to Netflix, but instead of the usual carousel of content, another commercial came on.

This one depicted a young girl, again about Kylie's age, lying in bed with a thermometer in her mouth. She looked very ill. Her skin was pale and her lips were blue as she shivered under the covers. Although she looked cold, sweat poured off of her, soaking the bedsheets.

A woman who was a dead ringer for Mom walked onto the screen, her face deadly serious as she looked directly into the camera.

"Poor Janet has a severe case of the Spanish flu. We noticed she was sick this morning and now her fever is up to one hundred and five degrees. Do you know what we do to cure this disease?" Her mom's doppelgänger paused for several seconds, as if waiting for Kylie to give her an answer. "Absolutely nothing. There's no cure, so Janet is going to die."

What the heck is this? Kylie thought, knowing damn well this wasn't any ordinary commercial.

In the background, Janet started hacking violently, her body spasming up off the pillow with each heaving retch. Spittle flew from her mouth, mingling with the sweat that had already stained the comforter. After several intense coughs, the saliva stopped, but blood came out in its place, droplets spraying everywhere. Kylie was horrified, but frozen, as she watched the horror on the screen in front of her. Finally, the girl's fit stopped and she collapsed back in the bed, her head falling to one side and her eyes rolling into the back of her head as a trickle of blood poured from her gaping mouth.

"See? No more Janet. That cemetery sure is getting crowded!"

The Mom-thing on TV's eyes turned pure white and its mouth expanded impossibly wide in a rictus grin that literally stretched from ear to ear.

Kylie put one hand to her mouth to stifle a scream, not wanting to alarm her parents, while grasping for the remote with her other. She found it with some effort and mashed the power button to no avail as the television remained on and yet another ghastly image filled the screen.

It was a face. It was shaped like a human and had a similar structure, but the features were that of a serpent. The visage was covered in scales, but they seemed to be made of skin, giving it a grotesque, melted look. The eyes were red and slits took the place of pupils. It opened its mouth wide and a long, forked tongue ran over its lips, which glistened with viscous saliva that dripped from long, curved fangs.

"Kylie," the thing hissed, each letter interminably drawn out. "Come play with us."

Tears in her eyes, she ran to the set, taking an angle that put her off to the side, too terrified to head for it straight on for fear that the monster may very well leap from the screen and bite her. She reached around the back and pulled out the plug, thanking God that it turned off and took the horrible image with it.

She slowly backed away, one step at a time, until she felt the back of her legs press against the edge of the bed. Slowly lowering herself down, she concentrated on her breathing, trying to slow it back to its normal rhythm. Just as she calmed down, she heard something strike her window. It was small, not enough to crack the glass like the bird's beak had, but noticeable enough to get her attention.

She didn't want to look, but did anyway. For several long seconds, nothing else happened, but just as she was about to turn her attention away from the window, a small rock bounced off the glass with a *tink* sound.

Hesitantly, she stood and slowly made her way to the window, dreading each step, but willing herself forward. Halfway there, another stone bounced off.

Tink.

When she reached the window, she immediately shut her eyes, not wanting to look down.

Tink.

With the next impact, she opened them and saw what she feared below.

Emily was standing in her backyard, staring up at her. She grinned and waved as soon as she had Kylie's attention. Kylie stood still, waiting for the girl to make the first move. She said something, but she couldn't hear her through the glass. When she didn't respond, Emily raised her hands in a gesture to mimic opening a window. Kylie shook her head and Emily frowned, making the gesture again.

Still unconvinced it was a good idea, but needing to know what she wanted, Kylie opened the window a few inches, focusing on the crack where the bird had killed itself only a few nights before. When it was open about three inches, she crouched down so her eye level was on par with the gap and looked at Emily.

"Come play with me!" the girl shouted cheerily.

"What do you want?" Kylie said, trying not to be too loud. Emily heard her perfectly.

"I want to play."

"I'm not going to play with you!" Kylie said, louder this time. Emily looked wounded.

"That's mean, Kylie! You're my favorite!"

"Go away!"

Emily scrunched her face in disappointment.

"You're not being nice. I don't like it when people aren't nice. It makes me mad." Kylie swallowed hard. This girl, if it was even a little girl, had gone from odd to downright terrifying. Everything about her was wrong in every way. "I'm going to go now. But you should really think about how you talk to your friends. I was there for you when you didn't have friends, Kylie. And this is how you treat me?"

"I'm not your friend!" Kylie shouted, no longer caring if her mom heard her.

"I see that," Emily said. "That's too bad. I think you're going to be sorry you said that to me. Yes. You're going to be sorry very soon."

180

The threat burned into Kylie's mind. She couldn't just go down there and go with her. She clearly didn't have good intentions, but now she feared what else she might do. It had to be her who had put those scary images on the television. What else was she capable of?

Kylie watched as Emily slowly turned and skipped back into the woods and out of sight. When she was gone, Kylie closed and locked the window before running to her bed and jumping under the covers, drawing them up to her chin as her body shook in fear.

CHAPTER 21

The quartet sat outside the deli, contemplating how to proceed. Kayla and Desiree each leaned against the wall, sneaking pulls off their vape pens between peeks in the window to make sure Big Al wasn't looking. Jasmine and Ben were seated on opposite sides of one of the small, circular tables shaded with an umbrella to accommodate outdoor dining. They each had food, but while Jasmine eagerly devoured her sausage, pepper and onion sandwich, Ben had barely touched his buffalo chicken cutlet.

"You okay, babe?" Jasmine asked.

Ben didn't answer right away, his silence drawing the attention of Kayla and Desiree as well.

"Ben?" Desiree asked.

The second time got his attention, and he looked up as if in a daze.

"You okay?" Jasmine asked again.

"You think there really is a demon?" he asked, his voice shaky.

Jasmine looked like she wanted to say no. For someone who grew up in a family of believers, she was, surprisingly, the most skeptical of the bunch. But she also knew that Kayla wasn't convinced that there wasn't something supernatural going on, and she didn't want to contradict her.

"I don't know if it's a demon," Kayla said, understanding full well that this was her show and that her friends were just along for the ride. She knew if she delved too far into the absurd, she would lose the support of which she was already testing the limits, especially considering she had only known this crew for a short time. She had a feeling that, if it wasn't for Desiree, they wouldn't have humored her this long. "But it's not something natural."

"What if..." he trailed off, as if afraid speaking the words out loud would lend them legitimacy. But the question still needed to be asked.

"But Kayla saw a bunch of fucked-up shit."

"We don't know what Kayla saw," Jasmine said before looking up at her as her tone iced over. "Kayla doesn't even know what Kayla saw."

At first, Jasmine's stern reaction surprised Kayla. She had heard everything her aunt told them about the playground and her great grandmother's involvement with it. But she also hadn't seen the same things that Kayla or Kylie had. Kayla hadn't considered that maybe she didn't buy into her family's obsessions. That maybe the Hoodoo stuff was something she wanted to distance herself from. Yet, here was the new girl diving right in to something she'd just as soon forget about. More than that, her boyfriend's brother was sick and, if Ethel was to be believed, may actually be in danger from something more than the common cold.

Kayla's guilt intensified. Her focus was on Kylie, and she was ashamed to admit that she hadn't even considered that this whole thing could have exacerbated Ben's concern for his brother.

"Ben, I'm sure it's just a cold," she said unconvincingly.

"See?" Jasmine said.

"Don't get your head all twisted up with this nonsense." She dropped the last quarter of her sandwich onto the wrapper and crinkled it up, turning and depositing it into the trash can behind her before standing up. "In fact, I think that's about all I can handle for today."

As if Kayla couldn't feel any worse.

"Jazz..." Desiree started as Ben wrapped his sandwich to take with him.

"I'm sorry," Kayla interrupted.

Jasmine held her hand up as a warning not to continue. "It's all good. I've just had enough of ghosts and demons for today." Ben stood up and walked around the table to join his girlfriend. She put her arm around his waist, and he held her around her shoulders.

"Give us a call when y'all are done playing Ghostbusters." Ben still looked rattled, but he threw up a peace sign as the couple turned and left.

Kayla released a heavy sigh as she claimed the seat Ben had vacated. Desiree walked around and gave her shoulder a gentle squeeze as she passed by.

She took the seat across and asked, "So what now?"

Kayla rubbed her temples. She wasn't one to get headaches often, but she felt a doozy coming on. Probably because she hadn't eaten or had anything to drink outside of a cup of coffee. Plus, she still felt guilty about dragging her friends into this. She knew she was on thin ice with Jasmine and Ben was mostly aloof outside of his concern for his brother. So, she looked to Desiree for reassurance.

"Do you believe me?" she asked.

"I believe you believe in whatever it was you saw,"

Desiree replied, reaching across the table and taking Kayla's hand. She squeezed it. "That's enough for me to see this through with you." Her smile offered Kayla the comfort she sought. It didn't matter if she believed in the supernatural or not, Desiree was here for her. For the first time in a long time, she didn't feel alone.

"Thank you," Kayla said.

"So, what now?" Desiree asked.

Kayla squeezed Desiree's hand before releasing it and leaning back in her chair, raising her arms and clasping them behind her head as she considered just what the hell they were going to do now. "I guess we need to find someone who knows about demons."

"You know anyone?" Desiree asked jokingly.

Suddenly, Kayla shot up in her chair and leaned forward, grabbing Desiree's hand again, but this time guiding her up and out of her seat.

"Actually, I do!"

Desiree let her friend lead her but said, "I swear, if I get possessed by a demon, I'm eating you first!"

"I'm not sure what I was expecting, but I should have figured," Desiree said as they ascended the steps to St. Ann's church. It was a large building, adorned with pointed arches and ribbed vaults and an ornate stained-glass window just above the grand wooden doors of the main entrance. A bell chimed from the tower above, signaling the turning of the 3 p.m. hour as the girls stepped inside.

The interior nave was lined with rows of wooden pews on each side. The vaulted ceilings gave a sense of grandiose scale that was apparent from the exterior. The focal point at the front of the sanctuary was a marble altar with candles surrounded by wreaths on either side. The light filtered in through more stained-glass windows, each depicting an apostle engaging in various activities from delivering sermons to feeding the hungry. Below them, the portraits of the Stations of the Cross told the story of the passion of Jesus Christ from his arrest to his execution to his resurrection. An elaborate fresco depicting the ascension covered the ceiling.

Kayla wasn't what anyone would call a practicing Christian, especially given her mother's overzealous piousness in recent years, but she could certainly appreciate the artistry and skill that went into designing a building like this. She looked around the room and saw two parishioners lined up in front of two wooden booths on the right side of the church toward the front.

"Must be time for confession," Kayla remarked.

"Is that where you go in and tell the priest you use bad language and shit?" Desiree asked, immediately cupping her hands over her mouth, realizing her mistake.

"Nice one," Kayla whispered. "I'm not sure I believe in any of this, but if we're going to ask for help to face a demon, maybe we should stay on God's good side."

Desiree stifled a chuckle behind her hands as she nodded.

"You good?"

She removed her hands and bit her lip, trying not to laugh. Kayla felt a surge of guilt at just how sexy she found the gesture. She gave her a look silently telling her to *knock it off.*

"Good," Desiree said. "Let's confess."

It took about twenty minutes for the other parishioners, a middle-aged woman with high bun hairstyle and horn-rimmed spectacles and an elderly gentleman who made it in and out of the booth only with great effort, assisted by his cane.

When it was Kayla's turn, she entered the booth, the stench of too much of the old man's cologne wafting out when the door was open. Kayla shut the door behind her and took her seat on the padded bench, feeling her heart race as she prepared to ask the priest something that may very well make her sound like a lunatic.

After a few moments, a small wooden panel slid on the other side of a mesh lattice, revealing the silhouette of a man on the other side.

"Please begin whenever you are ready," Father Lee said.

"Father Lee," Kayla said. "It's Kayla Macklin. From the house on Cornerstone Circle."

"Kayla?" the priest asked, sounding perplexed. "Are you here for confession?"

"I'm not sure. I mean I may have done something bad that I need some help with, but I'm not sure if that thing was actually as bad as it may have been."

"I'm not following."

"What do you know about demons?"

The priest went silent. Kayla could only imagine what he was thinking. After a moment, he asked, "Kayla, what is this about?"

"Please, Father, just humor me on this."

"This is very unorthodox for confession. Have you

been taking part in blasphemy?"

You don't know the half of it.

"I just... I need to know. Are demons real?" Another long pause. "Father?"

"The Church acknowledges the existence of demonic possession. Yes."

"Do you believe it?"

"I'm sorry?"

"The Church recognizes that it's a real thing, but have *you* personally ever seen it?"

"No, I can't say that I have."

"So do you believe in it?"

"I took a vow of faith in Catholic doctrine. Demons are a part of that, so, yes, I do believe there are demonic forces in this world."

He was choosing his words carefully. Kayla couldn't blame him. After all, it wasn't every day a girl burst into the confessional ranting about demons.

"How would you know if you were faced with an actual demon?"

"Despite belief to the contrary, the church has grown with the modern world. What we now know of mental illness has dispelled a lot of what used to be seen as symptoms of demonic possession."

"Can demons possess the dead? Like a ghost?"

"Kayla, this is a strange line of questioning."

"I know. I know. Just a few more. Please."

"There isn't any record of ghosts, as you put it. A demon typically possesses a living soul."

"So what happens when the demon hasn't possessed someone? Say they're just walking around in their demon form?"

"A demon in its pure, hellish state would theoretically

be hideous to gaze upon. It may have humanoid features, but it also may appear like an animal, say a goat, or a boar, or—"

"A snake?"

"Yes, that's possible. The devil himself took the form of a serpent if you recall your Bible study."

She didn't, but the story of Adam and Eve in the Garden with the serpent and the apple was pretty common knowledge. "Could it shift forms? Say between the snake and the person?"

"For a demon to take a human form would require possession."

"What would you do in that case?"

"In that case, an investigation would be opened and, if evidence of true demonic possession was found, a request would be made to authorize an exorcism."

"How would you stop it if it wasn't in human form?"

"A trained exorcist would perform a ritual to banish it back to hell."

"Are you a trained exorcist?"

"No. I am not. There's not much call for that here in Alabama."

That's what you think.

"Thank you, Father," Kayla said before adding, "but I have one last question." His silence beckoned her to go on. "If it can't be banished, could it be killed?"

"I honestly don't know. They say that a blessed weapon, a blade, for example, could be used to kill a demon, but there's not much record of that happening and, if so, it's certainly above my pay grade."

Now it was Kayla's turn to fall silent. The priest had given her a lot of information, but she had no clue how she'd be able to use it.

"Do you wish to make a confession now?" the priest asked.

Kayla thought about it. She felt a sudden, compelling urge to just unload, but wasn't sure if she should. "I don't even know where to start."

"Let's start like this. Repeat after me—Forgive me, Father, for I have sinned."

"Forgive me, Father, for I have sinned."

"It has been—state how long it's been since your last confession—and then say *These are my sins.*"

"It's been *forever* since my last confession. These are my sins."

She went silent again.

"Go on, Kayla. It's okay."

"I've resented my family. I've resented them for so long. My sister got sick four years ago and, since then, it's been all about her. Even after she got better, it's all about Kylie. No one cares what's going on in my life. No one cares who I am or what I want in life. And it's not Kylie's fault. She didn't want to get sick. She didn't deserve any of what she went through, but some days I wonder if she had died..." Saying that out loud, she started to cry, struggling to choke the next words out. "...would my parents be able to give that love to me? Then I feel like an asshole... sorry, Father."

"It's okay. A lot of people think profanity is a sin, but that's bullshit." Kayla laughed out loud through her tears. She wondered if Desiree could hear that and what she must be thinking about what was going on in here right now.

"Just don't use the Lord's name in vain. That's where it becomes a sin."

"I didn't want my sister to die, Father. Please believe

that."

"I do."

"It... it just felt like there was no love for me. I was an afterthought. Kayla's healthy, so she'll figure it all out on her own. She has no problems. Yeah, no problems except feeling so damn alone all the time. Sure, I had friends back home, but they didn't really know me. Not the real me. And I'm not sure they would still be my friends if they did."

"That must be very difficult. I'm sorry. But your thoughts alone aren't a sin. It's when you act on them that it becomes sinful."

"I just want to feel like someone sees me."

"And you feel that there's no one like that?"

The light switch flipped in her head. There was somebody like that. She was sitting outside waiting for her. She had only known her a little over a week, but when everything started going haywire around her, she hadn't abandoned her or written her off as crazy. When she showed an interest in her as maybe something more than a friend, she didn't recoil like her supposed lifelong BFF had. Desiree had been there for her since this weirdness started. That caring she was looking for in another person was right in front of her. She smiled as she sniffled and wiped away her waning tears.

"There actually is," she whispered. "I don't know if you guys would approve, though."

"It's not for me to approve or disapprove. God gave us free will. You're free to exercise it in the way you think best comports to his gospel."

From what she knew of religion, she doubted it comported to any gospel she knew of, but she appreciated the sentiment.

JAMES KAINE

"Thank you, Father."

"You're welcome, Kayla. By the way, you know the sacrament of penance is usually anonymous, right? You didn't need to announce yourself when you walked in here."

Fuck.

She got up to leave when another question came to mind.

"Aren't you supposed to give me an assignment of prayers or something? Like ten Hail Marys and ten Our Fathers?"

"I'll put it on your tab. I wish you well, Kayla."

"Thank you, Father."

She exited the booth and smiled when she saw Desiree a few pews back, her feet up as she thumbed through a songbook. When she heard the door open, she straightened up and returned it as if the priest were about to come out too.

"Did you get answers?"

Kayla looked her over and smiled. "Not a lot. But some."

CHAPTER 22

I t was a little before midnight when Kylie scurried back to her bedroom. She was relieved that her bladder, which had urged her awake a few minutes before, was empty, but not very keen on returning to the safety of her room via the darkened hallway. Making it back unscathed, she quickly, but quietly, shut her door and climbed into bed, pulling the covers up to her neck. Even at her young age, she knew the blankets didn't provide any actual protection, but she felt a sense of security with them covering her.

As she lay there trying to fall asleep, she heard voices outside. Coming from that damn window that faced the back of the house. They were low and quiet, but they didn't sound like kids. Nor were they deep and gruff and menacing. They just sounded like normal girls.

She got back out of bed and crept over to the window, stealing a look down and feeling immediate relief when she saw the voices belonged to Kayla and Desiree. They were standing off to the side on the deck, talking about something. They were trying to be inconspicuous, but their voices were raised enough that she could hear them, even if she couldn't make out what they were saying.

She saw the girls blowing smoke out while they talked.

That made her nervous. If Mom caught Kayla smoking, she'd be in a ton of trouble. Kylie thought maybe she should sneak down and warn her sister but, more than that, she could find out if they had learned anything about what was going on.

While she contemplated, she heard a whisper behind her, causing her to jump.

"Kylie!"

The small voice sounded like it came from the direction of her closet. She looked toward it and saw the door was ajar. She felt every muscle tense as fear gripped her. There was no way she was going to open that door.

Kylie looked down again and saw the tops of Kayla and Desiree's heads as they reentered the house. Good. She would run out and meet them and they could help her.

She backed against the wall and started sidestepping to her left. She edged around the room carefully, as if she were making her way along the ledge of a skyscraper with no harness.

At no point did she take her eyes off the darkened gap leading into her closet.

She only dared turn away when she reached her door. She gripped the brass doorknob but immediately recoiled. It was freezing to the touch. Kylie glanced again at the closet. The door looked to be open even wider this time.

Cold be damned. She grabbed the knob again and twisted. Panic set in when she realized it turned less than a quarter of the way. She examined the lock, and it looked like it was in the right position, but she flipped it and tried again. Nothing. She turned it in the opposite direction, but it still didn't budge. Did her door even lock from the outside? If so, who had locked her in?

On the other side, she could hear movement up the stairs. It was quiet and deliberate. Kylie could hear it because she was right there, but to anyone asleep—like her parents—it would go unnoticed. She hoped if she could mirror that volume, she could get Kayla's attention without rousing their parents.

"Kayla!" she whispered as loudly as she could, with it still qualifying as a whisper while simultaneously tapping on the door.

Her heart sank as her pleas for help went unheard. She listened in defeat as she heard Kayla's bedroom door open, then gently shut.

"Kylie!" the small voice called again, itself straining the criteria for what could be defined as a whisper.

This time, she dared to look. The door was open even wider this time. Not only that, but a child's head poked its way out. To Kylie's surprise, the face was familiar. And friendly.

"Drew?" she asked in bewilderment. "What are you doing here?"

The boy motioned for her to join him. In her confusion at seeing her friend in her room, she didn't consider that it may be unwise to take his presence at face value. He pushed the door open wide enough to accommodate her as she slipped inside before he shut it tight.

The closet was a small walk-in, so there was more than enough room for the two of them. Kylie pulled the string and flooded the area with light from the overhead bulb. It was only then that she worried this may be another of Emily's tricks. If it was, it was too late now. The light flickered, making the illumination sporadic and unreliable, but what it revealed horrified her.

Drew, if it really was him, looked awful. He appeared

195

to have lost a great deal of weight, and his Minecraft pajamas looked way too big for his current frame. His eyes were sunken deep into his sockets, which were a deep purple. The eyes themselves were so bloodshot they looked almost completely red. He winced with each painful blink. His color was a pallid gray and lined with darkened veins that protruded from under his skin. It looked like his flesh itself was molded around his skeleton. Kylie noticed the oppressive heat inside the confined space lacking in air vents and felt herself sweating. Drew was positively drenched as the light green of his pajamas was darkened around his neckline and armpits.

"What's wrong?" Kylie asked, her fear growing with each second. "What are you doing here?"

"You can't let them find me!" Drew exclaimed, desperation permeating his demeanor. "Please!"

"Who?" Kylie asked, even though she had a good idea.

Before Drew could answer, his eyes went wide and his body trembled violently. He scooted back against the wall, pushing the hanging garments with him as he curled into a fetal position.

"He's here!" Drew whispered, his voice low and shaky. "Turn off the light!"

Kylie jumped as she heard a crash downstairs. It sounded as if it had come from the kitchen. Specifically, the back door.

Instinctively, Kylie reached up and pulled the string to extinguish the light. She moved over and pressed herself against the wall next to her petrified friend.

As the terrified children huddled together, they heard heavy footsteps navigating the first floor of the Macklin house.

The Caretaker was here.

"Ka—" she started to call to her sister, hoping she and Desiree could help them, but Drew clasped a bony hand over her mouth.

"Shhh," he whispered desperately. "He'll find us!"

Kylie felt helpless as tears pooled and fell, dripping down over Drew's frail hands as they listened to the footsteps stop briefly, only to change in pitch as they started ascending the steps. The volume crescendoed at the top of the steps before pausing again. There was no respite, though, as they started again only seconds later, until the man was right outside of Kylie's bedroom door. The knob turned and the door opened effortlessly. It had never been locked. Kylie just hadn't been able to open it for reasons unknown.

She hugged Drew, who did his best to embrace her as well, but the boy had no strength. Kylie did her best to hold him tight enough to comfort the both of them, but she was too scared to provide any type of reassurance.

The steps started up again, deafeningly close as the man moved with purpose and confidence toward the closet. A thin slit of moonlight that had poked through the bottom of the door blackened as the enormous feet blocked the light from getting through. Immediately, the heat dissipated, and a sharp chill developed in the surrounding air.

He didn't open the door. He just stood there for a long time. It was long enough that Kylie started to think that maybe he didn't know they were in there. Maybe he saw that the room was empty and he would leave without investigating further.

Please God, don't let him find us.

The prayer went immediately unanswered as the door

flung open and the sinister, massive frame of The Caretaker filled the doorway, the black abyss under his hood still hiding any distinguishing features. Kylie opened her mouth to scream as loudly as she could, but no sound escaped, not even a grunt or a sigh. She tried again and still couldn't get any words out.

Holding on to Drew, she tried to drag him toward the back of the closet, his slight frame providing little resistance as he cried, apparently unable to scream. The giant man ducked to enter the closet, also not making a sound as he reached out a mammoth hand toward the children.

The Caretaker gripped Drew's arm and pulled him toward him. Kylie tried to hold on, but he was too strong as he wrenched her friend away from her. She was surprised his brittle bones didn't snap under the force of his pull. She didn't know what else to do so she suddenly lunged forward in an attempt to bite the man's hand, but her mouth passed right through it, causing her to unintentionally bite Drew instead. Kylie lessened the pressure at the last second but she'd clearly still hurt the boy, as his mouth widened and his eyes shut in soundless pain.

Stunned, she fell backward on her haunches, barely bracing herself to prevent falling completely on her back. How was that possible? How could he grab and hold Drew, but she couldn't touch him? It didn't make sense and the helplessness and dread consumed her as she watched The Caretaker sling the sick boy over his shoulder and turn to leave the room.

Kylie got up and ran after them, but it felt like she was dragging her feet through heavy mud and she couldn't keep pace, even though the man was just walking. Muddy footprints stained the carpet in patterns going to and from the closet to the door. She tried to scream again, but still no sound came out. As he crossed the threshold from the bedroom to the hall, Drew finally found his voice and screamed, "Kylie! Don't let him take me!"

Finding her own ability to speak, she screamed, "Drew!" as the door slammed shut. She ran over and turned the knob, devastated to find that it again resisted letting her open it. "Kayla! Help me!" She bellowed as she pounded on the door as hard as she could. "Kayla! Mommy! Daddy! Please!"

It was no use. Inexplicably, no one else in the house was alerted to the commotion. She listened as the footsteps receded through the house again, exiting the same way he'd entered through the back door.

Kylie ran to her window and watched helplessly as the man lumbered through the backyard with Drew slumped over his shoulders, too weak to fight anymore. She tried to open the window, but, like the door, it wouldn't budge.

She cried as she saw Drew use the last of his strength to lift his head and look up toward her. His fight was gone, but his fear for his life remained. He mouthed her name as she put her hands against the glass pane.

"I'm sorry," she said as she watched The Caretaker disappear into the woods with Drew.

Kylie opened her eyes, having not realized she had shut

them. She was lying in bed, the covers a disheveled mess at her feet. She felt hot and sticky from perspiration and her mind was disoriented from the loss of time. Remembering the terrifying events, she bolted upward in bed and looked around her room. It was empty and there was no sign of anyone having been in there. The muddy footprints were gone and her door was open a crack. In fact, the only thing out of the ordinary was that the closet light was on, peeking out from under the door frame. The rest of the room remained dark, although the moonlight filtering in through the trees cast eerie shadows along the walls.

Cautiously, she got out of bed and opened the door, both relieved and disappointed to find it empty. Had the whole thing been another dream? The one thing she was understanding was that her dreams may not have exactly been real, but they also seemed to be predictors of things that were going to happen.

That's how she knew Drew was in grave danger.

CHAPTER 23

While Kylie was in the midst of her nightmare, Kayla and Desiree sat beside each other cross-legged on the bed with Kayla's laptop open. Her web browser had dozens of tabs open as she researched demons. The priest had given her a greater degree of confidence that they were in fact dealing with a demon, but what kind of demon and, more importantly, how to stop it were still questions that needed answers. All she knew was that it had a snake-like appearance and was somehow connected to the playground.

Her searches had revealed names like Ophiomorphos, Sakatal, Stheno and Euryale. But none of those seemed to fit the description of anything they were dealing with here. There was of course Medusa but, to her knowledge, kids weren't being turned to stone so she could at least cross that one off the list.

She also looked into the child murders in Huntsville back in 1962. There were a number of articles and a few YouTube videos on true crime channels. They were interesting in a morbid way, probably more so if they weren't reliving the whole thing right now, but they didn't shed a whole lot of light.

Kids had disappeared from around town starting in late 1961. Most of them had vanished in the middle of the night with little or no trace of any type of break-in. Authorities were perplexed and instituted county-wide searches and curfews, but to no avail. Eventually, in 1962, a witness saw Abel Hargrave, a mute who served as the caretaker of Maple Hill Cemetery, walking into the woods with a local child, who later went missing. A few days later, the police announced they had found the bodies of the missing children in the abandoned Hermitage Quarry. Abel Hargrave committed suicide by hanging himself from a tree not far from where the corpses were discovered.

With the main suspect dead, the case was closed and there were no reported cases of missing children outside of the occasional runaway in the time since.

Kayla rubbed her eyes, the blue light of the laptop screen starting to get to her. She gently pushed it closed and leaned back against the headboard, letting out a heavy sigh as she did.

"I don't even know what we're doing here."

Desiree scooted back to position herself next to Kayla. She arched her back and raised her hands over her head while simultaneously extending her legs to give herself a good stretch. As she did, Kayla saw her shirt ride up to expose her stomach to just above the belly button. Her skin was smooth and tight, but she couldn't help but notice a small scar at the top of her navel.

She must have been too tired to be subtle about it because it did not go unnoticed by her companion. Kayla felt her face flush when Desiree caught her staring. She wasn't upset, though. In fact, the smirk that spread across her face registered her amusement as she raised her shirt up even higher, her full stomach on display now as she ran a finger across the tiny disfigurement.

"Looking at this?" she asked coyly.

"What's it from?" Kayla asked, curiosity winning out over embarrassment.

"Had my appendix out when I was fifteen. Thank God they do it laparoscopically now, because I'd hate to be laying out in a bikini with a big ole' scar across my abdomen."

"That must have sucked," Kayla said.

"Hell yeah, it sucked," Desiree confirmed. "I always thought when people got appendicitis that it was some really sharp-ass pain that doubled you over, but it was like a dull ache for a day and a half before I finally went to the doctor. He did this test called a *rebound test* where he pushed his fingertips into my right side. That was uncomfortable, but when he quickly released it, I screamed and nearly fell over. I swear I wanted to punch him in his fucking mouth!"

They both laughed at that.

"You didn't, right?" Kayla asked.

"I thought about it, but he said I needed to go to the ER and that scared me enough that I put thoughts of violence aside. They took me into surgery right away and a few hours later, I was in recovery. All in all, it could have been worse, but you know what really sucked?"

"What?"

"They told me the whole time that appetite loss was a symptom of appendicitis, but I was hungry the *whole* time. They kept me overnight and I couldn't eat until the morning. They brought in jello and chicken broth, telling me I had to start with a liquid diet before moving on to solids. By the time they brought me lunch, I devoured it. That shitty hospital turkey sandwich may have been the best meal I ever ate!"

They laughed again as Kayla looked back at the scar, realizing that Desiree had not yet lowered her shirt to cover it.

"Does it feel weird?"

"You tell me," Desiree said with a wicked grin as she grabbed Kayla's wrist and started guiding it toward her navel.

"Ew! No!" Kayla exclaimed as she feigned putting up a fight.

"Don't be a pussy!" Desiree laughed as she pulled on her hand, finally managing to place it right over the scar.

Kayla tentatively extended her index finger and let it brush over the damaged skin. It felt a little strange, but it wasn't unpleasant. When she moved past the scar onto her unmarred flesh, she felt warmth spread throughout her body. She opened her hand so each fingertip could make contact with the other girl's stomach. When she didn't protest, she pressed her entire hand down and rested it there. When she looked up, she realized just how close their faces were. She met Desiree's eyes, which seemed to burn a hole into her own.

She felt like she should say something, but knew that anything she uttered would make things awkward. Desiree's lips parted slightly and Kayla accepted the invitation to kiss her. Her lips were soft and tasted faintly of the vanilla from her ChapStick. The lip lock was gentle and exploratory. Kayla left her hand on Desiree's stomach while Desiree reached behind her and softly grasped the back of her neck, running her fingers through Kayla's dark hair. She pulled her in tight and Kayla opened her mouth as the kissing intensified to include their tongues.

Kayla's first real kiss was better than she could have

ever hoped. She had kissed a few boys at parties, but was never really into it, having just figured that was something to do. But it was usually awkward and unsatisfying. Kissing Desiree made her understand why. Everything about it felt right and, to top it all off, the girl was a damn good kisser.

She couldn't help but wonder how far this would go, but figured she'd let Desiree take the lead. Kayla tentatively started sliding her hand up Desiree's stomach until she reached the hem of her bunched-up shirt. Her fingertips started to slide under as the kiss again increased in intensity.

That was when Kylie burst into the room.

Startled, the girls broke their kiss and straightened up on opposite sides of the bed, Desiree quickly pulling her shirt back down over her stomach. Kayla cursed silently for forgetting to lock the door. She was going to have to explain a lot to her little sister, from what she saw them doing to why she was doing it with another girl, an aspect of her life she had not yet shared with her family.

But Kylie didn't seem bothered by or interested in any of that. She looked absolutely terrified and that, in turn, scared Kayla.

"Kylie?" she asked, noticing her sister's tear-streaked cheeks. "What's wrong? Did you have another bad dream?"

"Drew," was all the girl could say.

"Drew?" Desiree asked, also brushing aside the awkwardness that this child had just caught them making out. "What about him?"

"He's in trouble. Really bad trouble."

Kayla held out her hand and beckoned for her sister to join them. Kylie took a few hesitant steps forward and took her older sibling's hand. Kayla pulled her close and grasped the other one.

"What makes you think that?"

"The man. The Caretaker. He was here."

Kayla felt a shudder run through her. She and Desiree had been awake the whole time they'd been home and they hadn't seen or heard anything to make them think anyone could have been in the house.

"Kylie," she said. "It was just a bad dream."

"Can you call Ben again?"

Kayla looked at the clock and saw it was close to midnight. Ben might be awake, but it wasn't really appropriate to bother them right now. Especially as pissed off as Jasmine had seemed after their visit with her aunt.

"He's probably asleep. I'll call him first thing in the morning."

"No!" Kylie said, tears flowing anew. "Please."

The plea came out as the slightest of whispers, Kylie's desperation palpable. This newest dream seemed to have rattled her sister to her core. Kayla turned to Desiree who looked sympathetic to the young girl's plight.

"I'll call him," she said, sparing Kayla the awkwardness.

As Desiree stepped off the bed to retrieve her phone from the dresser, the trio jumped as the screen lit up and A Day to Remember's song "All I Want" blared from the speaker. Desiree picked up the phone and held it up for Kayla and Kylie to see. The display read *Jasmine* as the green-haired girl's picture filled the screen. Desiree answered, opting not to put the call on the speaker.

"Jazz?" she asked nervously.

Kayla couldn't hear what Jasmine was saying but didn't

need to as Desiree's face told the story.

First, her eyes widened. Then, her hand cupped her mouth as it fell open. Her eyes reddened and watered and the tears started as her face scrunched into an expression of sorrow.

Kayla turned to her sister and pulled her in, hugging her tightly as they started to cry too, not needing to hear the words to know the news that Jasmine had just delivered.

CHAPTER 24

K ylie felt numb.

It was a beautiful day at Maple Hill Park. The sun was shining and the temperature, despite being in the low eighties, was tempered by a lack of humidity and a slight breeze that danced through the trees. Yes, it was a beautiful day and that very beauty mocked the throng of mourners gathered under the canopy at the freshly prepared gravesite.

It had been exactly one week since Drew Gatto died. While Kayla hadn't shared the details of exactly what had happened, Kylie overheard conversations between her and Desiree and pieced together that his *cold* had turned into something more severe and his condition had deteriorated so quickly that when his mom found him when she went in to check on him before she went to bed, he looked as if he had been sick and emaciated for years. The doctors were stumped. They had performed an autopsy, but the results were still pending.

Now Kylie stood in front of the small coffin that was draped in the velvet cream-colored pall embroidered with a cross and gold fringes that reminded her of the stole that Father Lee had worn when he came to bless her house. She, like the other mourners, held a single red rose in her hands. She absent-mindedly flicked her fingertips over a thorn about halfway up the stem. Not enough to draw blood or even to hurt that much, but just enough that she felt something.

Fat lot of good that blessing did, Kylie thought to herself, allowing herself to wallow in her growing cynicism.

She wasn't registering what Father Lee said as he droned on about things like sorrow, community and God's kingdom. She couldn't take her eyes off the box, knowing that her friend would be in there forever. Knowing that it could very easily have been her in one of those had her cancer had its way.

Kayla stood behind her with her hands on her little sister's shoulders. It was a small comfort; the one thing that could be considered a positive throughout this whole situation was that it had brought the two of them closer and seemed to have given Kayla a purpose. She wasn't as angry as she used to be. Some of that must have had to do with her friend Desiree too. The night she had burst into the room, she had been so terrified for Drew that she didn't stop to think that her sister was kissing another girl. She knew that sometimes girls liked girls and boys liked boys, but she didn't know her sister had those feelings. Still, it didn't feel weird to her. If Desiree made her sister happy and that made her nicer, that was a-okay with her.

Unsurprisingly, her mother hadn't wanted her to attend the funeral. She had continued her trend toward reasonability by not being mean or over the top about it. Instead, she conveyed her concerns that Kylie would be traumatized attending a classmate's funeral considering her own brush with death. Dad was neutral on it, but acknowledged that Mom did have a point, although he did seem more willing to let Kylie consider her own choice. Ultimately, it was Kayla who convinced their parents to let her attend, promising that she would remain close to her and, at the first sign of any distress, would remove her from the area.

So, yeah, she and Kayla were okay for the first time in a long time. What wasn't okay with her was what was happening here in her new town. Drew was dead, but she was scared that he was just the start of it. The ghosts seemed to have disappeared from the playground. She had seen the girl in her doorway and Kayla had mentioned the one in the graveyard, but it was like they were hiding from The Caretaker.

What was he? He had to be a ghost too. How else could he move about without alerting people? And how could she not touch him but he could touch Drew? Was it because Drew had been a ghost too by the time she found him in her room? There were so many questions with no answers in sight.

Her ruminations were interrupted when Kayla gently squeezed her shoulder. She looked back over it and saw her sister, who was wearing dark sunglasses, nod in the direction of Father Lee, prompting her to pay attention.

"Now, we say our final goodbye to our brother Andrew," the priest said somberly. "Though his physical body has died, his spirit lives on in fellowship with our Lord Jesus Christ. Eternal rest grant unto them, O Lord, and let perpetual light shine upon them. May their souls and all the souls of the faithful departed, through the mercy of God, rest in peace. Amen."

The tears flowed at the words. Thinking back to how he had been carried away by the monstrous spirit, she wondered if his soul was gone too. That broke her heart. If the monsters that haunted this town could not only kill, but also steal their victim's souls, who could possibly stop such horrors?

Father Lee continued, "This concludes our service. The Gatto family would like to thank you all for your attendance and your support during this most trying of times. Please approach the coffin and place your rose on top. The family invites you to join them at Grace's Diner and Restaurant for a repast luncheon following the service."

The procession started toward the coffin and Kayla guided Kylie along. When they rounded the corner, she saw the front row filled with Drew's family. His parents were front and center. His dad, a tall, burly man with a bald head and bushy beard held his mom, who melted into his shoulder as she sobbed, her face a mask of emotional agony. Ben sat to their right, his posture stiff and upright as he stared straight ahead, sunglasses hiding his eyes. Jasmine rested her head on his shoulder, her arms hooked in his.

As she reached the coffin, she gently placed the rose among the myriad of others that had already been deposited. She placed her hand on the pall and felt the softness of the velvet material.

"I'm sorry I couldn't save you," she whispered.

She didn't want to move, having already felt like she failed the boy once. She didn't want to leave him alone. But Kayla gently ushered her along, not wanting to hold up the crowd behind them. As they passed, Kayla and Desiree both hugged Ben and Jasmine, providing what little comfort they could.

While the older girls offered their condolences to their

friends, Kylie took notice of her classmates. Both Jessie and Trina were present with her parents. They each looked sad, but there was something more than that. They looked sick too. Maybe it was from crying, but they both looked as if they were coming down with colds, with runny noses and glassy eyes. Other kids that she didn't know as well had similar affects about them. A horrid thought intruded on her. Were they all about to end up the same way as Drew? Could it somehow be stopped?

She froze, lost in her thoughts, when Kayla again ushered her forward. She turned to face her sister who asked, "What is it?"

"I don't think this is over," Kylie said. "I think the other kids are in danger."

Kayla looked around the crowd. Kylie could tell by her expression that she realized what she was talking about. Turning her attention back to her sister, she said unconvincingly, "It'll be okay. Come on."

Kylie walked with Kayla and Desiree to her father's Cadillac Escalade. Big Al and his wife, Marie, had also attended the funeral, but had hung back to give the girls their space. They had been some of the first to the coffin and were now back at the car, waiting for the trio to join them.

As they walked to the car, the sun mockingly shining down on them, Kylie caught movement from the corner of her eye. She focused in that direction and saw Emily skipping around a tombstone in the distance.

When the girl realized that Kylie had seen her, she stopped and stared directly at her. The evil little girl pointed to the funeral canopy and then brought her fists to her eyes and rubbed them underneath in an exaggerated crying gesture.

Kylie felt rage boil over as she clenched her fists. She abruptly started in the direction of the girl, her sister and Desiree unaware that she had broken away.

A cruel smile spread across Emily's face as Kylie approached, not the least bit intimidated by the girl. She shrugged and started skipping again, this time toward a maple tree off to the side. Kylie broke into a run to catch up, but couldn't get to her before she vanished behind the trunk. *Vanish* was an appropriate way to put it because when Kylie looked behind the tree, Emily was, once again, gone.

Kylie wanted to scream. She wanted to punch the tree trunk until her hands were bloody. She felt so helpless and like such a failure that emotion needed to escape, but now wasn't the time. Heading back toward the car, she saw Kayla looking around in a mini panic to see where her sister had gone.

"I'm here!" she called to alleviate her sister's concern. From the distance, she saw the tension release from Kayla's posture as she waved her over in an impatient *Come here* gesture.

As she passed the tombstone Emily had been circling, she stopped again when she saw the etching in the stone. It wasn't like a normal grave maker with one or two names with birth and death dates below them. This one contained about fifteen names, each one with a birth date of 2014 or 2015; all listed a death date of *TBD 2024*, except the first one, which was dated one week ago. Upon closer scrutiny, she started to recognize the names. It was her fourth grade class. The first name was *Andrew Gatto. May 14, 2014 – September 19, 2024.* The other names all had the *TBD* designation. She saw Jessie and Trina were the next entries, followed by the remainder of the class roster. There was one name missing though.

Kylie's name wasn't on the tombstone.

Why? Why is she tormenting me if she doesn't want to kill me?

She stared in shock at the foretelling slab. Unable to move until she felt someone touch her shoulder from behind. She jumped startled and saw Kayla standing there with Desiree.

"Are you okay?" Kayla asked. "Desiree's parents are waiting for us."

Kylie couldn't muster the words so she turned back to the tombstone and pointed, only now it no longer had the names of her class. Instead, a singular name was engraved:

Heather Freeling
1975–1988

"It... it was... different," Kylie said perplexed.

Kayla pulled her in for a hug. "It's okay. We'll figure this out."

Kylie squeezed her big sister tight as they embraced. When they finally let go, Kayla led her by the hand to the car. During Kylie's detour, the mourners had dispersed and the canopy was empty save for the workers who were breaking it down. The workers and Emily, who was seated cross-legged on Drew's coffin, somehow unnoticed by the attendants, one of whom flipped the switch to lower the casket into the hole where her classmate would rest for eternity.

Emily was calm and flashed that malicious grin and waved as if she were atop a parade float rather than a child's coffin. Kylie didn't bother to alert anyone else to her presence. She knew they wouldn't see her.

She just watched as Emily descended into the ground

with the box containing Drew Gatto's body.

CHAPTER 25

T he repast had been over for an hour. Desiree's parents had dropped Kylie off at home before taking the older girls with them to the diner. None of them were in the mood to eat much. Big Al and Marie had left shortly after it ended with Desiree telling them she would either walk or Uber home. Now, Kayla, Desiree, Jasmine and Ben were all hanging around the side of the diner.

Ben was sitting on a parking bumper in an empty spot taking a swig from a bottle of vodka concealed in a paper bag. He offered some to Jasmine, who declined while continuing to rub his back. He held it out to Kayla and Desiree who were leaning against a Ford Explorer, even though none of them knew who it belonged to. They also declined, opting to use their vapes to alleviate their stress.

"I can't believe my little brother is dead," Ben said morosely before taking another swig of the vodka. "How can a ten-year-old kid catch a cold and die?"

He looked toward Kayla. The question wasn't rhetorical.

"I don't know," Kayla admitted.

"You don't know," Ben said, his head bobbing up and now in slow nods as he mulled the response over. Then,

216

without warning, he stood, pivoted and chucked the bag with the bottle against the wall, the glass within shattering upon impact as the alcohol poured down the diner's exterior. "Well, who the fuck does know something? What kind of a fucking monster would kill a little boy?"

"Ben," Desiree said, "this was just some fucked-up illness."

"No," he said, pulling his glasses off and chucking them to the side, baring his bloodshot eyes. "No kid gets eaten alive from the fucking inside like my brother did. That isn't fucking natural." He pointed to the girls. "And you fucking know it."

Jasmine came up behind him and gently pulled him back, stepping in between him and Kayla and Desiree. "Babe," she said calmly, placing her hand on his cheek. "It's not their fault. They're trying to help."

He looked back down at his girlfriend, trying hard to push back the tears, but as he said, "They didn't help fucking fast enough," the dam broke and he collapsed back onto the curb and buried his head in his hands as he sobbed. The trio of women stood by, unsure of what they could say. Knowing that there were no words to relieve his anguish. "I'm sorry," he said without looking up.

The three took positions around him—Jasmine in front, Desiree and Kayla to each side. While Jasmine cupped his face and brought it up to meet hers, the others put their arms around him on either side. Jasmine was crying now too.

"You don't have to apologize, baby. You feel every damn feeling inside of you right now. It's okay."

He broke again and she pulled him in for an embrace. Kayla and Desiree released their own hugs, but rubbed his back as Jasmine held him. They were so caught up in their sorrow and attempt to comfort Ben, they didn't notice that someone else had joined them.

"Jasmine, baby," an older voice said. They looked up to find Aunt Ethel standing over them. Jasmine stood and her aunt surprised her by giving her a hug. Kayla noted that she didn't seem like quite the same curmudgeon they'd been sparring with.

Ben composed himself and stood in time for Ethel to shock him by putting her arms around him too. "I'm so sorry, Benjamin," she said with sincerity. "I'm so very sorry for your loss."

He gave the old woman a gentle squeeze. "Thank you," he said as he pulled away.

Ethel regarded the group, a sadness in her eyes, but something else as well. Resolve.

"Now, listen y'all. I know some of you believe more than others. But I think you done seen enough to understand that what's happening here ain't natural."

Kayla looked to Jasmine, who didn't offer protest this time, her skepticism having waned in the wake of her boyfriend's brother's sudden death. "I know, Auntie," she admitted. "But what do we do about it?"

"Something happened last night that may point us in the right direction."

"What?" Ben asked eagerly.

"Mama managed to break through. Don't ask me how cause I'm not rightly sure, but she came to me in a dream."

"Auntie..." Jasmine started, doubt creeping back in. But she saw Ben and knew that some type of explanation, no matter how far-fetched, would be preferable to their current lack of answers.

"I know, Jasmine. I know you don't fully believe, but I'm telling y'all the truth. I woke up in the cemetery. Or I was there in my dream, I don't know. But Mama's rocking chair was there. It was all taped and put together. It looked like shit truth be told, but it was intact. I walked over and sat down, half afraid it was gonna break the minute I sat down, leading to me busting my ass."

Kayla suppressed a laugh, knowing that it would be highly inappropriate but, even through the tragedy, the visual struck her as humorous.

"So, we need to put the chair back together?" Desiree asked.

"Don't know," Ethel replied. Kayla glanced over at Ben. The answer was clearly unsatisfactory to him and he looked to be growing impatient for Ethel to get to the point. To his credit, though, he stayed silent. "When I sat in it, it didn't break. But I saw Mama walking in the distance. She looked toward me and waved. I called out to her, but she didn't answer. She couldn't talk. But what she did do was hold up a piece of paper. She placed it on a tombstone. I got up and tried to catch up to her, but she was gone."

"Did you see the paper?" Kayla asked.

Ethel nodded. "I did. It was a page from her recipe book. A Hoodoo spell."

It was Ben's turn to ask the follow-up. "What kind of spell?"

"The kind that'll let us talk with the dead. As soon as I woke up, I jumped out of bed and damn near fell and broke my hip running to get a piece of paper to write it down before I forgot."

The quartet exchanged confused glances. "Who would we talk to?" Kayla asked. "The ghosts in the cemetery?"

"Naw, them kids is so scared, they be hiding. They ain't gon' wanna come out. Even if they did, they couldn't help us. Mama made her way back to somehow to give us a way to communicate with her and that's what we gon' do. We gon' talk to Mama. And she gon' tell us where the rest of her recipe book is. And maybe there we can find something to stop all of this."

"How'd your mother find her way back without her tether?" Kayla asked.

"Sweetie," Ethel said, the endearment sounding odd coming from her. "Like I done told you — my mama was a special lady. A powerful one. If anyone could find their way back from the other side, it would be her."

"Okay," Jasmine said, the resolve now in her voice. "Then what do we need to do to talk to Great-Grandma Eunice?"

It was just before eight o'clock by the time they had gathered everything they needed for the one spell they actually had. They had split into pairs to procure the items Ethel had listed. Kayla and Desiree teamed up, as did Jasmine and Ben. The ingredients were pretty simple. They needed a white candle and incense, which Kayla and Desiree bought from East Meets West in the Parkway Place mall. Ethel said they also needed something from the deceased of which she had several choices in her home as well as mundane items such as a glass of water, a pen and paper which Ethel had at home as well. The last piece of the puzzle was dirt from the graveyard which had to be obtained respectfully. Being that Jasmine was kin, she agreed to go fill a bag from around the Weeks family crypt.

With the supplies in hand, Kayla and Desiree walked up the path to Ethel's house. Before they reached the stoop, Desiree's phone buzzed. She checked it and informed Kayla, "Jasmine and Ben are about fifteen minutes behind us."

Kayla was anxious to get this over with. She prayed that this spell wasn't just bullshit from an old lady with dementia. She hoped they could actually communicate with Eunice who could somehow get this monster back in its cage.

They realized something was very wrong as soon as they reached the front porch. The first sign was that the door was open. But it wasn't just open, the wood frame was cracked as if it had been forced open. A large boot print was imprinted just below the knob, which was twisted to one side from a heavy impact.

"Ethel?" Desiree called, not wanting to go inside. "Are you okay?" There was no answer so she turned to Kayla. "What do we do?"

It was the last thing she wanted to do, but they couldn't just stand there if Ethel was in trouble. Never mind the fact that she was their only hope of stopping the monster that was preying on the local children, it was the right thing to do.

Kayla carefully pushed the door open and took a tentative step inside, not prepared for what she was about to find.

The place was completely wrecked. The couch they

had sat on the last time they were here was overturned and every cushion was ripped apart, with polyurethane foam strewn about the room, making it look like it had snowed inside. Ethel's leather recliner was in the same condition. Every hutch and cabinet was open and the contents emptied without any regard for keeping them intact. The walls were smashed full of holes as if someone had taken a sledgehammer to them. Insulation was ripped out and spread around with the foam from the coach cushions and a strong, musty smell permeated the air.

"What the fuck happened here?" Kayla asked.

This question *was* rhetorical because she knew damn well Desiree didn't know either.

"Ethel!" Desiree called, lowering her voice at the last second as if realizing it wasn't wise to be too loud in case the perpetrator of this vandalism was still in the house.

Again, there was no answer. Kayla grabbed Desiree's hand and the terrified girls moved toward the kitchen.

If the living room was bad, the kitchen was even worse than they could have imagined. Every cupboard and cabinet was open, with some of them ripped from their hinges. Glasses and plates were scattered everywhere, mostly shattered; glass was spread across the tile floor which itself was in bad shape, having been ripped up in multiple spots. The kitchen table was upended and three of the four legs were broken off. The chairs were in the same condition; one had been flung clear across the room and now rested on the counter. One of the pipes under the sink had been ripped out and water sprayed everywhere, flooding the kitchen.

But the most horrible sight of all was Ethel.

The elderly woman was impaled against the wall

adjacent to where they had entered the kitchen, one of the broken table legs driven through her stomach. The stump of the wood was stained with bloody handprints as the woman had no doubt tried to extricate it from her abdomen before it was too late. The floor below, wet from the busted pipe, was colored red from the blood that had slowed from a gush to a trickle from both the entry and exit wounds.

Her head hung obscenely to one side; her eyes wide, frozen with the terror of her final moments forever etched on her face. Her tongue lolled out of her mouth which also leaked out what was left of the blood in her body.

Kayla and Desiree both screamed at the horrid sight, no longer thinking about whether the culprit was still in close proximity. Kayla couldn't fathom who or what could have done this. Everything they had seen thus far pointed to ghosts. The big bastard that she saw in the cemetery had walked right through her so he couldn't have done this, could he? Was it the snake thing? She stepped cautiously around and, when she got to the other side, something caught her eye. Written in blood on the wall next to Ethel's body was a single word:

LAMIA

Desiree had her phone out to call the police, but stopped when Kayla grabbed her arm and pulled her to her vantage point so she could see the word too. Ethel's right hand hung next to the word, her fingers covered in her blood. A streak of crimson stretching from the end of the *A* to where the hand hung limp indicated that Ethel had been the one who'd written it in what must have been a last-gasp effort to help Kayla.

"What the fuck does that mean?" Desiree asked.

"I don't know," Kayla said. "But it's gotta be something."

"We have to call the cops," Desiree said the panic evident in her voice.

"Do it," Kayla said.

As Desiree dialed 911, Kayla looked around for anything else that may clue them in to what had happened. She saw that the back door, much like the front, was also knocked off its hinges. She cautiously stepped over the debris, both in an effort to preserve the evidence and to avoid hurting herself. She looked into the backyard which, like her house, backed up to a wooded area.

That's where she saw him.

The large man in the yellow rain slicker, The Caretaker, stood between the trees, staring at her as his chest rose and fell with heaving breaths. Things about him were different than the last time she had seen him in the cemetery. Most jarring was that his coat was covered in blood. Ethel's blood.

That seemed impossible. He was a ghost. *He can't interact with the living*, she thought. He passed right through her in the cemetery and Kylie told her how she had tried to bite him but her mouth also went right through him. If he had somehow become corporeal than the danger he presented had increased exponentially.

"Dez..." Kayla started, her voice cracked and low as she took two steps back into the kitchen. Desiree didn't hear her; she was on the phone giving the dispatcher the address and describing the scene in a teary, choked tone.

"Desiree!" Kayla shouted, finding her voice.

"Hurry!" Desiree told the 911 operator as she hung up and turned her attention to Kayla's scream. She joined her at the back door in time to see the assailant staring her down.

"That's him!" Kayla said. "That's the man from the cemetery."

"He did this?"

"He had to. Look at the blood."

"We gotta get out of here," Desiree said. This time it was her turn to grasp Kayla's hand. As they prepared to run, The Caretaker lifted his head as if someone had called to him. He turned his head and looked in the direction opposite Ethel's house, before heeding whatever call beckoned him.

The monster turned and, once again, disappeared into the trees as the sound of approaching sirens grew louder.

CHAPTER 26

S chool shut down the week after Drew's funeral. Every day, more kids called out sick to the point where the officials had no choice but to take things remote in an effort to slow the spread of whatever virus was going around. It wasn't just Alexander Elementary either. It was every school in Huntsville. While it seemed that it was mainly elementary and middle-school kids getting sick, they took the high schools remote too. It felt like the Covid days all over again, only this time, the adults seemed unaffected while it was the children who were becoming deathly ill. There were even reports that two more children had passed away from the mystery illness in different schools across town.

Kylie felt horrible, mainly because she didn't feel sick at all. For all her parents' worry about the fact that she was immunocompromised, she remained healthy without so much as a sniffle while everyone around her seemed to be falling ill. She wasn't ungrateful for that, but it also didn't make sense to her. She knew Emily was the source of this disease and she had been in close contact with her on multiple occasions, so why didn't she make her sick like the others? She wasn't naive enough to think that she was immune to this. She was afraid that this thing that looked like a child had darker plans for her.

The school shutdown wasn't the only issue in town. The night after the funeral, something had happened with Kayla and Desiree that involved the police. She wouldn't tell Kylie what, only that her friend Jasmine's aunt had died. She said they went to check on her and found her like she had a heart attack or something. But the police were involved. They had come to the house a couple of times to ask Kayla questions, which made it seem like it was something more than just an old lady dying. Mom and Dad had actually been quite supportive and sat with her each time the cops came calling. They were all very hush-hush about the whole thing, though.

Kylie didn't believe it, but she also didn't push. Kayla had earned her trust and she knew her big sister was working on her behalf.

She asked Kayla if they should finally bring their parents into the loop as to what was happening, but Kayla was adamant that they didn't. She said Mom would think they were crazy. She'd freak out and Kayla wouldn't have the flexibility she needed to figure things out. Dad would just analyze and dismiss it as always. Her sister said she didn't like it either, but they only had each other right now.

As Kylie paced her room, sparing an occasional nervous glance out her window to ensure there was no one there, she was startled by a knock at her door. Without waiting for her to answer, Mom opened it and entered.

"Kylie, honey?" she asked as she walked in. "There's someone here to see you."

She didn't know who to expect, but it certainly wasn't the priest who had blessed their house when they'd moved in. The same one who had presided over Drew's funeral. If she was shocked to see Father Lee walk in, she was floored to see Kayla behind him.

"What's going on?" she asked.

"Father Lee is here to perform a blessing of good health for you."

"Mom!" Kylie protested.

"It was my idea," Kayla said. Mom looked at her sister in a way that she hadn't seen in years. She looked... proud. "With everything going on, maybe a little faith is the key here."

The words had multiple meanings and Kylie was smart enough to pick that up. It wasn't just about the Catholic faith, which, given that they were dealing with ghosts and evil spirits, seemed as good an option as any, but also it was Kayla's way of reminding Kylie to have faith in her as well.

Kylie walked over and sat on the bed, ceasing her protests.

Father Lee pulled up a chair and sat in front of her, holding the same book and wearing the same stole as when he'd come in for the blessing the first time. He smiled warmly at the weary young girl and asked, "Are you okay to proceed?"

"Yes, sir," Kylie answered while looking at Kayla.

The priest made the sign of the cross and the Macklin women followed suit. He started the blessing.

"Heavenly Father, we come before You today seeking Your blessing and healing. You are the source of all goodness and mercy, and we trust in Your loving care. Look upon us with compassion and grant us the gift of good health."

When he finished, Kylie thought he was done, but no such luck. He opened his book and read a passage from within. He said it was from the Book of Matthew, chapter eight, verses sixteen and seventeen.

"That evening they brought to him many who were possessed with demons; and he cast out the spirits with a word, and healed all who were sick. This was to fulfill what was spoken by the prophet Isaiah, He took our infirmities and bore our diseases."

He reached into his pocket and produced a small vial of water. He opened it and pressed his finger to the spout while turning it to wet the digit. He then reached out and made the shape of a cross on Kylie's forehead. As he did, he said, "May this holy water remind you of your baptism, through which you were united with Christ. May it be a sign of His healing power and love. In the name of the Father, and of the Son, and of the Holy Spirit. Amen."

A few more prayers followed and, just when Kylie thought this may never end, he indicated that the next blessing would be the final one of this ceremony.

"Holy Mary, Mother of God, pray for us. St. Joseph, patron of the sick, pray for us. St. Raphael the Archangel, patron of healing, pray for us. All the angels and saints, pray for us. Amen."

He stood when he was done.

"Thank you, Father," Gretchen said.

Kylie wasn't mad at her. She knew her mother loved her and only wanted her to be safe. Whether or not this blessing made a difference remained to be seen, but it put Mom somewhat at ease and she supposed that wasn't a bad thing.

Kayla mouthed the words "thank you" from where she stood, unseen by both her mother and Father Lee.

"I wish you well, Kylie. Please keep yourself safe," Father Lee said before turning to Kayla. "It's admirable that you're thinking of your sister in this way. I wish more young people would turn to their faith in dark times."

"I'm trying," Kayla said.

"Often, that's all we can do," the priest confirmed.

"I'll see you out, Father," Gretchen said, beckoning toward the door.

"Thank you, Gretchen," Father Lee said. "Goodbye, Kylie. Kayla."

When he left, Kayla pushed the door shut behind her and took a seat next to her sister on the bed.

"Do you think that will help?" Kylie asked.

"I don't know," Kayla admitted, "but it's all we have right now. Things have gotten out of hand and I think I know what we're up against, but I need you to stay safe, so I'm going to use every resource at my disposal to keep it that way."

"So, what now?"

"Now, I have to go see Jasmine. I think there's a way for her to help us."

"I want to come with you!"

"Kylie," Kayla said, her tone emphasizing just how unrealistic the request was. "You know you can't."

"I know," she said defeated. "Just please be careful."

"I will," Kayla said as she got up and walked toward the door. She reached for the knob but didn't turn it. Instead, she released it and turned back to her sister.

"Did you know I was thinking about applying for college before we left Florida?"

Kylie shook her head. "No. I didn't think you wanted to go."

"I don't know if I really did, I just wanted to get away from Mom, ya know? In case you couldn't tell, we don't always get along the best."

"No shit," Kylie said.

Kayla laughed, her sister's casual use of profanity throwing her off.

"No shit," Kayla repeated as she made her way back to the bed and reclaimed her seat next to Kylie. "When you apply for college, they sometimes make you write an essay, usually some bullshit, but this question was kind of intriguing. They asked me who my hero was."

"What did you say?"

Kayla shrugged. "I didn't have an answer and, you know me, I get an idea then I give up on it and move on to something else. But I've been thinking about that question a lot these past few weeks and I can say for sure that I know who my hero is."

"Who?"

"You are." Kayla looked at the shock register on her sister's face before her eyes misted up. "You got dealt the shittiest of shitty hands in life. For a kid to get diagnosed with cancer at five years old, to have surgery and chemotherapy and all the other stuff that comes with it is beyond unfair. But you know something?"

"What?"

"You handled it better than any adult would have—sure as hell better than I would have. All you wanted was to go back to school. You weren't afraid of dying, you just wanted to live."

"I was afraid of dying. I was really scared that I was going to die."

"Then that just makes you all the more heroic. You faced this thing down with courage. Bravery is not being afraid. Courage is being afraid and doing it anyway. That's why you're the most courageous person I know. That's why you're my hero. Because not only did you

231

fight cancer, but now you're fighting something that might be even worse. And you're still showing that same courage. I'm so damn proud of you."

Kylie threw her arms around Kayla and hugged her tightly. Kayla reciprocated.

"I love you, Kylie."

"I love you too, Kayla."

They held each other for a long time until Kayla finally broke the embrace, wiping her eyes as she stood up.

"I need you to stay here and stay safe," Kayla said. "If you see anything even the least bit strange, you go tell Mom and Dad. I don't care how they react. Understand?"

Kylie nodded in acknowledgment. "Where are you going?"

"I'm going to go find out how to kill this fucking thing."

CHAPTER 27

Gretchen stopped Kayla as she made her way to the front door. Kayla braced herself for a fight, but was shocked when her mother pulled her in for a hug.

This feels... odd, she thought.

"Thank you, Kayla," Mom said. "I know you've never been big on faith, but I appreciate you considering your sister in all of this. And me."

"Of course," she said. "I know I can be a little self-centered at times—"

"A little?" Gretchen said, cocking an eyebrow as she cut her off.

Kayla searched her mother's face and was surprised to see the hint of a smirk. "Was that... was that a joke?"

The smirk widened into a grin which turned into a laugh. "You may not remember, but I do have a pretty good sense of humor."

"You're right," Kayla replied. "I don't remember that at all!" Now it was her turn to smirk. But beyond the banter, it felt really good to share a warm moment with her mother again. It had been so long that she hadn't thought it possible.

"Where are you off to?" Gretchen asked with genuine interest as opposed to her usual interrogatory affect.

"I'm meeting Desiree," she said trying not to sound

nervous. "We're going to catch a late movie."

"That's great, sweetie," Mom replied. A silence hung between them for a few moments before she added, "You know, your father and I just want you to be happy, right?"

It did feel like that in this moment, even if it hadn't for the past few years. But it also seemed like Mom was alluding to something else.

"I know, Mom."

"Just because I've embraced my faith more in these past few years doesn't mean you can't tell me things. I hope you realize that."

Kayla realized that her mother was more observant than she gave her credit for. She shouldn't have been surprised. She'd been a pretty damn good lawyer when she was still practicing. You don't get to where Gretchen Macklin got by not seeing the world around you. As happy as it made her to hear her mom being supportive, though, now wasn't the time. Maybe when all this was over she could really pursue her relationship with Desiree and not having to worry about judgment from her parents would go a long way toward her happiness.

But right now, there was the little matter of the demon wreaking havoc on their lives.

"Here's what I found on Lamia," Kayla said from the driver's seat of her father's Tesla. Her dad had let her borrow it so she and Desiree could *go to the movies*.

"Either she's the demon from that old movie *Drag Me to Hell*, according to Wikipedia, or a monster from Greek mythology according to every other source I found."

"Let's go with the second one," Desiree said.

"According to the mythology, she may have been the daughter of Poseidon. She was also apparently drop-dead gorgeous to the point that she was seduced by Zeus and had a bunch of kids with him. That didn't sit too well with Hera, Zeus's wife."

"I don't imagine it would," Desiree said bluntly.

"Yeah, well, Hera was so pissed that she made her kill her own children."

"Wow. That is fucked up."

"No shit. The stories go on to say that her being forced to murder her own children drove her mad to the point where her hatred and anger melted away her beauty and left her a twisted, hideous demonic figure. A demon who was half serpent."

Desiree took her eyes off the road long enough to give Kayla a knowing look.

"The crypt."

"Exactly. It wasn't a damn *coral snake* that I saw in the crypt."

"So why didn't it, like, eat you?"

"I don't think it was after me at all. I think it used me to break the chair. Eunice Weeks had some kind of power to keep this thing at bay, even after death. If that chair really was a tether keeping her soul tied to the human world, by breaking it, Lamia was now free to do what it wanted to."

"I'm afraid to even ask."

"Lamia's grief turned to an insatiable desire for revenge. What do you think would be the best way to pay the world back when you've been forced to kill your own children?"

Desiree swallowed hard. "You take it out on their kids. Jesus Christ."

"I don't think he's going to help us out on this one."

"There was one more thing about her that I don't quite see how it fits in."

"What's that?"

"Lamia was also said to be a seductress, but as far as I've known she's only taken the form of that snake demon. I think The Caretaker is something different."

"You think she seduced him into helping her out? Like she was banging him or something?"

"I don't think so. But there're other ways to seduce someone besides sex."

"No good ones," Desiree scoffed. Kayla glared at her in silence until she turned and winced when she saw how annoyed that comment had made her. "Sorry, I say stupid shit when I'm scared."

Well, that made two of them. "May I continue?" Kayla asked.

"Yeah. Sorry."

"She may not be banging him," she said putting some extra stank on *banging*. "But I do think she's controlling him somehow. And that's not even the worst part."

"I don't want to ask, but I guess I will. What's the worst part?"

"I think with Eunice gone, she's able to feed. The more you feed, the stronger you get. And if she's getting stronger, I think she's able to make The Caretaker stronger. That's why he's not just a spirit anymore. That's how he was able to do that to Ethel."

The mention of the scene made Kayla want to vomit.

It was like experiencing the horror all over again.

"Fuck, Kayla," Desiree said as she turned onto Jasmine's street. "How are we going to stop this thing?"

"We have to ask Eunice."

CHAPTER 28

Kylie saw them as soon as she turned out her light. One minute she was in her room by herself, the next the two girls were standing at the foot of her bed. This had happened enough that she didn't bother to scream, though she still felt the same paralyzing fear to see two of her classmates seemingly materialize in her room.

"Hi Kylie," Jessie and Trina said in unison. The greeting sounded drawn out and mechanical as if the girls were in a daze. They certainly looked it. They were mostly still, although they swayed side to side, the movements jerky and awkward.

They looked sick, but not quite as bad as Drew had. Their skin was pale, save for the red on their noses. Their lips were dry and flaky, and purple veins were starting to show prominence on their necks. But the truly disturbing part was their eyes. Each girl's pupils and irises had been replaced by black opal orbs.

"You ready to come play yet?" a voice came from Kylie's left.

She both was and wasn't surprised to see Emily by her closet. The girl wore the same clothes she had every time that Kylie had seen her thus far. Like Jessie and Trina, her eyes were different too, but they weren't black. They were red, with black slits in the center. They looked like the eyes of the monster she had seen on her television. She blinked and when she opened them again, they were back to a normal human variation.

Kylie looked toward her door and Emily, as if she could read her thoughts, said, "If you try to call to your parents, I'll kill your friends before the words finish coming out of your mouth."

"How did you get in here?"

"Kylie," Emily said with a *Come on, let's get real* tone. "I can do lots of things. Always could. Well, I couldn't do as much when that old bitch was up my ass all the time. But, she's gone now, so I'm remembering new tricks every day."

"What do you want?"

"I just want you to come play. That's all I ever wanted. Does that sound so bad?"

"Why did you kill Drew?"

"Ugh," Emily said rolling her head back. "You and all your questions. Just come with me and I'll show you."

"No way!"

"Sigh, Kylie, you know you don't have a choice. It'll be so much better for everyone if you just come with me."

Fifteen minutes later they approached the clearing that led to the cemetery gates. In just a few more minutes, they'd be at the playground. Kylie hadn't wanted to go, but she knew she had no choice. Kayla wasn't home, she couldn't call to her parents, and who knew what Emily would do to Jessie and Trina if she didn't go with her. She was terrified, unsure of what awaited her. But all she could think of was one of the last things Kayla said to her:

Courage is being afraid and doing it anyway.

Emily skipped the whole way, happy as a damn clam. Jessie and Trina shuffled behind her, their gait reminding her of the mummy from that movie she had watched with Kayla and Desiree. Only they didn't walk with their hands in front of them. Kylie brought up the rear, dreading each step and trying to delay the inevitable as long as she could.

They made it to the cemetery gates and moved around the outside of the fence. At one point, Kylie thought she saw a small head quickly pop up from under one of the tombstones before quickly ducking back down. That was the only thing unusual she saw. Until she reached the playground.

When the swings came into view, they were full. But it wasn't ghosts. It was living children. Kids from her class.

They were all over the playground. They were swinging, sliding and playing tic-tac-toe. A group of four darted around, avoiding each other in a game of tag. Three girls off to the right were playing double Dutch. Every one of them looked very sick with pale or ashen skin and each had eyes as black as Jessie and Trina, who had now joined the group on the slide, waiting their turn to descend.

"What are you doing with them?" Kylie asked.

Emily grabbed her shoulders and turned her around, her eyes were back to their red, serpentine version. "Whatever the hell I want!" she hissed, her voice deep and modulated. It took all Kylie had not to scream.

"What do you want me to do?"

The demon child released her and smiled, blinking her eyes back to *normal* again. "That's the spirit, Kylie. Because what I want most... is *you*."

"Why me?"

"I told you, silly. You're special."

"I'm not!" Kylie screamed, her voice cracking. "I'm just a regular kid!"

Emily paused and looked her over, her expression one that resembled genuine curiosity. "Oh, Kylie," she said. "You're so much more than regular. A human could live a hundred years and not meet anyone like you."

"I can't help you," she said quietly.

"Oh, you can. And you will."

"And what if I don't?"

Emily stepped forward until she was almost nose to nose with Kylie. She was taller than her. Kylie didn't think it had always been that way, but it was noticeable now. Emily looked down on her.

"If you won't play with me. *They* will."

CHAPTER 29

"I can't believe we're actually doing this," Jasmine said as she punched in the code to enter the Weeks family crypt. "We all need to see a shrink or something."

"You're not wrong," Kayla said as she stepped inside the one place she thought she'd never be again. It was early evening and the moon was full, so the light from the small window provided a lot more illumination than the last time they were there. The remnants of Eunice's rocking chair still lay in the corner of the room.

"Let's make this quick," Jasmine said.

They went to work immediately. Desiree and Ben lit incense and started waving it around the room, making sure they reached every corner in their attempt to cleanse the area. Once they were satisfied they had enough coverage, they placed the incense sticks on the window ledges in opposite sides of the room, letting the aromatic smoke continue to waft about.

Kayla placed the white candle in the center of the room. The one she had chosen was large and thick but unscented; she'd doubted that *Clean Linen* or *Lavender Dream* would enhance the ritual. With the candle in place, Jasmine retrieved a small bag and poured the contents slowly in a circular radius around the candle until it was surrounded by the grave dirt she had picked up for the previous attempt prior to her aunt's murder. She also placed a glass next to the candle and filled it with water from a plastic bottle that she also retrieved from her bag.

"Now, we just need a personal item," Kayla said.

Jasmine produced an old, faded photograph of Eunice with a young Ethel and a boy of similar age that Kayla could only presume was her grandfather, Martin.

"That's good," Kayla said, "but I think I have a better idea." She grabbed a jagged leg from the pile of wood that used to be Eunice's rocking chair and placed it on the side of the candle opposite the water glass. "If this chair was some type of spiritual object, it makes sense that this would be the best item to use, right?"

Jasmine shrugged. "I think you know more about all this than I do at this point, so I'll go with your gut."

With the preparations complete, the four of them stood in a circle around the candle, glass, dirt and broken chair leg. Kayla reached out on both sides, taking Desiree's hand in one and Jasmine's in the other. Jasmine took Ben's and Ben took Desiree's to complete the circle.

"Okay," Kayla said. "Everyone focus. Breathe deep and try to calm your minds."

"Yeah. That'll be easy," Desiree muttered. Kayla and Jasmine both shot her looks. "Sorry," she said sheepishly.

After a few minutes of silence, with the group breathing in and out until they were in unison like some type of absurd workout video, Kayla retrieved a piece of paper and a pencil from her pocket. On the piece of paper, she wrote:

Eunice Weeks
How do we stop Lamia?

She held the paper out and instructed her friends:

"When I read this, focus on the candle and visualize Eunice. Pay attention to your thoughts and look out for any sensations that feel different because they might be messages." The group all nodded their acknowledgment and Kayla spoke the words of the ritual, "Spirit of Eunice Weeks, I call upon you. With respect and reverence, I seek to communicate. Come forth and speak, let your presence be known. In the light of this candle, through the water's reflection, guide me to your wisdom, your voice I wish to hear."

She shut her eyes and listened, hoping and praying for a response. For a moment, she felt it odd that she was mentally invoking the Christian God to allow a pagan ceremony to work. She wondered if the conflicting ideologies would cancel each other out.

That's not calming your mind, Kayla, she thought.

After almost two full minutes of standing there with her eyes closed, not hearing anything other than the ambient noise of the crypt and the cemetery beyond it, Kayla grew frustrated. The spell wasn't going to work. They were screwed.

She opened her eyes and looked at the makeshift altar. The candle was lit, the water was full and the dirt and chair leg were undisturbed. But her friends were gone.

Oh no! she thought as the panic set in. The door was shut and the room was completely dark once again, save for the small flickering flame of the candle. It danced in an unfelt breeze and she was terrified it would go out. Almost as terrified as she was of the demon once again making its presence known.

"Don't fear, child," a voice that was both familiar and alien at the same time said. It came from the corner of the room. It was accompanied by a creaking noise that sounded like pressure being put on a piece of wood. Like a rocking chair.

Kayla carefully picked up the candle, taking great care to move slowly lest the flame extinguish, and pointed it in the direction of the sound. The light shone on Jasmine sitting in Eunice's chair, which had been fully restored somehow. She rocked back and forth with her arms draped over the rests as she surveyed Kayla with eyes that weren't her own.

"Jasmine?" Kayla asked.

"Oh, I'm just borrowing my great-granddaughter for a spell. It's easier to do with kin."

The realization hit her. "Eunice?"

"Yes, young lady. That's my name. You went through a lot of trouble to get me back here. For someone who ain't a trained practitioner, you done a good job."

Kayla was stunned. She had hoped the spell would work but now that it had, she realized that she never thought it actually would. Jasmine/Eunice smiled as she watched her understand the full scope of what she'd managed to do.

"Can you help us? Can you do whatever it was that you did to keep the kids safe all those years?"

"I don't think so, honey. I'm no longer tethered to this world. I been fighting like hell to get back, but it ain't gon' be long before I move on forever."

Kayla felt the desperation rise. "So, what can we do?"

"Well, first you gotta understand what you up against. Lamia is a powerful, ancient demon that feeds on the souls of children. There's all kinds of stories about where it came from, but I reckon it don't rightly matter. What does matter is what it wants."

"What does it want?"

"Demons ain't all that different from people in some respects. They got needs and urges. This particular one needs to feed. The more it feeds, the more powerful it gets. That thing was drawn here by the souls that rest in that cemetery. From the time they had kids working the quarry up to the Spanish flu, there was plenty of souls for it to feed on."

"Does it matter if they were alive or dead? I've seen it attack both ghosts and humans."

Eunice continued to rock as she nodded her head up and down, letting Kayla know that it was a good question. Kayla thought it odd to hear the old woman's voice coming from Jasmine's twenty-year-old form with its modern clothing and dyed green hair.

"It feeds on the soul after a child passes. But in its stronger forms, it can spread its sickness across large swaths of land, infesting and infecting the children, making them sick and eventually killing them."

"Was it the cause of the Spanish flu?"

Eunice shook her head. "No, but that was a welcome development for the beast. Like getting a coupon for an all-you-can-eat buffet."

"How did you get involved?"

Eunice didn't answer immediately. The question seemed to make her sad. She sniffled and wiped her nose with her arm before continuing.

"My daddy's family came from Ghana. They was brought over like so many in the early days of this country, forced into slavery. They kept up with their traditions, though, practicing and praying in their quarters away from the watchful eye of the plantation owners. They knew Hoodoo like none other, passing it down through generations. Daddy showed me and my mama different ways to use it for good. I never really considered that it would be a calling for me. I just wanted to play and go to school. I loved the outdoors. Down a little ways from my house was a small creek. I used to go there and play after my lessons was done for the day. See, I didn't go to school so I never really had any friends. We lived in a small farmhouse with our nearest neighbor near half a mile away so I was on my own a lot. I'd make up all manner of fanciful scenarios involving pirates and knights and princesses. I'd go have these adventures in my head."

"But one day that all changed. I was walking along the creek when I saw a big ole white kid on the other side. He was trying to skip rocks, but to be honest, his technique was kinda shitty." That almost made Kayla laugh, but she stifled it. "I was a bit nervous to go up to him, not knowing who he was and all. He looked about my age, but he was already big as an ox. I was thinking about turning back when he seen me. He stood up and waved at me. He looked real happy to see me, like he ain't never seen no other kid in his life."

"Who was he?" Kayla asked.

Eunice's eyes narrowed and she said, "Damn, missy, ain't you got no patience? I'm getting to that!"

I guess that's where Ethel got it from, Kayla thought but didn't say. Instead, she offered a meek, "Sorry."

"Anyways, I didn't realize it at first but the boy couldn't speak. You can imagine that made things tough seeing as he couldn't even tell me his name. But we managed to communicate in our own way. I showed him how to skip his rock properly. He jumped up and down and clapped like he were a damn toddler or something. That's when I realized the boy had some, let's say, deficits. But that didn't matter none. He didn't have no friends neither, so we hit it off."

"Every day after my chores was done, I would go down to the creek and my friend was there too. We would play, mainly the stories I made up, him being unable to communicate and all. But he was happy to go along. I tried to bring paper and some crayons one day and asked him to write his name, but I should have known he couldn't spell neither. So, I just called him "friend." He seemed okay with that. Right up until the day I learned his name was Abel Hargrave."

Kayla was shocked. "The Caretaker? The serial killer from the 1960s?"

"Serial killer? Girl, you seem smart, but you ain't smart enough to know not to believe everything you been told?"

"I've seen things that give me reason to believe otherwise."

"Well, you can't always believe what you see neither. But, yeah, me and Abel Hargrave was friends. Best friends in fact. We was the only friend either of us had with neither of us going to school." That was a sad notion for Kayla. It reminded her of Kylie's struggles being isolated from her peers due to the combination of her cancer battle and the pandemic. "But even something as pure and beautiful as a friendship between two children can get snatched away in an instant."

"What happened?" Kayla asked, her natural curiosity overcoming her fear of getting chastised for interrupting again. This time Eunice didn't rebuke her.

"We was playing down by the creek one day, just like we had for months, having a fine time of it when a white man came storming out the trees. He looked mighty cross with us for some reason. I had no idea who he was. He shouted at my friend and grabbed him by his arm hard. He said, *Abel Hargrave, what in the hell are you doing? Why are you cavorting with her?* He called me something else. I'm not about to debase myself by repeating it, although I'm sure you can imagine what it was."

Kayla could and it made her angry to think there was a time where a black child and a white one couldn't even play together. "I'm sorry."

"Some folks just got hatred in their heart, dear. Ain't no cure for it. But the day I learned my friend's name was Abel was the last time I saw him."

"So, what happened to him? What made him into a killer?"

"He weren't no killer, Kayla. My friend Abel was just a pawn of the demon Lamia. It took the form of a little girl. He was working at the cemetery when it befriended him. I guess years after the Spanish flu ended, its food supply was running low. It wasn't strong enough to spread its sickness, so it needed the kids to come to it. It got in Abel's head. Pretended they was friends. He was told that if he brought more kids to Lamia, they could all play games and have fun and be just like kids. Abel grew up and got real big, but his mind was never more than that of a child himself, so he was easily manipulated."

"That's horrible," Kayla said. "Everyone thought he was the killer?"

Eunice nodded somberly. Kayla could tell that recounting this tale caused her great pain.

"Someone seen him going into the woods with a kid. They hunted him down and beat him senseless. I was there that night. I couldn't do nothing but watch as the townsfolk brutalized the poor man. When they strung him up from the tree, I did the only thing I could. I got into his head and brought him back to the place we used to play. I let him sit by the creek and be at peace while the life drained out his body as he hung from that noose."

It took a second for her to compose herself. Kayla stepped forward and crouched in front of the chair and put her hands over Eunice's as she stopped rocking. "You were a good friend to him, Eunice."

"I just wish I could've saved him. A few nights later, I went back to the cemetery and performed a banishing ritual. It wasn't easy and the demon nearly managed to get to me, but I was able to push it back. I just wasn't able to kill it, even though it was weakened."

"How come you couldn't kill it?"

"Hoodoo is a spiritual religion and, believe it or not, it's infused throughout with Christianity, using a lot of the same psalms and prayers, but demons aren't really our department, so to speak. That's more a Catholic thing. From what I could gather, a silver knife blessed by a priest could possibly kill it, but I don't know for sure."

"You didn't try?"

"Sweetie, not a lot of Catholic priests would be willing to bless a silver knife for a black woman to kill a demon in the 1960s."

Good point.

Eunice continued, "The only thing I could do was sit in that cemetery and make sure that beast never got strong enough to prey on them kids again. I watched every night while the ghosts of those poor souls flocked to that playground. It made me happy, but also sad. I knew then that my purpose would be to keep these kids safe by keeping that demon from ever returning. I had children of my own, but they was practically grown at that point. I knew that I couldn't put this burden on them, so I made preparations that I could continue to stand guard even after my mortal body died. But I never let my own children participate in Hoodoo. That's why I found something that would keep me tied to this place long after my death."

"The tether?"

"It took a lot of research into the most obscure parts of Hoodoo to accomplish it – nothing you kids is going to find searching on your computers – but I managed to. I wrote them all down in what I called my recipe book which I hid far away, so Martin and Ethel never felt compelled to get into this fight. There's just too much that could go wrong."

"Why didn't you just burn it?"

"Because I wasn't one hundred percent sure that we wouldn't need it again someday. I just didn't want my kin involved if I could avoid it."

"Can the recipe book help us now?"

Eunice nodded. "If you can recreate the banishing spell, I believe you can weaken Lamia enough to kill it. But you're gon' need some help from the Christian side of things as well. Get a silver knife and have it blessed by a priest. That can kill it if you can weaken it. But getting differing faiths to work together ain't always the easiest."

No, but Kayla had the second part covered. They just needed the book.

"Where is your recipe book?"

"The quarry," Eunice said. "The leftmost cave, forty-four paces in just under the formation of three large rocks jutting out the wall. Dig down about two feet and you'll find it in a small burlap sack. The spell is titled

'Banishment.' But you also got another problem."

Of course they did.

"What?" Kayla asked hesitantly.

"From what Abel did to my daughter, you must know he's become flesh and blood again, right?"

"Yes. How?"

"As the demon feeds, it gets stronger. It can exercise its power. It can imbue strength and abilities into its servants. He's got flesh and blood again, but he's more than a man. Think about what he did to my Ethel." Her voice cracked on that one. "Please be careful."

Kayla squeezed Jasmine's hands, connecting with the spirit that currently occupied her body. "Thank you."

"I wish you well, Kayla. I truly do."

Suddenly the flame went out and the crypt was in total darkness once again.

This time there was no demon emerging from the darkness. The candle ignited itself once again and the light filled the enclosed space. It was back in the center of the room while Desiree, Jasmine and Ben all stood where she had last seen them.

Kayla was disoriented at first as she observed her surroundings. The rocking chair was once again broken and piled in the corner. She looked to Jasmine, who was standing there with her eyes closed, but seemed to be herself. Ben opened his eyes and said, "I don't think it worked."

The others followed suit, all wearing looks of varying disappointment. All except Kayla.

"Yes, it did," she said. "And I know what we have to do."

CHAPTER 30

"**A**re they all going to die?"

Kylie felt cold as she asked the question while watching her classmates play on the playground seemingly without a care in the world even though they all looked very sick.

"Yup," Emily said callously. "I have to stay strong and unfortunately, this body has run its course. Even though I'm stronger than I was before we got rid of that meddlesome bitch, I'm not able to maintain without feeding more often."

"Why kids?" Kylie asked.

"What's your favorite food?"

That was a weird question. "Kids are your favorite food?"

"You took health class, right? Didn't they teach you the difference between eating an apple and a candy bar? The apple will sustain you and make you feel good. Give you energy and make your body healthy overall. The candy bar, on the other hand, may satisfy a craving or give you a quick boost of energy, but it's not good for your overall health."

"So, kids are your apples?"

"How biblical of you!" Emily said with a laugh. "But yes.

Something like that."

"Why me?" Kylie asked again. "Why do you need me?"

Emily walked over to one of the swings and Kylie followed. Trina had taken her spot on the one Emily usually favored, so Emily shoved her off when she got there. The zombified young lady hit the ground hard, but didn't protest. She simply got up, dusted herself off and made her way over to the slide as Emily took her place on the swing. As she swung, she addressed Kylie's question.

"I came to this land following the scent. There were so many young souls to feed on. More so than a lot of places. But, when your food source is children who have died, there's only a finite amount out there, so you have to ration. But when I ration, I'm not as strong as I could be. My normal form is not meant for this world. Sure, I can inhabit the earthly plane in small bursts but, to really stay, I need a human host, but it has to be one I've drained enough to get inside. Unless they let me in willingly, but there's not many like that. Kids are so fucking weak. Most of them, that is."

"I still don't get it," Kylie said, her frustration evident.

"Emily was strong. When the Spanish flu was wreaking havoc on this town, somehow she managed to avoid getting sick. Even though she was exposed countless times. I don't know why, but something in her gave her the ability to fight off the sickness. It made her strong. It made her the perfect host."

It was starting to come together, but there was something Kylie still didn't get.

"If she was so strong, how did you take her over?"

"She let me."

"Why would she do that?"

Emily's grin widened to that unnatural width again.

255

"She was strong, but those she loved weren't. Her mom and her older brother got very sick with the flu. I told her that if she let me in, I would help them. Dumb little bitch believed me. I actually felt her soul die inside of me when the virus took her family. Even her dad couldn't sustain the grief and died of a broken heart only a few months later."

Kylie thought back to when Emily had told her that her family died in the *pandemic*. She had assumed that she meant Covid, but now she understood that she had chosen her words carefully to hide the truth.

"But I'm not all bad. Honest," Emily said, taking one hand of the swing chain and placing it over her heart in mock sincerity. "If I had a body strong enough to sustain me, I wouldn't need to feed as much. Maybe not at all!"

Kylie didn't buy it but played along. "And that's me?"

"Yes!" she said excitedly. "It may have been Emily, but she wasn't quite strong enough. Then when that meddlesome woman kept me from my food supply for all those years, it made it a foregone conclusion that this body was on borrowed time. But I think you're even stronger."

"What makes you think that?"

"Because you survived cancer. You had something in your body that was dead set on killing you and you beat it. Not only that, but when I spread this plague across your town, you didn't get so much as a sniffle. You're the one, Kylie. You're the one that can stop all this."

"If I just let you in."

"Yup."

"I'm not stupid."

"Oh, I know you're not," Emily said as her voice turned deep and serpentine. "You're very smart. Smart enough to know that I'm going to kill every single kid in this town. And that's not going to be the end for them. Because I'm going to eat their souls once they're dead. Death will only be the beginning of their torment. And when I'm done feeding, their souls will be cast into the pit of hell because there will be nothing left to grant them entry to heaven." Emily jumped off the swing and held out her hand to Kylie. "But you can save them all. The only thing you have to do is take my hand."

Kylie had never been so scared in her life. She knew Emily wasn't telling her the whole truth, but she also knew the part about killing all these other kids was true. But, still, she couldn't just let her in. Could she?

"No," she said defiantly, keeping her hands at her sides.

Emily didn't move. "Oh, Kylie," she said. "You really have no choice in this matter. I'm not killing you right now because I have more use for you alive. But just because I can't make you sick doesn't mean I can't take my true form and rip your head off. Then I'm going to kill all these kids anyway. And when your sister comes to visit your grave, I'll rip her fucking head off too."

Kylie swallowed hard. She knew this monster was telling the truth. There was only one way she'd have a chance to save her classmates and every other child in Huntsville. Maybe if she went along, it would buy Kayla enough time to find what she needed to stop her. Maybe this was like the *Avengers* movie where Dr. Strange willingly let Thanos win temporarily because he knew it was the only way to stop him for good. She couldn't let this thing kill anyone else.

Courage is being afraid and doing it anyway.

She felt the tears run down her cheek as she nodded and extended her hand toward the monster. Emily was ecstatic as she took it, her fingers having extended into scaly claws, her eyes back to their red, demonic state.

"Say it," she hissed. "Say you accept me."

"I accept you," she said.

With that, lightning streaked across the skies as dark clouds enveloped the moon, eliminating what little light there was. They opened and unleashed a torrent of rain along with deafening cracks of thunder as an intensifying wind blew through the trees.

Lamia had taken a new host.

CHAPTER 31

A few minutes before Kylie made her choice, Kayla and her friends left the Weeks family crypt. Kayla led and told them just to follow her and that she would explain later. As they made their way through the cemetery to the exit, Jasmine stopped suddenly and started to wobble on her feet. Fortunately, Ben was behind her and managed to catch her before she collapsed.

"Jasmine!" he shouted, both to ask if she was okay and to get the attention of Kayla and Desiree, who stopped and rushed back to gather around their fallen friend.

Jasmine shook it off and sat up on her own. "I don't know what happened. I just got light-headed for a second."

Kayla knew exactly what it was, but explanations of what she saw in the crypt would only slow things down, so she felt it was best saved for if and when they survived this ordeal.

"Are you okay?" she asked.

"Yeah," Jasmine said as she retrieved the half-empty water bottle from her bag and took a sip. "I just need a minute."

"Ben," Kayla said, "stay with her while Desiree and I go ahead."

"Where are you going?" he asked.

"We're going to the quarry. Leftmost tunnel. If she feels up to it, you can meet us there. If not, we'll be back once we have what we need."

Jasmine nodded to Ben and Kayla and Desiree ran off, leaving the other two behind.

The storm started just as they entered the quarry. There hadn't been rain in the forecast, but the skies opened up and immediately started drenching them as thunder boomed and lightning streaked across the sky.

"Well, that's fucking ominous," Desiree observed, her now familiar defense mechanism of humor on display.

"That's not natural," Kayla observed.

"Maybe it is," Desiree said. "Huntsville has had some pretty gnarly weather events. Back in 2011, we got hit with sixty-two tornadoes in less than twenty-four hours. Killed about two hundred and fifty people."

"Either way, something feels very wrong about this. Let's get the book and get the hell out of here."

Desiree grabbed her hand as they navigated their way down the slope, taking care not to slip as the rain soaked the terrain, making the descent that much more treacherous. They made it to the bottom and saw the three cave mouths ahead, but also saw a bigger problem.

The Caretaker emerged from the right-most tunnel, moving with purpose. Kayla pulled Desiree behind a cluster of rocks off to the side and the girls ducked down, hoping that the large man didn't see them. For the moment, it appeared he didn't, turning and entering the middle cave, disappearing into the darkness within.

"Let's move!" Kayla whispered as she pulled Desiree heading for the cave Eunice mentioned. She was scared to death that Abel would continue his pattern and exit the middle and go to the left, but they couldn't wait to find out. She needed that book now!

The girls ran, keeping as far away from the center as they could, terrified that Abel would emerge at any moment, but they made it to the left cave without incident, ducking inside and getting a respite from the torrential downpour outside. Another ear-splitting thunderbolt announced their entry as they both turned on their phones' flashlights to look around.

"Forty-four paces," Kayla instructed. "Then look for a formation of three rocks jutting out of the wall."

"Got it," Desiree acknowledged as they counted their steps until they had taken forty-four. While probably not exact, accounting for different heights and gaits, they did see a formation of three protruding rocks that looked like Ethel described.

"There!" Kayla pointed. "Come on!"

The girls hurried over and both looked at each other dumbfounded as they simultaneously realized they'd forgotten one very important detail.

"What the hell are we going to use to dig?"

"Fuck!" Kayla shouted, disgusted with herself that she hadn't thought of it. She crouched down and rubbed her hand along the dirt surface. It didn't seem too solid, kind of like regular garden-variety soil. She dug her fingers in and pulled out a handful of dirt. "Looks like we're using our hands."

Desiree joined her and immediately started digging frantically, neither of them verbalizing their fear that the man in the next cave might enter this one at any moment.

Kayla hit a particularly hard section about three-quarters of the way down. She needed something to break it up, so she looked around and found a decent-sized rock. She grabbed it and slammed it forcefully against the hardened soil, breaking it up and allowing them to continue digging. They had made it just past a foot when another crack of thunder sounded and a bolt of lightning lit up the sky. The illumination at the mouth of the cave revealed a silhouette. The silhouette of Abel Hargrave.

He was here.

Kayla was too busy digging, but the thunder had caught Desiree's attention and she saw the ominous figure flash at the cave mouth. "Kayla," she said, her voice shaky and not nearly as loud as she wanted it to be as fear paralyzed her body. Kayla continued to dig as Desiree reached back and tapped her arm. She looked up and Desiree turned to her. "It's The Caretaker," she said through trembling lips.

Kayla only saw darkness toward the front of the cave, but she heard the heavy footsteps approaching. She was about to raise her flashlight to see, but another streak of lightning did the work for her. The cave lit up and Abel Hargrave was close. Too close.

Kayla grabbed the rock she had used to break up the dirt and threw it as hard as she could, striking the man in the face, which as always was obscured beneath his hood. Although he'd passed right through her on their last encounter, the rock did strike home, confirming that the man had somehow become corporeal again. He staggered back and raised his hands to his face as he bellowed in pain.

That wouldn't buy her nearly enough time and Kayla was sure that the attack would only serve to piss him off, but she had no other choice but to keep digging. She manically scooped dirt out but hadn't reached the necessary depth when she felt Desiree grab her collar and pull her up.

"Kayla!" she screamed desperately, "We're out of time!"

"No!" Kayla shouted as she tried to resume her task, "We need that book!"

"We need to not be fucking dead!" Desiree shouted as she pulled Kayla away, just barely avoiding a swipe from Abel which drove the point home.

The girls ran toward the back of the cave, doing their best to keep their lights out in front of them. They had no idea how far back it went, or what hazards awaited them, but they had no other option. Abel was just walking, but somehow keeping pace; his ponderous footsteps would fade into the background only to pick up again without warning.

Kayla's heart sank when they hit the back wall of the cave. They scanned quickly with their flashlights only to find that they had nowhere else to go. They were trapped. Desiree put her arm around Kayla and pulled her close as they both trained their lights toward the direction from which they had come. For a moment, they didn't see nor hear their pursuer, but it was only a moment.

Abel Hargrave. The Caretaker. He stood before them, blocking their path to escape. It was over.

"I'm sorry," Kayla whispered to Desiree.

"No," Desiree said. "*I'm* sorry." She kissed her and said, "Save your sister."

Kayla didn't register, but screamed, "Desiree! No!" when the other girl lunged toward Abel and tried to knock him off balance, failing spectacularly as he barely budged. The large man reached down and closed a meaty hand around her throat and lifted her off the ground with inhuman strength. He pivoted and slammed her hard against the cave wall, knocking the wind out of her.

Kayla had the chance to run around him, to head back and dig the rest of the way to get the book for the opportunity to save Kylie and the rest of the children. She could have done that, but she couldn't let Desiree die. She searched the ground and found another medium-sized rock. Without taking too much time to consider her plan, she grabbed it and rushed The Caretaker but instead of going high, she went low. She slammed the rock into the large man's patella, causing him to buckle and drop to his knee with another wail of agony.

He hadn't released his grip on Desiree, so she took the rock and drove it into his elbow joint. It gave with the impact but somehow he held on to the girl's throat. Another lightning strike outside lit up the cavern enough for Kayla to see that Desiree's face was turning blue as the air escaped from her lungs.

She raised the rock, intending to hit his elbow again, but his free arm snaked out and grabbed Kayla's neck, the pressure sudden and startling as she lost control of her limbs and dropped the only weapon she had.

The Caretaker got back to his feet and slammed Kayla into the wall next to her rapidly fading friend. She tried to call to her, but the man's grip on her throat made speech impossible. It was as if he were taking revenge for his own inability to communicate. Kayla felt helpless as she watched Desiree losing consciousness while she felt her own lucidity fading. She knew they were going to die in this cave. If this was her deathbed, all she could do was make amends.

I'm sorry, Dad.

I'm sorry, Mom.

I'm sorry, Desiree.

I'm sorry, Kylie.

The thought of her sister both saddened and comforted her as she felt her vision blacken. It wouldn't be long now.

"Abel!"

The voice woke Kayla slightly, bringing her back from the precipice of darkness. It must have caught the big man's attention as well because, while he didn't release her, she did feel his grip loosen enough for her to suck in a little of the stale air of the cave and give her burning lungs something to work with.

"Let them girls go!" Kayla recognized the voice as Jasmine's. But the words weren't her friend's. They belonged to Eunice Weeks.

Kayla felt the grip release and she fell to the ground along with Desiree. The very first thing she did after the shock of the impact was to reach over and try to rouse the other girl. She was unconscious, but Kayla was relieved to feel her chest rise and fall when she placed her hand over it. She was alive. They could assess injuries if they got out of here but, for now, that was enough.

She struggled to her feet and another thunder and lightning combo showed Jasmine standing in front of them, Ben right behind her, looking confused as all hell. Jasmine was holding the white candle they had used in the ritual, casting enough light in the cave for her to see what was happening.

"Jazz," he said, "what the hell are you doing?"

Eunice, in Jasmine's body, turned and shoved him back with surprising strength, causing the tall boy to stumble back on his butt.

"Don't have time for your sass, boy," she told him. "Just stand back and let me handle this." She turned her focus to Abel, who surveyed her curiously. "Now, Abel. I know I don't look like you remember, but you know me."

Kayla felt that she should also heed Eunice's demand that she handle this, so she sat back next to Desiree and hugged the unconscious girl close to her as she watched the scene unfold.

Abel took a step toward Eunice. Then another. She held her ground, not showing any intimidation as the large man approached. He took two more steps until he was right in front of her, towering over the girl's slight frame.

"Kayla," Eunice said without taking her eyes off Abel. "Get Desiree and Ben out of here and get that book. Me and Abel gon' have a chat."

"Jas— I mean, Eunice—"

"Do as I say, girl. This ain't a negotiation."

Kayla knew it wasn't. "Ben!" she called as she slung Desiree's limp arm over her shoulder. "Help me!"

Poor Ben was mystified by all that was happening around him and he certainly didn't want to leave his girlfriend with the menacing figure that was The Caretaker, but he did as Kayla said and helped her lift Desiree off the ground. When he had her as well, Kayla said, "Take her." He again complied and scooped her in his arms as the trio edged around Abel and Eunice.

"Get her out of here," Kayla instructed as they ran toward the exit.

"What are you doing?" Ben asked.

"Just get her out! I'll meet you in a minute."

"Okay," Ben said as he carried Desiree out.

Kayla took a detour back to the hole and started digging with everything she had. She could feel the dirt packing under her fingernails, feeling as if it threatened to pull them up and off the skin. But she kept going until finally she felt a rough burlap material in the ground. She brushed off more dirt to allow her to pull the small sack out of the ground. Quickly undoing the string, she extricated a small leather-bound book with the word *Recipes* written across the front.

"I got it!" she called back, wanting to let Eunice know she'd been successful but she didn't wait for a response as she got to her feet and sprinted for the front of the cave, knowing she needed to move quick. She saw the exit. She saw Ben crouching over Desiree, who he had laid on the ground. Her lungs burned as she ran, having been strained from being choked just a few minutes earlier, but she managed to escape the cave just in time.

No sooner did she exit than a lightning bolt, accompanied by the loudest roar of thunder yet, struck the wall above the cave mouth she had just exited. Large cracks spider-webbed their way across the exterior before an avalanche of gravel collapsed in front of the entrance, piling up until the cave mouth was entirely blocked, trapping Abel and Eunice inside.

Trapping Jasmine inside.

"No!" Ben screamed as the realization hit him. He ran

to the collapsed entrance and started trying to pull rocks away, but to no avail. They were wedged in and not budging. He slammed his fists into them, breaking the skin and causing his knuckles to bleed as he collapsed in front of his girlfriend's prison.

Desiree was starting to come to and sat up groggily, rubbing her bruised neck. Kayla sat next to her, relieved that she had regained consciousness and that she had retrieved the book. But watching Ben's anguish at losing his brother and now maybe Jasmine too, made this feel like a Pyrrhic victory.

She rose and went over to Ben, placing a hand on his shoulder. "We'll call for help when we get to shelter. But right now, we gotta get out of here."

He had fallen silent, his despair having got the better of him. Desiree was more with it now and had joined the two of them. She didn't ask about what had happened while she was out, she just took Kayla's lead as they both hooked him under his arms and helped him up. Kayla grabbed his face and made him look at her.

"I promise. We will get her out."

She felt bad because she wasn't actually sure how they could do that, but the priority was to stop Lamia.

Judging by the rage of the storm around them, they didn't have much time.

CHAPTER 32

Bruised and battered, the former quartet, now a trio, ducked through the storm and back into Kayla's father's Tesla. Ben was shell-shocked, Desiree was beaten and Kayla was resolved as they prepared to engage in what they hoped was the final battle.

Kayla started the car and immediately the radar went haywire. Markers were all around them, indicating the presence of people, but a glance out the window revealed that there were none. The markers were moving away from their current position. Kayla suspected it was picking up the spirits of the children of Huntsville, fleeing from something, no doubt the demon Lamia.

Kayla pulled out her phone to call the police, but cursed when she saw there was no service. Even the SOS function created for just these types of situations wasn't working. She was going to ask Desiree or Ben to try, but they were also both angry at the failures of their respective phones. "We'll try the landline at the deli," Desiree assured Ben.

Before she started driving, Kayla flipped through Eunice's recipe book, looking desperately for the banishing spell. She found it after some examination. It was the last entry in the book. She quickly scanned the list of ingredients. They needed a white candle. The one they had used was now trapped in the cavern with Jasmine and Abel, but she knew where she could get another. That was already the destination they were heading anyway. They needed salt, holy water, an herb—the book said they could use rue, sage or rosemary—an obsidian stone and protection oil, which could be made by mixing olive oil, incense and rosemary.

She also needed a silver knife to be blessed.

"This is a lot of shit," Desiree said, her voice hoarse and scratchy. "Where are we going to get all of it?"

"You got your keys to the deli?"

"Yeah?" Desiree said, not sure where she was going with it.

"We can take care of the rosemary, olive oil and salt there." She paused, "And the knife."

"Daddy's fancy silverware set?"

Big Al had an old-style silverware set encased in a shadow box on display in the deli, including four big fancy-looking steak knives. They had been gifted to him by some family member who was descended from Italian royalty or something like that.

"Sorry, Des."

"He's going to be pissed, but fuck it. I think this is more important."

"That's the spirit," Kayla said as she shifted into drive while cursing herself for falling into the same disarming humor trap as Desiree.

She hit the accelerator and drove through the storm toward town.

To their dismay, the phone line at the deli was also inoperable. With no way to currently send help for Jasmine, the group quickly gathered the supplies and returned to the car. "Where to now?" Ben asked impatiently as he looked over the blades that the group had procured from the deli while Desiree was busy mixing the salt, olive oil, and a portion of the leftover incense with the rosemary in a plastic soup container they had also absconded with. Kayla was worried about the solubility of the salt in the rain, but she hoped that, with it being coated on the rosemary with the oil to bind it in, it would last long enough to serve their purpose. Not that they had any other choice.

"Church," Kayla said as she gunned it down the street. Rain pelted the windshield to the point where the wipers couldn't keep up. Thunder and lightning crashed through the sky at regular intervals and Kayla could barely see the road in front of her. She hoped no one else was crazy enough to be out in this storm and, if they were, the radar would alert them in time.

It took a little longer than usual, but they made it to the church. They rushed up the steps, taking care not to slip and fall, and were relieved to find it unlocked, but it was also unoccupied. Kayla ran toward the altar, shouting instructions to her friends.

"Desiree, fill the bottle with holy water from that font over there! Ben, grab one of those white candles from the altar!"

As she did, she ran toward a small door off to the side, hoping it led to the priest's quarters. "Father Lee!" she shouted as she ran. "We need your help!"

Before she could get to the door, it opened on its own and Father Lee stepped into the vestibule.

"Kayla?" he asked. "What's going on here?"

She ran up to him and put her arm on his shoulder while she caught her breath.

"Father," she said. "I really don't have time to explain, but we need your help."

"With what?"

Kayla reached into her bag and pulled out the knife set, not having considered that the priest may consider it a threat; he took a startled step back. "I need you to bless these knives."

"Kayla! This is really unusual."

"Look outside, Father," she said. "There was no rain in the forecast today and suddenly we're in the midst of the storm of the century. Do you think that's natural?"

The priest hesitated, knowing damn well it wasn't. "What are you trying to say?"

"There is a demonic force at work in this town. I know you can feel it."

"Perhaps, but—"

She cut him off just as she had on the first day they had moved to Huntsville. "Faith? Right, Father?"

With everything set, Father Lee stood behind the altar in his vestments with three silver knives from Desiree's father's deli laid out in front of him. He made the sign of the cross and prompted the small congregation to do the same, after which he instructed them how to respond.

"The Lord be with you," the priest said.

"And with your spirit."

He opened his Bible and quickly found the passage he wanted, reciting it aloud, "Finally, be strong in the Lord and in the strength of his might. Put on the whole armor of God, that you may be able to stand against the schemes of the devil. For we do not wrestle against flesh and blood, but against the rulers, against the authorities, against the cosmic powers over this present darkness, against the spiritual forces of evil in the heavenly places. Therefore, take up the whole armor of God, that you may be able to withstand in the evil day, and having done all, to stand firm. Stand therefore, having fastened on the belt of truth, and having put on the breastplate of righteousness, and, as shoes for your feet, having put on the readiness given by the gospel of peace. In all circumstances take up the shield of faith, with which you can extinguish all the flaming darts of the evil one; and take the helmet of salvation, and the sword of the Spirit, which is the word of God, praying at all times in the Spirit, with all prayer and supplication. To that end keep alert with all perseverance, making supplication for all the saints."

Does that make us the saints? Kayla wondered. None of them would fit the classic definition of saintly, but it took all kinds. And, if they succeeded, they were about to pull off a miracle.

The priest continued the ceremony, uncorking a small

273

vial of holy water, probably the same one he had used to bless Kylie earlier that day. Before doing anything with it, he recited another prayer: "Almighty God, grant that this blade, your creation, may be sanctified by your grace. May it serve as a protection against the forces of evil and be a sign of your power and presence. May all who use it with faith and righteousness be safeguarded and victorious over the powers of darkness. Through Christ our Lord. Amen."

"Amen," the trio parroted.

With that, he sprinkled the knives with holy water and made the sign of the cross over each one. When he was done, he returned the vial to his pocket and imparted the final blessing.

"May the blessing of Almighty God, the Father, the Son, and the Holy Spirit, descend upon you and remain with you forever. Amen."

Again, the three friends repeated, "Amen."

Kayla gathered up the knives and handed them to Ben.

"Thank you, Father," she said.

"Kayla," the priest replied. "There's no guarantee that this will work."

"I know that," she acknowledged. "But right now, it's all we have to go on. I have to have faith that it'll work."

The priest gave her a tight-lipped smile and nodded his head, patting her on the shoulder. "I wish you well, Kayla," he said. "God be with you."

Twenty minutes later, as the storm continued to rage, they pulled up to the cemetery. Before they exited, Desiree realized something. "Wait!" she said. "We don't have any obsidian! How are we going to do this if we're missing an ingredient?"

Kayla pushed the button to pop the trunk.

"I got that covered, but it's going to be a little distasteful."

Desiree and Ben were confused as they watched Kayla stomp through the rain around the side of the car and retrieve a tire iron. They followed her through the cemetery gates as she scanned the rows of gravestones until they found one that stood out from the rest. While most were stone gray, this one was black. Obsidian. Kayla held out the tire iron to Ben.

"You want to do the honors? We need four pieces."

Ben took the object, not feeling great about it, but also realizing they didn't really have any other choice. Kayla watched as he used it to strike the tombstone. It stayed mostly intact save for a small chip that fell from the top corner. Ben's rage at everything he had been through propelled him forward as he struck the stone again and again until finally pieces started to break off. He finally stopped when he had four decent-sized chunks to serve as stones for the ritual.

They gathered them up and returned to the car to retrieve the rest of the supplies. As they did, Desiree asked the obvious question.

"Isn't the rain going to wash all this away? Will this even work?"

"We don't have a choice, Des. It's all we got."

They reentered the vehicle to take stock of everything. Just as they were about to confirm and head out to lay their trap, Kayla's phone went off, apparently working again. She looked at the screen and saw that it was her mother. She considered not answering but, being that it was getting late, she thought she'd better take the call. She was probably calling to check and see if she was okay in the storm. No sense in having her worry.

Gretchen's voice was distorted and faded in and out, but Kayla could still pick up the panic in her voice when she answered.

"Kayla! Are you okay? Is Kylie with you by any chance?"

Kayla's whole body tensed and her blood froze.

"No, she's not with me. She's not in her room?"

Gretchen sounded like she was crying now. "No! I can't find her anywhere! We've checked the whole house three times! Do you have any idea where she could be?"

I know exactly where she is, she thought but didn't say. "I'll find her, Mom. I promise."

"Do you know where?"

"I have an idea, but I'm not sure. You and Dad just stay there in case she comes back. I'll find her."

"Oh, Kayla, please be care—."

The phone cut out before Kayla could say, "I will." She looked at the lack of bars on her screen. Again, the SOS function was useless. It was as if the demon had allowed that one call to go through, just to taunt them.

She hung up and looked at Desiree. She and Ben were both trying their own phones again to no avail. More than that, the situation had just gotten infinitely more complicated.

"It has my sister."

CHAPTER 33

Kayla approached the playground with Desiree and Ben by her side. She wasn't sure how they could do this now. Not only had the storm not slowed, making it impossible to light a candle out in the open but, if Lamia had her sister, it may not be as easy as just stabbing it. Not until she knew Kylie was safe.

When they stepped into the playground, they saw it was empty. There was no sign of any type of presence—human, ghostly or demonic. Everything was still outside of the storm raging around them.

Kayla looked toward the slide and saw that there was an area underneath where they could crawl for cover. That was their only option to light the candle. They had discussed their plan in the car, so they were ready. They poured the mixture of the salt, rosemary, incense and olive oil around the entirety of the perimeter, leaving a small portion for the next part. The rain soaked them immediately, but there was no other choice. They had to just hope that enough would remain to do the trick.

Once they met back up in the middle, Kayla poured the rest of the protection mixture over her fingers and quickly used her thumb to spread it on each of their foreheads and hands. "Please spirits, protect us from evil," she said as she did.

Next, they ducked under the slide to allow them to do the next part with as much shelter from the rain as they could get. Kayla took the rest of the rosemary and combined it with remaining incense in a glass jar they had "borrowed" from the deli. They had used the knives to poke holes in the lid as if they were about to catch fireflies, but instead, she took a lighter from Ben and ignited the contents, causing smoke to rise and pour out of the holes when she replaced the lid.

While she did this, Ben and Desiree placed the four chunks of obsidian from the tombstone at the four corners of the area in the rapidly moistening ring of salt and rosemary. With her makeshift smoke bomb, Kayla exited her sanctuary from under the slide and started waving it around. As she did, a familiar voice mocked her from behind.

"You all look ridiculous right now."

She turned and her stomach dropped as she saw Kylie on the swing set, swaying back and forth as if she didn't have a care in the world. Even though it looked like her sister, the thing had glowing red eyes with serpentine slits. Its fingers were gnarled into reptilian claws that twisted around the swing, and her skin was cracked, revealing leathery scales underneath.

"Where's my sister?" Kayla demanded.

"She's in here. With me," the thing said. "She's my favorite playmate."

Desiree and Ben joined Kayla and looked on in horror at the creature that was mimicking Kylie's appearance.

"Let her go, you fucking bitch!" Kayla bellowed.

The Kylie-thing twisted its mouth into an exaggerated O shape, revealing the curved fangs jutting from her upper gums.

"Such intensity!" the thing mocked. "But I'm going to have to say no."

Kayla couldn't worry about the candle right now. She went into the ritual and had to hope it would work. She recited the psalm as detailed in the recipe book.

"He who dwells in the shelter of the most high will abide in the shadow of the almighty." The demon laughed, a deep, chortling mockery of her efforts. "I will say to the Lord, 'My refuge and my fortress, my God in whom I trust.'"

"Yes! Trust him all the way to your grave, you stupid girl!"

Undeterred, Kayla continued, "By the power of the most high and in the name of all that is holy, I command you, Lamia, to leave this place. You are not welcome here. Be gone and never return!"

The demon continued its derision. "If it's all the same to you, I think I'll stay."

Kayla didn't know what to do. The spell wasn't going to work. They had failed. She turned to Desiree and they looked at each other in desperation, neither knowing what to do. As they did, they heard Ben say, "I'm sorry, Kayla. You had your chance. Now I have to end it."

They turned to see Ben brandishing his knife, starting toward the thing that looked like Kylie Macklin. Desiree reached out and grabbed his arm.

"Ben, no! We don't know if it'll kill Kylie too!"

He wrenched his arm free.

"I'm sorry, but that thing's gotta die. We can't fuck around with it anymore."

With that, he charged the demon. It never stopped laughing as he approached, his knife held high. Kayla and Desiree ran after him, but he was too fast and too

279

dead set on stabbing the thing. The demon swung back and when it propelled itself forward, it released the chain it held in its right hand and flicked its wrist to the right. Even though she didn't make contact with Ben, the motion took him off his feet and sent him careening clear across the playground, sending him tumbling over the slide. He hit the ground hard, the impact knocking him senseless.

"Whoops!" the demon said chuckling in amusement.

Kayla felt the defeat sink in. Not only couldn't they release Kylie, but they weren't going to be able to kill it outright either.

"Why are you doing this?" Kayla asked.

"It's just what I do," the creature hissed. "You can walk away, you know. I don't need you. I've already got what I want."

"Why her? Why Kylie?"

"I needed a strong host and your sister is one of the strongest children I've ever smelled. I don't think your family truly appreciates just how special she is. Not like I do. That's why she was so willing to let me have her."

"Take me instead!"

That comment made the demon let out its hardest laugh yet.

"Kayla, Kayla, Kayla," it said. "You're just a weak sack of flesh. You have nothing to offer me." It suddenly turned very serious. All humor in its demeanor disappeared as it stopped swinging, but didn't dismount yet. "Now listen to me carefully. This is your last chance to walk away. Go, live out the rest of your useless fucking life and leave me be. Do that and I won't flay the flesh from your bones."

Kayla hung her head as she thought about what she told Kylie about courage.

Be afraid but do it anyway.

She raised her head back up and stared down the demon that wore her sister's body and pulled the knife from her bag, letting it fall to the ground. She turned to Desiree, who gave her a look. It told Kayla that even though they had cheated death once tonight in the cave, they wouldn't be so lucky this time. Seemingly resigned to her fate, Desiree drew her own blade and stepped up next to Kayla. She reached out and grabbed her hand, giving it a squeeze before they rushed toward the instrument of their death.

Lamia hopped off the swing and shook its head. "You fucking humans and your drama." She opened her mouth wide, displaying her fangs, and her claws extended further, each one looking like it could slice through just about anything. "Don't say I didn't give you a chance to live."

The demon roared and the girls screamed, but it wasn't a shout of fear. It was a war cry. The combatants rushed toward each other, but something unexpected happened.

Lamia made it only a few feet before it collapsed into the mud underfoot. Kayla and Desiree managed to pull back, unsure of what just happened. They watched as the creature struggled to get up, collapsing back down as if it were trapped. The girls exchanged glances, unsure of what had felled their opponent. Sensing someone behind her, Kayla turned and was nearly floored by what she saw.

Jasmine, or more accurately, Eunice Weeks, was walking toward them, the white candle in hand. Towering above her was Abel Hargrave. He had removed his raincoat and had it draped over her, using it as a makeshift umbrella to keep the candle lit. Seeing his face for the first time, Kayla saw a normal, albeit bigger-than-usual, man. His eyes displayed an innocence that she wouldn't have thought possible recollecting the way he snatched up the ghost that night in the cemetery or, worse, the massacre at Ethel's. The way he held that coat over Eunice, making sure to stay close, showed the love that he held for her. Kayla didn't know what she had done to bring him back, or how they got out of the cave for that matter, but she was damn glad to see them.

"You!" the demon hissed incensed. "How?"

"You ain't the only one with powers, you foul bitch!" Eunice said. "But I got friends too. Something y'all can't say for yourself."

"I'll kill you!" Lamia bellowed.

"Not today." She walked over to the slide, Abel by her side the entire way, until she could duck under to keep the candle lit. She placed it in a dry spot and found a broken piece of tree branch which she plunged into the ground around it. After that, she instructed Abel to lay his coat over the makeshift spikes to keep the wind and rain from extinguishing the candle. It wouldn't protect it for long, but it would do for now.

With the final piece of the ritual in place, Eunice emerged from under the slide and made her way toward the downed monster. She circled it along with Kayla and Desiree. Ben, having been able to get back up, but still shaky, limped over when he saw Jasmine was okay. They formed their own circle around the thing that looked like Kylie Macklin as it tried manically to get up or at least lash out to get them.

"Kayla," Eunice said. "You need to know what's about to happen ain't gonna look pleasant. But you gon' have to trust me. We've come this far. We can't stop now. Do you understand?"

She didn't understand, but she knew she had to trust her. There was no other way she could see. This was it.

Eunice turned to Abel and stroked his arm before taking his mammoth hand in her dainty one.

"Abel, honey," she said. "It's time."

Abel nodded and, without hesitation, grabbed the demon girl by its head and pulled it back. It took everything Kayla had not to try to stop it. The thing was an evil monster and, even though Kayla knew it was an evil monster, it still retained portions of her sister's appearance as well. Her sister who she prayed was still in there somewhere. She felt sick as she watched Abel reach his hand into the demon's gaping mouth and plunge it down its throat.

She screamed, not knowing how Kylie could possibly survive this, but she stood back, letting the bizarre events in front of her unfold. An ear-shattering screech emanated from Kylie's expanded mouth, but it didn't come from her. It came from the monstrous snake demon that Abel extracted from her sister's body. Its upper half was a humanoid form, but its lower half was that of a snake, just as the writings had detailed. When its tail, the last part of it, exited Kylie's mouth, she collapsed to the ground, no longer containing any part of the demon. Somehow, despite the massive trauma Kylie's body had experienced a moment ago, it now looked somehow intact. Kayla didn't know how that was possible.

With Kylie now free of the demon, Kayla rushed over and picked her up off the ground, getting her even further away as Abel slammed the writhing creature hard into the dirt like a professional wrestler. The beast wailed in agony and defeat, bested by a bunch of filthy humans.

Like she had with Desiree in the cave, Kayla put her head to Kylie's chest and felt immeasurable relief when she heard her breathing. Even more so when she coughed. She was alive. Kayla held her sister tight as the group watched the demon flail. It looked up at her with the same hideous face she had seen in the crypt the night this all started.

"This isn't over," the demon hissed. "I'm going to kill you all."

"No, you're not," Kayla said as she hugged her sister close. "You're going back to hell where you belong." She looked to Ben and gave him the nod.

Ben took a step forward, knife drawn, and grabbed the thing's stringy, matted hair, yanking its head back so he could look it in its eyes.

"This is for Drew," he said as he plunged the blade directly into its chest.

Another inhuman scream pierced the night, louder than any of the thunderclaps they had heard yet, as viscous yellow blood seeped out of the wound and over the handle. The creature lurched back and fell on its back, writhing around as it gripped the handle, trying in vain to extricate the knife from its body.

Suddenly, an eruption of flame burst from its chest, quickly enveloping the demon's entire body as if it was a piece of paper thrown into a fireplace. Its body quickly immolated. The ashes held their form for a few seconds before the entire frame collapsed like a house of cards, the rain and wind carrying the remnants away into the night.

The demon Lamia was dead.

Kayla felt her sister stir. Kylie lifted her head off of Kayla's shoulder and regarded her with groggy eyes.

"Is that really you, Kayla?"

Kayla pulled her in tight for another hug. "Yes! It's me! It's over!"

"Did you... kill it?"

"We killed it," she said as she watched her friends gather around. "We did it together."

She felt Kylie squeeze her tight as her little body started to convulse with sobs. "Thank you," she said. "I knew you'd save me. You're *my* hero."

The words broke Kayla and the sisters cried together. "I love you, Kylie."

"I love you too, Kayla."

A lightning bolt shot across the sky, reminding the group that, while they had just defeated the monster, they were now in a different kind of danger. The wind was picking up again, getting stronger with each gust.

"The demon's dead!" Desiree shouted. "If it brought the storm, why hasn't it stopped?

"A storm this fucking big doesn't look like it's going to just disappear in a minute! It doesn't look like it's going to let up!"

"We need to get inside," Ben said. "It's getting bad out here."

Kayla concurred but, as they went to leave, she saw Abel and Eunice out of the corner of her eye.

"Wait," she said as she put Kylie down.

The group turned their attention to the old friends, one a spirit, the other channeled into the body of her great-granddaughter. Abel was kneeling on the ground but, even then, was still almost the same height as Jasmine/Eunice. She had her hand on his cheek, gently stroking it.

"Abel, honey," she said. "You done good."

The simple man's eyes lit up like those of a puppy who had just been called a good boy. It broke Kayla's heart because he had truly been an innocent pawn in all of this. She saw his tears flowing as he held his old friend's hand against his cheek.

"You know it's time to go now, though, right?"

The man shut his eyes tight, fighting to keep from breaking down as he nodded his acknowledgment.

"But you gon' be somewhere where you'll always have friends. You ain't never gon' be alone again."

Abel Hargrave broke into full sobs, his large chest heaving as he hugged Eunice close. She was crying now too.

"Goodbye, my sweet friend."

With those final words, Abel's skin turned gray and the texture turned gritty. He kept his eyes closed as he dissolved into dust, scattering across the ground and into Eunice's clothing.

When Abel was gone, Jasmine held her hands out in confusion and asked, "What the hell is all this over me?" she said confused.

"Jazz?" Desiree asked.

"What the hell is going on?"

Ben ran up and hugged her tight before planting a kiss on her lips. "We'll tell you later. Right now, we gotta get the hell out of here!"

CHAPTER 34

K ayla hit the curb as she turned into her parents'
driveway, almost all visibility gone at this point. She
killed the engine and they all exited the car and made a
mad dash for the front door.

Gretchen and Roger jumped up from the couch when
they saw their daughters and their friends come bursting
into the house.

"Kylie! Oh, my God!" Gretchen exclaimed as she ran
over and scooped her youngest daughter into her arms.
Kayla thought briefly how that would have bothered
her only a few short weeks ago, but Gretchen almost
immediately pulled Kayla in too, something she wouldn't
have done then. Roger came over and embraced all the
women in his life as relief washed over the Macklin
family.

Suddenly there was a loud bang outside as the sky lit
up before the house went dark as it lost power.

Roger rushed over to the window and looked outside.
"Looks like the transformer down the street blew," he
said. "Come on, we should head to the basement."

The Macklins, Desiree, Jasmine and Ben all sat around the finished basement while the storm raged outside. There was a good deal of light from the candles and the flashlights they had set up. Service had returned to the phones and, though the calls were spotty, Kayla's friends were able to contact their families to let them know they were safe.

Kylie had explained she'd seen a stray dog looking scared in the back yard and she had chased him into the woods, but got lost when the storm started. She said she came across the playground and had taken shelter under the slide, not knowing what else to do as she didn't want to chance trying to make it home. She credited Kayla with finding her. Kayla didn't think her parents had bought it, but they didn't argue in their relief to have their daughters home.

Jasmine explained away her dirty clothes by saying she fell in the mud. Desiree sat next to Kayla on the small couch, but they kept a bit of distance so as not to raise questions.

Dad asked anyway. "So, what's the deal? You two dating or something?"

"Dad!" Kayla exclaimed. "Inappropriate!"

"I'm a dad," Roger said. "Embarrassing you is my job."

Kayla looked at her mom, trying to dispel the idea, but Gretchen just gave her a wry smile. "Parents can be very observant, you know."

Considering they had no idea that they had just saved

a possessed Kylie from a child-eating demon that they had managed to kill, she questioned the validity of that statement, but she also understood that maybe her parents knew her a little better than she liked to admit.

She didn't give them a verbal answer, but she did reach over and scoot closer to Desiree, taking her hand in her own.

Kayla looked to her sister, who was sitting on the floor with her tablet. Mom had warned her that once the battery died, they'd have no way to charge it, but she didn't seem to care. She looked up at her big sister and smiled.

For the first time in a long time, the Macklin family and the town of Huntsville was at peace.

CHAPTER 35

The storm passed as all storms eventually do. There was some damage and more than a few power outages but overall, it didn't take the town long to get back to normal.

Over the next few days, all cases of the mystery virus that had plagued the town of Huntsville had stopped abruptly. There were no new cases and, within a few days, all the sick children had recovered. As a precaution, school was still out for the rest of the month but as they got to the middle of October, classes had resumed in person. Gretchen, of course, still had her concerns but she didn't protest when Kylie went back with the rest of the class.

Kylie was happy to see Jessie and Trina, but felt a great deal of sadness looking at Drew's empty chair. She threw some hints in there but it seemed like both girls had no recollection of showing up in her room that night nor anything at the playground. She was glad for that. No one should have to remember the terrible things that had happened that night.

Kayla had gone back to the quarry with Desiree, Ben and Jasmine. The left-hand cave was still collapsed. Jasmine had no idea how they had gotten out that night with Eunice having been in full control. They got their answer by venturing into the center cave. About two-thirds of the way in, the wall that had separated it from the adjacent cavern was collapsed, allowing free movement between. Whether it had collapsed from the storm or if somehow Abel had been able to break through would likely forever be a mystery.

They retrieved the broken pieces of the rocking chair and managed to crudely reassemble them one weekend in October. It looked like shit and it definitely wouldn't stand up to anyone sitting on it, but it was back together. They didn't know if by repairing it, they would enable Eunice to stay and watch over the kids again but with Lamia gone they weren't in danger anymore. At the very least, repairing it was the right thing to do.

They returned the chair to the crypt and added one last touch, draping Abel's rain slicker over the back of it. Even though the two friends had been separated by bigotry and death, Kayla hoped they would find their way to each other in the next life, wherever that was.

Kayla relinquished Eunice's recipe book to Jasmine, who had declined at first, with the rationale that Kayla had been a much more effective practitioner of Hoodoo than she, but Kayla insisted. She felt that Eunice's book belonged with the family.

To her surprise, Kayla found herself attending church semi-regularly. Not every week, mind you—that was a little much to ask—but she would go with her mother and Kylie. Heck, sometimes even Dad and Desiree went too. Father Lee had played a big role in defeating the demon and, although he never asked about it, he would sometimes give Kayla a knowing smile during a particularly relevant portion of the gospel.

Mom and Dad did better. Not great, but better. The blow-ups and tension were mostly gone, but Kayla was starting to understand that sometimes a marriage can lose something. There may still be love there and, with the right communication, they could still manage an effective partnership but, unfortunately, it seemed like the romantic aspects of her parents' relationship was gone. It made her want to try that much harder in her own relationship, which she was grateful was going well.

It was a little after ten p.m. on Halloween night when Kayla snuck into Kylie's room and woke her up. Her Scarlet Witch costume was crumpled in the corner and there were a few discarded candy wrappers on her dresser.

Kylie was groggy and confused to see Kayla in her room but she'd been roused from sleep enough by ghosts and demons to know that it certainly wasn't the worst-case scenario.

"Kayla?" she asked as she rubbed her eyes. "What are you doing?"

Kayla held her finger up to her lips, signaling her sister to be quiet.

"Come on," she whispered. "Get your shoes."

The girls hurried down the path to the cemetery, Kayla leading her younger sister by the hand. She was still confused.

"Kayla? Are you going to tell me what you're doing? Mom'll kill you if she finds out you brought me here at night. Probably both of us."

"Will you just trust me?" Kayla said with a grin. "We're almost there."

Kayla led her to the edge of the cemetery, just out of view of the playground, before she stopped and stood in front of Kylie, crouching down in front of her.

"Listen, I had to make sure of something before I brought you here."

Kylie regarded her with confusion. "What?"

"I know after everything you went through you weren't sure if we did any real good. I'll be honest, I didn't know either. But I came out here last night to see for myself. And now it's time for you to see it too. Come on."

She grabbed her hand and led Kylie around the corner. When she saw it, she felt as if she would break out into happy tears.

The playground was alive with activity. The swings were all moving back and forth and the sound of children laughing echoed through the night. The slide squeaked and dust kicked up as the spirits landed at the bottom. The kids, no longer having to fear the demon, were back and having fun. Kylie walked to the center of the playground and felt the spirits dancing around her. She was elated as she basked in their presence as glowing orbs floated through the air. Everything they had suffered and fought for hadn't been for nothing. They had saved the spirits of the children who called Maple Hill Park home.

"You did good, kiddo," Kayla said, putting her arm around her little sister.

"You too," Kylie said.

Kylie looked over to the swings and one of the spirits materialized. Drew Gatto swung back and forth and a big smile stretched his face when he noticed Kylie. He didn't speak, but he waved at her. She returned it and felt a single tear drop down her cheek.

"Someone familiar?" Kayla asked.

"Yeah," Kylie said wiping away the tear. "They'll always have a place to play."

"Thanks to you," Kayla said. They took in the scene for a few more minutes, not speaking as they watched the spirits find a happiness that may have eluded them in life. "You want to stay for a bit?"

Kylie could see them all now. Drew, the two other kids that died from other schools. And all the kids from the past. Off in the distance, she saw a rocking chair. In it sat Abel Hargrave. He wasn't wearing the raincoat, but it was draped over the back of the chair. A small smile stretched across his face and he looked at peace as he watched the children play.

"No," Kylie said with a smile, "let's go home."

EPILOGUE

K ayla watched as the movers loaded the living room furniture onto the back of the truck. They'd been working all morning and were mostly finished. It was almost time to leave the house on Cornerstone Circle.

She stepped back inside and took a look around at the mostly empty interior of the house that she had called home for the past two years. She thought back to the day they moved in. Mom and Dad arguing, Father Lee showing up out of nowhere and Kylie being caught in the middle of it all. She recalled the fight with her mother at the family playground and the awkward family dinner that followed. So much had happened since then that she didn't even feel like the same person.

Mom came down the stairs, carrying a box marked *Kylie's Room*. She placed it at the bottom of the stairs and looked at Kayla. "Did you get all your stuff out?"

"Yup," Kayla said. "Al drove the U-Haul we rented to the apartment with my furniture. I got everything else in my car." She'd saved up over the past few years and bought herself a used Ford Mustang. It had a ton of miles on it, but the previous owner had maintained it well and it drove without issue.

When the house went up for sale, she talked it over

with Desiree and they finally decided that after being in a relationship for the past two years and with them both being twenty-one, it was time to give living together a shot, so they signed a lease on an apartment in downtown Huntsville two weeks ago. Al was a big help in getting the furniture out and she was going to be meeting them over there as soon as everything was wrapped up here.

She just needed to talk to Kylie before she left.

"You good, Mom?" she asked.

Gretchen nodded. "I will be."

When Kayla arrived at the playground, she headed right to the swing set and sat, but didn't actually start swinging yet. She needed to have this conversation first.

"I know all this happened really fast, Kylie," she said to her little sister. "After all the shit we went through, this is not where I thought we'd end up. Well, I mean I always kinda figured me and Des would get a place together once we got serious." She paused. "Who am I kidding? We were pretty much serious from the start. Even without the near-death experience thing bonding us.

But I never really saw Mom and Dad getting divorced. Sure, I thought that before we moved out here. I'm sure you saw it too. But after everything that happened, I thought maybe they'd just kinda see it out. But after you got sick again, I guess it was a foregone conclusion."

Fuck, she thought as the tears started sooner than she expected. She didn't even try to fight them.

"I'm so sorry," she said. "I thought we beat it. But I guess that thing was in you long enough to take whatever it was that let you beat the cancer the first time. Even when they said it was back, I thought you'd beat it again."

She turned to the empty swing next to her.

"I'm so sorry you died, Kylie."

Kayla brought her hands up to her face as the sobs racked her body. She let it all out. The sorrow and the guilt. Deep down she knew it wasn't her fault, but she'd felt so goddamn helpless watching the cancer eat away at Kylie for a second time.

Just after Christmas that first year in Huntsville, Kylie had started experiencing stomach pains again. She went to the doctor and the tests confirmed the Macklin family's worst fears. Kylie's cancer had somehow returned. This time it was stage four. They started treatment and her sister again faced it down with bravery, but, unlike last time, it wasn't enough. The doctors told them it was terminal six months ago and two months after that, she went into hospice.

Two weeks later, she passed away with her family by her side. They opted for cremation rather than burying her in Maple Hill Cemetery. Mom struggled with the decision, cremation being frowned upon in the Catholic faith but, ultimately, she couldn't bear the thought of her daughter not being with her, so they moved forward. Most of her remains were kept in an urn, but the three surviving family members each got a necklace with a vial containing a portion of her ashes.

Kayla pulled the necklace from her shirt and ran her fingers along the small vial. She almost broke down again but managed to keep her composure.

"When you died, Mom and Dad really had no shot of staying together. The funny thing is they weren't as mean about it. They stopped being cruel to each other, but they couldn't stay together. I actually told them that they shouldn't feel obligated to keep trying for me. I love them both whether they're together or not. I think that gave them the okay to move on. They needed to. I need to."

She took the necklace off and held it out in front of her.

"You lost so much, Kylie. You lost your chance to be a kid. To go to school. To have friends. It's so unfair that it makes me angry." She took a breath to compose herself and stifle the rage that was building inside. "But I know you wouldn't want that.

I'm staying in town. So is Dad. Mom is moving back to Florida to be closer to grandma and grandpa. I told her I'd go visit. Me and Des got an apartment. I'm kinda nervous about living with someone other than you, Mom or Dad for the first time, but I'm excited too. I really love her. And, honestly, she liked you from the start, but she grew to think of you as a sister too. I hope you knew that."

Kayla's sadness hit her again as she remembered the times the three of them would hang out. Kayla and Desiree would let Kylie watch scary movies that their mother would never approve of. But, after facing down a real-life demon, *Candyman* wasn't that scary, no matter how creepy Tony Todd's voice was. They would eat popcorn and too much ice cream and laugh at scenes that would probably terrify the average ten-year-old.

Kayla shook the memory away. It was time to go, but she had one more thing to do.

"I know that there were times you thought that your

illness drove our family apart. But that's not true. You were the one that held us together. Without you, I think Mom and Dad would have split up long ago. You were so special, Kylie. And so very loved. But now it's time for us to move on. All of us.

I think you deserve a chance for the happiness that you didn't always get when you were alive," she said as she carefully unscrewed the vial in her necklace. She held it out to the side and let the ashes fall out onto the gravel under the swings. "You deserve to be with your friends."

Kayla screwed the top back on and tucked the necklace back into her shirt. She pushed herself back on the swing then scooted herself forward. She repeated the process, building momentum until she was swinging back and forth at a good pace.

She continued like this for a few minutes until she felt something to her left. She turned and saw the swing next to her starting to wobble. It stabilized after a second, but then started to move back and forth on its own, picking up the pace until it matched Kayla's. Soon they were in sync and Kayla smiled through her tears.

As the afternoon sun shone down on the Dead Children's Playground, the Macklin sisters played together one last time.

AFTERWORD

Thank you for reading The Dead Children's Playground! This has been very different from anything I've written to date, being lighter on the blood and gore and also my first time delving into a ghost story. Also, sorry about the Epilogue. That was always the way I felt this story needed to end and I didn't write it, nor can I reread it without tears in my eyes. If you're really mad about it, you can always pretend the book ended with Chapter 35.

That aside, now that you've experienced this first chilling chapter in my *American Horrors* series, I want to give you a little info about where I got the idea for the series and some background on the *real* Dead Children's Playground in Huntsville, Alabama.

Experience a Nation of Horrors

One day, while I was wasting time instead of writing, I was scrolling Facebook and saw an article titled something like, *The Scariest Urban Legend From Each State*. My immediate thought was, "Nice! I just got fifty book ideas!" I went through them and, like any list, they were hit and miss, but a lot of them were really cool. I may not follow that list exactly (I can't even find that original article), but it was a good starting point. I don't feel like all of them can sustain full-length novels, so I'm also thinking there may be some short story collections in the series too.

You'd think the obvious place to start would have been my home state of New Jersey. Not only do we have the infamous Jersey Devil, there's also a bunch of other stuff I could use—Annie's Road, the woman in white my dad said he saw while working the Turnpike when he was a state trooper, or the crazy old man we saw chopping something in a field when three of my best friends and I were driving lost in the woods in a broken-ass red Ford Escort ZX2 that would stall if someone farted too hard only to have the dude disappear into thin air after we made a U-turn to get the hell out of there.

That last one technically happened to us in Pennsylvania, but it is a one hundred percent true story. It's also one for another time.

So, anyway, yeah. After two books set in Jersey, I was ready for a change in locale. The one entry that I kept going back to was called The Dead Children's Playground in Huntsville, Alabama. The name itself elicited such a sense of dread and heavy sadness that it really stuck out to me. So, I dove into my research.

My intention with this series is to give you, the reader, some background on the actual urban legends and folklore that inspired these books as well as a bit of insight into the writing process and how I developed it into the story you just finished. Think of it as bonus content!

So, what's the actual story here?

Come Play at The Dead Children's Playground

A lot of my information came from a couple of articles. Keep in mind that this book was never intended to be a fully historically accurate detail of the playground, it's a fictional horror story inspired by the legend.

The main articles I used were:

- *The Legend of Alabama's Dead Children's Playground (Al.com)*

- *Dead Children's Playground, Huntsville, Alabama (Factschology.com)*

Most of my info came from the second article. Here's a brief summary of the true story:

Maple Hill Cemetery is the oldest and largest cemetery in the state of Alabama. It was originally founded in 1822 by a man named Leroy Pope and expanded from about two acres of land to over a hundred.

Between 1945 and 1955, the surrounding area was home to a limestone quarry. When they extracted the limestone, it created large pits which were perfect for hidden secrets (*like a hoodoo recipe book maybe?*).

As I looked more into the quarry, I also learned about a place called the *Three Caves*, which was a former limestone mine known as the *Hermitage Quarry*. Now, I'm not quite sure of the proximity of the caves to the cemetery and playground, but I probably took the most liberties in this story with the geography. For the purposes of Kayla and Kylie's tale, all three locales are in close proximity (although I leave enough ambiguity that I hope it doesn't take people who live in the area out of the narrative).

Both the *Al.com* and *Factschology* articles talk about the ghostly activity there at night—Orbs, swings moving on their own, dirt being kicked up at the bottom of the slides, a chill in the air and the sound of ghostly laughter. *Al.com* also mentioned the large number of children buried there who died in the 1918 Spanish Flu pandemic.

I recall another article that spoke of children being used to work in the mines, resulting in several accidents and deaths, but I can't seem to find it again and, honestly, this being a work of fiction, it's not terribly relevant whether or not it was true.

Reading further into the *Factschology* article, there was talk of a serial killer abducting children in the 1960s. This part I take with a grain of salt because I couldn't find anything anywhere else about this. The article says *Local legend has it that during the 1960s, a string of child abductions terrorized the city of Huntsville. With no ransom requests for any of the children, many believed the perpetrator was not just abducting, but also killing the children.*

It then goes on to say that a child's skull was found in the quarries along with more skeletal remains. Once the bodies were discovered, the abductions stopped, but the killer was never identified or apprehended.

So, that part may not be true, but never let the truth get in the way of a good story, right?

Another part of the *Factschology* article that struck some inspiration in me was a picture of a man standing behind a tree wearing a yellow rain slicker, his features obscured in darkness. It also talks of people reporting a ghostly figure of a man staring down at the playground.

Hence, Abel Hargrave a.k.a. The Caretaker was born.

There was another article, again one I can't locate, that mentions a crypt with an old rocking chair that people claimed moved on its own. I thought that was another cool touch, so I added the character of Eunice Weeks.

Lastly, I came across a couple of facts that I thought would make cool Easter Eggs. First, I learned that Huntsville is the birthplace of none other than David Howard Thornton, none other than Art the Clown from the *Terrifier* film series! That's why I gave him the little cameo in Chapter 1 with Kayla's shirt. Also, when I was researching which exits are off the highway to get to Huntsville, I saw one of them was *Wall/Triana* with Kristopher Triana being one of my all time favorite horror writers. I've seriously read almost everything he's written. When Kayla asks if Triana was where "that crazy cheerleader butchered all those people?" it was a direct reference to my favorite Triana novel *Full Brutal*. If you haven't read it, I highly recommend it, although be warned it is *not* for the squeamish!

Those are the facts as I could find them. There wasn't a lot as far as one specific incident or legend, just a bunch of disconnected stories around the playground. With as much info as I could gather, it was time to put it all together.

Crafting a Ghost Story

Once I started putting the pieces together, I realized that this was unlike anything I'd written before. I'd done werewolves, serial killers—alive and undead—and evil clowns, but this was the first time I'd done a genuine ghost story. My first step was to understand that I had to pull back some of my impulses when it came to blood and gore. It's just not that kind of story. Ethel's unfortunate exit was the exception, but I also felt it was an unexpected shock that really raised the stakes, giving her such a brutal death and adding an additional problem of Abel becoming corporeal putting our protagonists in even greater danger.

I also cut down on the profanity. I don't know if I'll ever write a book free of F-bombs, because that's how a lot of people talk and I always strive for authenticity when it comes to my characters because I think it's important to ground a genre as fantastical as horror into reality as much as possible.

If you ask me where I came up with the idea of two sisters as the protagonists, I honestly couldn't tell you. Sometime things just come to me and that's just how I saw them.

Kylie's battle with kidney cancer because of a rare genetic condition was a little more personal to me. My son James was diagnosed with hemihypertrophy, which is an enlargement of one half of the body that also makes a child prone to kidney and liver cancers, when he was six months old. Honestly, you wouldn't know to look at him, but my wife, being ever diligent, noticed something that no one else would have and we were able to get him into the monitoring protocol of blood work every three months until he was four and abdominal ultrasounds every three months until he was eight. Thankfully, he was cleared in 2019 without ever having developed any tumors or other complications.

But writing is often a game of scenarios and this scenario was what if parents didn't notice the slight enlargement and the worst-case scenario came to life? That had a domino effect that irrevocably impacted the

Macklin family.

I had my protagonist in the sisters and a villain in The Caretaker. I came up with some supporting characters in the form of Kayla's friends, including a potential love interest in Desiree. But I knew Abel wasn't going to end up as the primary antagonist. The problem with ghost stories is that ghosts can scare you, but they really can't hurt you. So how do you reconcile that?

With a demon, of course!

I went back to my research, looking for child-eating demons (*I swear my FBI agent must have an ulcer by this point trying to monitor my search history*) and found a few, but the one I settled on was Lamia from Greek Mythology. I came up with the concept of the demon being drawn to a place where children died in greater numbers so it could feast on their souls. As I worked out the plot, I had the idea that it would take the form of a little girl who it possessed because of her resistance to the Spanish Flu. That made Kylie, a cancer survivor, the perfect new host to the demon who had been weakened by the many years Eunice prevented it from feeding.

The last thing I needed was a foil for the antagonist, who would serve as the Obi-Wan Kenobi for our heroes. I didn't want to just do Catholics versus demons, so I looked into different practices. My first thought, being set in the south, was that maybe voodoo would be an interesting angle, but it really wasn't prominent in Alabama. Hoodoo, however, was. And, when I looked into it, I saw it incorporated elements of Christianity, so it ended up being the direction I went.

I did some research on it, and I think I got a good amount right, but I also subscribe to Stephen King's philosophy that he detailed in his seminal memoir/how-to book, *On Writing* (which any aspiring writer absolutely should read). King believes—and I'm paraphrasing—that you should do just enough research to make it plausible, but don't overdo it. So, hopefully I got it close enough that no one will think I just made it all up out of the blue.

With the story beats in place, I set out writing and was pleased with how everything tied together. There's a meme floating around about how people are impressed with a writer's meticulous foreshadowing while the writer is just as surprised as they are to find it! That was the case with two scenes here.

One, I had no idea why I decided Desiree's dad owned a deli, but it certainly came in handy when the group needed to steal some silver knives, didn't it? Two, I used the image from the article to guide my description of Abel wearing that rain slicker. I knew there was going to be a storm at the end, but, until I actually wrote it, I had no plan to have him, now released from Lamia's control, using his coat to shield the candle the group needed to perform the ritual to trap the demon. I thought that ended up being a cool visual in my head. Kinda like my own small-scale version of the portals scene from *Avengers: Endgame*.

On your left.

I'm typing this on Wednesday morning, June 5, 2024. The only two people who have copies of this are my editor and my beta readers. As it stands now, when Kayla and Kylie return to the playground and Kylie sees Drew and the rest of the children playing, they also see Eunice and Abel sitting in rocking chairs watching over the kids hand in hand. That scene wasn't in the version you just read. I changed it because I think that was a bit too neatly wrapped. Eunice's tether is broken, and it wouldn't be true to the story if she didn't move on to another realm now that Lamia is defeated. Plus, the hand holding is nice, but Eunice and Abel's relationship was pure innocent friendship between children. I don't want to imply anything romantic between them. And, lastly, I think it's very poetic and fitting to the story I told that Abel takes over as the true *caretaker* of the Dead Children's Playground. The man was shunned in both life and death, and all he wanted was a purpose and friendship. And now he finally has it.

Before I wrap this up, I know some of you are probably mad at me for the epilogue. I get it. I'm mad at myself too, but that doesn't mean it wasn't the right way to end things.

Life doesn't always have happy endings. And unhappy endings aren't always unsatisfying. I knew very early in development that Kylie was going to die after the events of the story took place. The final line of the book was always going to be a variation of *the sisters played together for the last time.* Kylie was always a brave little girl. She fought her cancer head on and she let Lamia take her over to save the other kids. That's why it always felt fitting that her choice at the playground would end up costing her life. But, by Kayla leaving part of her ashes at the playground, she was free to do the one thing she missed out on—being a kid.

If she wouldn't get to grow up, at least she would always have somewhere to play with those whose lives were also cut short way too soon.

One last thing I want to mention about the writing of this book is a part I struggled with.

I'm not a political guy. I have my opinions like everyone

else, but I personally don't feel it's my place to inject my own opinions into my writing or how I conduct my business as an author or a publisher. There are some that do and others that don't and I'm not saying either is right or wrong. This is just how I personally handle things. I try to stick to universal themes of family and relationships in my work without delving into contentious topics.

That said, it's difficult to write a story about real-life places and times in history without at least touching on things that are either political or adjacent to it.

The first thing is that, by having a story with portions set during the civil rights era in the south, it's hard not to at least mention themes with race relations, most prominently here, the friendship between Abel and Eunice and how it was severed when they were children.

The second instance, and one that is still fresh in all our minds, was the mentions of Covid. I've seen many comments about books and movies and TV shows when the topic of the pandemic and everything surrounding it gets incorporated and I very much understand that many of us dive into fiction to escape those real-life problems. However, I also believe a story has to be genuine and I couldn't write a book that dealt with one historic pandemic in the Spanish Flu without incorporating the Covid-19 pandemic when an illness was spreading through a town. We all now know what would happen in that case and to avoid it completely wouldn't be authentic. I tried to keep it minimal and without bias or judgment and I hope that came through to all of you as you read. We all have different views and I want my work to bring horror fans of all kinds together.

That's how I came up with the story based on the information I gathered in my research. I hope you found it informative. If so, I'd love to hear from you whether or not you liked it, or if you have any other questions about the writing process.

A Creepy Tidbit

I couldn't not share this last part with you.

Early on, I knew what I wanted my cover concept to be. A creepy little girl on a swing surrounded by ghosts. The cover designer I use has an online form to fill out, describing what we want. I was doing that one Saturday afternoon while my wife and son were out and my daughter was in the other room drawing.

I typed everything out and hit submit. A few minutes later, my daughter comes in and shows me this drawing:

For those of you listening to this on audio, it's a drawing of an evil-looking little girl with black eyes on a swing with a man in a long coat with a hood and a skull face standing behind her with a knife.

I didn't tell *anyone* out loud about my cover idea. There is *no* way she would have known about it. Not only that, but the final cover doesn't have the guy in the background who looks mysteriously like The Caretaker, who didn't end up on my cover, but she also had no idea about.

So...yeah...that's freaky. I think I'm going to call a priest.

A Final Word

Thank you again so much for reading this book and for your continued support! I hope you enjoy this series because I look forward to bringing you more *American Horrors* soon!

Next up in the series, we'll be heading up the East Coast to Salem, Massachusetts and back home to New Jersey (although I haven't decided in which order yet).

Either way, I hope you come along for the ride.

If you enjoyed this book and have a few minutes to spare, please consider writing a review. Reviews help indie horror books like this get in the hands of readers and are very much appreciated.

Review The Dead Children's Playground on Amazon

Review The Dead Children's Playground on Goodreads

ACKNOWLEDGEMENTS

The author would like to thank the following:

Thank you to my editor Louis Greenberg for making my words coherent and pointing out those little inconsistencies I always seem to miss.

Thank you to Stephanie Evans for beta reading and making sure I got the local details right.

Thank you to all the amazing authors in the indie horror community for inspiring me and for being so generous with your time and advice helping to make me a better writer and publisher.

And, as always, thank you to my wife Jessica for always supporting my dreams and for picking up the slack when I disappear into my office for days on end every time I get close to a deadline and realize I'm way far behind. I love you more than words can express!

ABOUT THE AUTHOR

James Kaine picked up a copy of *The Scariest Stories You've Ever Heard* at a scholastic book fair when he was a kid and hasn't looked back since. Now an active Member of the Horror Writers Association, James, as he puts it, "lives his dream to give you nightmares." His work includes novels such as *My Pet Werewolf, Pursuit* and *The Dead Children's Playground*.

Born and raised in Trenton, NJ, James still resides in the Garden State with his wife, two children and a loveable Boston Terrier, named Obi. When not writing about horrible things, James enjoys reading, movies, music, cooking and rooting for the New York Giants. Well, maybe he doesn't enjoy that last one.

Visit www.jameskaine.com for news, merch and to join the James Kaine VIP Readers Club, netting yourself two free eBooks instantly!

f JamesKaineWrites

⃝ JamesKaineWrites

♪ @JamesKaineWrites

𝕏 JamesKaineBooks

▶ @HorrorHousePublishing

BOOKS BY JAMES KAINE

STANDALONE
Pursuit
Black Friday

MY PET WEREWOLF SERIES
My Pet Werewolf
Gunther

AMERICAN HORRORS SERIES
The Dead Children's Playground

Made in the USA
Coppell, TX
30 September 2024

37680504R00187